Boles Shuddered,

naked fear beginning to etch itself across his consciousness. He tried to ignore the terror, control the trembling in his legs, the shaking in his hands, but he could not. The trio of things had obviously seen him, had their attention focused on him. One by one they opened their maws, stretching their jaws to their fullest, flashing teeth and fangs and appetites that were not bound to mere hunger. Frothing drool foaming over their lips, the trio began to advance toward Boles.

They're coming for you, his mind whispered, terror frosting the words, the painful cold of them eating at him. What do you want? Why are you not moving? Run you idiot—run!

He did.

Thirteen tales of Supernatural suspense — some peppered with humor, most laced with unadulterated terror. Dare you accompany these intrepid adventurers — Blakely & Boles, Lai Wan the Dreamwalker, Lin Carter's Anton Zarnak, H.P. Lovecraft's Inspector Legrasse, and others — through some of C.J. Henderson's most chilling tales?

**Marietta Publishing Books
by or with C.J. Henderson:**

THE OCCULT DETECTIVES OF C.J. HENDERSON

LAI WAN,
Tales of the Dreamwalker

TO BATTLE BEYOND

WHAT YOU PAY FOR

THE REIGN OF THE DRAGON LORD,
Book One of The Dragon Lord Saga

BUT SERIOUSLY FOLKS,
The Comedy of C.J. Henderson

BREAKING INTO FICTION WRITING!
(with co-author Bruce Gehweiler)

Anthologies

WARFEAR,
A Collection of Strange War Tales

HEAR THEM ROAR

SUPERNATURAL INVESTIGATORS

of C.J. Henderson

MARIETTA PUBLISHING • GEORGIA

1-892669-31-5 (trade paper)
1-892669-32-3 (e-book)
1-892669-34-X (kindle)

Retail cover price $15.99

Admission Of Weakness — *New Mythos Legends*; 1999
To Cast Out Fear — *The Tales of Inspector Legrasse*; 2005
The Last Night Of The Lazarus Brothers — *Bad-Ass Fairies*; 2007
The Idea Of Fear — *Arkham Tales*; 2006
Memories — *The Nth Degree*; 2005
The Dungeon Of Self — *Cthulhu Codex*; 1999
The Questioning Of The Azatothian Priest — *Lost Worlds of Time & Space*; 2005
Ladies And Gentlemen, And Children Of All Ages ... — *Werewolves*; 2007
Eye To Eye — *Inhuman*; 2004
Cruelty — *Miskatonic University*; 2009
The Moment After Death — *Lai Wan: Tales of the Dreamwalker*; 2007
Folly — *Dark Wisdom*; 2007
A Puzzle Well Made — *The Supernatural Investigators of C.J. Henderson*; 2009

Printed and bound in the United States by Lightning Source, Inc.

10 9 8 7 6 5 4 3 2 1

Design: Rich Harvey
Cover art: Ben Fogletto
Frontispiece art: Ben Fogletto

Published by Marietta Publishing
Bruce R. Gehweiler, Publisher
677 Valleyside Road
Dallas, GA, 30157
www.mariettapublishing.com

GEORGIA, USA

TABLE of Contents

Dedication

I have been creating and reviving supernatural investigator
characters for quite some time now.

Lots of editors and publishers have encouraged me along the way,
of course. They have done so with encouragement,
and they have done so with checks.

One, however, stands out from the rest. This fellow certainly
published my work. And he gave me more in the way of
encouragement than could ever be catalogued or calculated.

What he did above and beyond all the rest was to open a fabulous
array of doors for me. I knew of H.P. Lovecraft, of course, but I did
not have the depth of understanding he would show me.

He led me to many other Mythos authors as well,
gifting me with scores of ideas and notions.

He also, as executor of Lin Carter's estate, granted me the privilege
of continuing his most wonderful character, Anton Zarnak,
an act for which I will always be grateful.

And thus it is that
I dedicate this book to:

~ Robert M. Price ~

A gentleman and a scholar,
in a world desperately
bereft of both.

One of CJ Henderson's most popular revitalization effort has been that which he put into bringing back the late Lin Carter's classic supernatural investigator, Anton Zarnak. With the passing out of print of the collection **Lin Carter's Anton Zarnak: Supernatural Sleuth,** *we decided it would be a shame for CJ's fans to no longer have access to his outstanding take on this character. Thus, as our first story in this volume, we proudly present the tale he designed to be the first in the Zarnak series ...*

Admission of Weakness

"Pride is an admission of weakness; it secretly fears all competition and dreads all rivals."
— Bishop Fulton J. Sheen

* Waterfront Terror *

Trevlin Fletcher ran, stumbling and gibbering, splashing through the puddled back streets of lower Manhattan. He did not waste time looking over his shoulder. He did not waste energy considering where he was going. He merely ran—straight and hard—his lungs heaving with arching pain, blood beating in his ears like a steel hammer pounding its way through mountains of ice.

Run, run ... have to keep moving, tell people what I've seen ... what's out there—what's coming! Run! Have to run, have to ... run—

His legs ached from the torturous distance he had already covered. Just his escape from the merchant hauler alone would have tired most men—crawling up through the dark hold over the calamitous towers of crates and bales, hanging suspended above the frigid harbor waters, grappling his way down the anchor—let alone once he had reached the dock. The mad dash toward the cliffs of the city, fleeing into its canyons, block after block in the choking, fetid summer heat—

"Watch it, you idiot!"

Trevlin dodged madly around the slow cruising jitney. Not a native of New York, he was not accustomed to automobiles being in the streets at such a late hour. Then, as he staggered around the vehicle, suddenly the portion of his brain still dully cataloguing events for his memory—the one tiny wad of tissue in all his skull that had not given itself over to hysteria—realized what it had seen.

"You—stop!"

He screamed the word with a bellow not brought forth from his aching lungs alone, but from the depths of his tattered, ill-used soul. Staggering after the cab, he screeched painfully, his throat tearing from the strain. Blood flecked the phlegm-thick foam bubbling over his lips.

"For the love of God," he wailed pitifully. *"Come back!"*

Brakes squealed. Trevlin dragged his throbbing legs forward, inching his way to the hackney. His hands clawing at the door handle desperately, he threw himself into the backseat of the vehicle, telling the driver;

"Go! Go—move! *Go!"*

The driver released the clutch and hit the gas pedal harder than he would have normally, his passenger's all too apparent desperation coaxing him onward.

"Where to, pal?"

"Anywhere, anywhere—just get me out of here. Far out of here." Throwing money over the seat, the driver watched a rain of crumpled bills splatter against his windshield as his sweating passenger bleated, "As far as we can go."

The large block engine roared and the taxi burst forward into Chinatown. As the driver steered away from the main streets bustling with activity, favoring the clearer side alleyways, he took note of the man's costume in his mirror, rightly guessing him to be a seaman.

Maybe a shanghai jumping port, he thought. Or a stowaway bolting the watch crew.

Wondering what kind of trouble his fare was seeking to avoid, he asked, "None of my business if you say so, pal, but ... you in the kinda trouble where you need the cops—or where you need ta avoid them?"

Gulping the city's thick, humid air into his burning lungs, Trevlin wondered, could the police help him? With what he had seen? He *had* to tell someone—but who?

"Who?" he wondered aloud.

Could he possibly be saved by men—mere men—armed with naught but clubs and knives and guns? Could anything save him? Protect him?

Was there any power on earth that could stop that which he had seen awakened?

no

The word was a darkened light that cut through Trevlin's brain with surgical precision. He felt his throat go dry and his bladder and bowels empty. And then, as the sailor's eyes flooded with tears, the shape appeared in the alleyway.

"What the hell is that?" muttered the driver. He hit his brakes even as the scarlet and black and gold form ahead raised its arms. Then, Trevlin screamed and fire filled the night.

* The Master Arrives *

Smug self-satisfaction pervading his frame, the man stepped into the dark mouth of the alley. He was tall but slender, with a fine-boned, but sallow face dominated by dark, hound-aggressive eyes. More arresting than those features, however, was his hair—sleek and midnight black, as well groomed as that of a cinema star. The man's deep, thick mane was obviously a thing of rightful pride to its owner.

He walked unerringly, his nimble balance unaffected by the greasy cobbles beneath his feet. Moving almost gracefully down the unfamiliar passageway, the summer's terrible heat not seeming to cause any discomfort, he stopped abruptly before the single door of a small, narrow, two-story structure—one shouldered on either side by far larger tenements.

Ahhhhh, he thought with a delighted contentment as he stepped up to the building numbered thirteen, this is where it starts. Noting the face of his pocket watch, he commented aloud.

"And this moment is when it starts—with a stroke. Now."

The man's hand reached up, his index finger stabbing the bell to the side of the imposing slab of solid oak that served for the old structure's door. As he waited, his eyes ran over the walls of crumbling brick, black with generations of grime, their few windows dim and smudged with congealing soot.

Excellent, he thought. Secluded, unimposing, dilapidated enough to put off all but the truly desperate ...

The door swung open noiselessly on well-oiled hinges. Cool air wafted into the alley from the building's interior, despite the horribly oppressive heat strangling the city. In the doorway stood a tall man, lean and rangy. A Hindu, he wore a tattered gray sweater and a pair of formless, baggy cotton pants. Indeed, he would have almost looked a beggar if not for the spotless white turban wrapped with careful precision about his head. His keen dark eyes locked with those of the man in the alley for only a moment.

"Sahib," he said with a slight bow. "You have arrived."

"You know me already, eh?" asked the man in the doorway.

"You are Dr. Anton Zarnak, sent to take over this post from your predecessor, Professor Guicet."

"And how can you be so certain I'm this Zarnak?" asked the man in the alley from behind a suppressed smirk.

"I am still packing the doctor's belongings to make space for your own. His demise was cruelly unfortunate. It left this city and thus by extension much of this world defenseless. You were sent to assume his duties. Neither of us has time to waste with games."

"But," chided the taciturn man, "you still haven't answered my question. How did..."

Without watching for a reaction the Hindu gave the massive oak door a subtle push, causing it to close abruptly in the man's face. When the bell rang again, the Hindu did not answer it, even though it chimed on endlessly. Finally, the door opened as the man from the alley let himself in.

"How *dare* you close that door in my face?" The man's normally waxen face was flush with anger. Dropping his bag in the middle of the foyer he stood with his arms folded across his chest, glaring at the Hindu as the man calmly continued packing a crate. "Did you hear me?"

"They have most likely heard you at Lo Fat's Duck House, I would imagine," answered the Hindu patiently. He threw the words over his shoulder, continuing his work, wasting as little time on the intruder as possible.

"This will not do!" growled the man. "I am Anton Zarnak! I've traveled halfway around the world to get here. I have studied for years for this moment—decades—and I will be treated with respect in my own home, by my own servant, no less!"

In the next chamber, the Hindu rose to his full height. His back to the angry man one moment, there was a blur that Zarnak could not actually follow, and then the Hindu was facing him, in the same room, separated by inches.

"I know who you are and where you have come from. Some time long ago, you made a trip to the far and cold East, seeking knowledge you did not deserve. You demanded it, loudly, foolishly, like a lout in a convent, seeking sex merely because you had discovered you had a penis."

Zarnak's face grew hot, his fine fingers clawing slowly at the seams of his trousers.

"With sad, head-shaking pity, and because they could see a use for you masked to most by your arrogance, those you accosted took you in and taught you. They gave you glimpses of other worlds and brought you slowly to the realization that the universe does not revolve around the human animal. Not even on occasion."

Zarnak found the part of his mind that had been trained to step past his reptilian cortex reaching out and hammering away at his hauteur. Suddenly realizing the man before him was no mere servant, the doctor replied slowly.

"You speak of my past as if well-informed."

"I was told only that you would arrive today," responded the Hindu. "But, I served Professor Guicet for fourteen years. The story I offer as yours, was his story as well. As it is mine. Seeing the same rude, self-important presumptuousness within your eyes which used to dominate both his—-and my own—I could only surmise that you were another who thought the secrets of existence could be discovered in a manner akin to children at Christmas ... tearing away ribbons, thinking they have found happiness rather than just another trinket."

Zarnak's manner collapsed inward, replaced by a more acceptable humility. Taken aback by his mistaken reading of the situation into which he had walked, he apologized.

"Please forgive me ..."

"Singh," the Hindu answered. "Akbar Ram Singh. At your service—in payment for my sins—as you now stand in service to the world for yours."

"It is as you say, Singh," Zarnak admitted. "I was tasked to hold this place against the dark elements of existence. Serving all men is new to me, though, even after my decades in A'alshirie. But I'm here to begin repayment for what I've been taught."

"I believe you are sincere in your words," answered the Hindu. Wearing a sad expression, he added, "Which worries me all the more. As Coleridge said, 'And the Devil did grin, for his darling sin, is pride that apes humility.' I wish you were only but trying to deceive me with your words. Sadly, Dr. Zarnak, in my humble opinion, the one you seek to deceive is yourself."

Turning, Singh walked into the interior of the building, beckoning his new master to follow.

"And that is always a dangerous business. Perhaps if Professor Guicet had not left us so unreasonably early, the monks would have had time to prepare you better. But, that is the way of things. Mankind takes what it can get. Now it has you."

Standing before the door of the apartment's study, the Hindu rested his hand on the latch, saying, "an inspector of police has been waiting for you for several hours now. Your work begins, Sahib Zarnak. Please strive to survive long enough to have dinner."

* The Scene of the Crime *

Lieutenant Thorner led Zarnak into the sweltering closeness of the police warehouse. He was a big man, thick-shouldered and barrel-chested. A derby sat forward on his shaved head, its brim slightly discolored from the constant cloud of cigar smoke the officer used to screen himself from the world. Thorner spoke as they made their way toward the back of the building.

"Sorry to get you like this, your first day in town an' all, but ... ah, what with Professor Guicet gone ... I mean, what happened last night, he would've ..."

"Please," Zarnak said with a wave of his hand. "This is to be my life. No sense taking a child's steps into the water. It will be just as cold no matter how long I take to acclimate myself."

Thorner wanted to turn, to run his eyes over the man behind him. He had gone to the oak door in China Alley a score of times in his career to enlist the aide of Dr. Zarnak's predecessor. The lieutenant had liked Guicet, admired him. They had dined together—in restaurants and each other's homes—on numerous occasions, closing many of the great island's taverns together as well.

But Thorner felt tall, hard walls growing between himself and the man behind him. Like most policemen successful in their work, the lieutenant was a shrewd judge of character. Sizing people up was no terribly difficult task for him. And so far, he did not like the size of Professor Guicet's replacement.

"But, well," said Zarnak in a soft but sharp voice, "luckily there's nothing saying that people who work together have to like each other."

"What?" Thorner let the one word escape, then went silent. Guicet had known what the big policeman had been thinking on occasion, but he had always made it seem as if the fact was only further proof the two were kindred spirits. Thorner knew that was not the case here.

Pulling in on himself as far as he could, the lieutenant hid his true self behind his badge and the character he had constructed over the years for presentation to the rabble in the streets. Suddenly he not only did not like Zarnak, he did not even feel comfortable around him.

"This is it."

The doctor moved forward toward the grotesquely misshapen arrangement of blackened steel resting in the back of the police warehouse. His hands gripped one the other behind his back as he approached the twisted blob. Zarnak had been told he would be inspecting a motor vehicle that had been subjected to some kind of great heat. As he stared at the unnaturally distorted tangle shimmering beneath a single light, the doctor was grateful for the clue Thorner had granted him as to what the thing before him had once been. Scrutinizing the contorted, melted frame, the globs of shapeless metal hanging in the air as if frozen, the doctor still found himself forced to ask the obvious.

"This really was an automobile?"

"Yes. A jitney cab." When his guest did not reply, the lieutenant added, "It's in such weird shape, it took us a while to even figure out what company it belonged to. Don't know what happened to the driver."

"Amazing ..." Zarnak mused aloud. "Just amazing."

"You've found something?" asked the lieutenant.

"No, no—sorry. I was merely thinking aloud about automobiles in general. The concept of them. Mechanical transport ... I've seen very few of them, actually."

"Seen very few?" repeated Thorner, absently pulling a cigar from an inside jacket pocket. "Good God, man—it's 1922. The streets are filled with them."

Zarnak did not turn from his inspection of the nightmarishly bent and boiled slag. Not yet daring to touch it, he responded absently to the policeman as he paced the ruin's circumference.

"I know. But I don't believe they had been invented when last I was here."

Thorner said nothing. The sallow-faced doctor appeared to him to be no more than thirty years old. Several questions ran through the policeman's brain, but he kept them to himself, staying behind his tall, hard wall. Answering them anyway, Zarnak said;

"No, I wasn't a child when I left the country. I'd just received my third degree. I'd had to wait for the war to end before I could graduate, of course."

"The World War disrupted things at a lot of the universities," the big policeman offered.

"World War?" Zarnak responded. "Oh yes, I heard someone on the boat mention ..."

And then, the doctor went silent. Climbing a free-standing ladder which had been used earlier by a news photographer to obtain an aerial shot of the unexplainable slag, the doctor investigated its uppermost strands and spires. He was not surprised to find that unlike the rippled, bubbling surfaces below, that the tops of all the upward reaching columns were not only smooth, but concave as well. Descending the ladder, Zarnak finally lay his fingers on the fused remains before him. Drawn to one horribly twisted shaft of dissolved steel, he felt along its spiral ridges.

"Yes, lieutenant," he whispered, "you were right to come for me. Notice how these wiry strands of metal look to have been pulled aloft— how much of the total mass seems to have melted upward, sideways ... and look here ..."

The doctor pointed up along a thick, inverted pedestal of metal. As the detective drew closer, Zarnak grabbed his sleeve and pushed his hand up against the cool, burned black steel. Shoving Thorner's fingers up the curving wrinkle, the doctor kept the big man's hand moving over the smooth surface until suddenly it ran against a slight, almost unnoticeable jagged edge bursting through the polished skin. The lieutenant jerked his fingers away with surprise. As he looked at the scrape marks that had been drawn across his flesh, Thorner asked;

"And just what the hell was that?"

"The upper half of a femur, I believe."

"What?" asked the big policeman.

"You were complaining that you couldn't find the driver of the automobile, lieutenant." Turning, the doctor stared directly into Thorner's eyes. "Congratulations. You've found him."

* A Discovery *

"So," said Zarnak, staring at the dark circle in the middle of the lane, "this is where the wreckage was discovered."

Two uniformed officers stood at each end of the Chinatown alleyway, barring both automobile and pedestrian traffic. Thorner stood halfway between them, off to the side on the thin sidewalk, a new cigar clenched firmly in his teeth. Several storefronts down from Zarnak, the policeman leaned against the cleanest building he could find, staying in what shade was present to avoid the blistering sun. Blowing out a cloud of smoke, he watched as Zarnak bent down on all fours, making his way around the black, burned bricks like some sort of gigantic, spindly crab. The lieutenant could not imagine what the doctor hoped to discover.

Hundreds of people and vehicles had gone down the lane since the police had removed the ruined cab earlier in the day. The area had been thoroughly trampled, the black dust the lieutenant had initially noticed scattered across lower Manhattan. Still, that was why he had brought Zarnak in—why he stuck with the doctor despite his personal feelings toward him.

"Ah, lieutenant, I believe we have something."

Thorner did not move from his position. Did not respond.

"I'm certain you noted the fact that the street buckles inward concavely from the blackened perimeter here. The jitney was not the only thing consumed. The cobblestones here have been sheered away, like fruit scooped up by a spoon." Standing, Zarnak indicated the wall next to Thorner, then the one across the street from the same spot.

"Notice the line of soot on the walls—near the sidewalk? Keep that in mind. But first ... look at this." Reaching into one of the inner pockets of his voluminous great coat, the doctor pulled forth a length of string with a metal sphere attached to one end. Centering the weight within the black circle, he extended the string to the edge of the darkness.

"You see, the street itself has been torn away in a curving line. Note how the string, extended from the midpoint of the disturbance does not come in contact with the roadway again until it gets beyond the burnt area. But now, observe this ..."

Leaving the center of the street, the doctor continued to stretch the string until he came to the curb. Motioning with his hand, he waved Thorner forward to his side. Pointing down, he said;

"Where the string comes in contact with the edge of the sidewalk, there is a thin ridge of soot, extending both down the curb toward the gutter, and over it, onward toward the buildings beyond."

Moving out of the street, Zarnak then extended the string all the way to the nearest wall. Holding it tight against the building with his thumb, he added, "And, if we follow the trajectory here, we see that again, the fabric of the street has been hurled outward and splashed against the surrounding buildings."

"Yeah, okay," Thorner answered, rolling his cigar around in his mouth. "But, so what? What's it mean?"

"It means, my dear lieutenant," said Zarnak as he reeled in his weighted string, "that most likely I have arrived here just in time."

* Explorations and Explanations *

Zarnak sat at the desk in the study found on the first floor of the grimy little building at number thirteen, China Alley, sifting through the contents of a score of books. Some were texts he had brought with him. Others had been found among the volumes he had inherited from Professor Guicet.

Which, he thought, will all some day fall into the hands of whomever walks through the front door after I've been destroyed in my own unpleasant manner.

Sitting back in his chair for a moment, Zarnak closed his eyes. Reaching inside himself, he sighed audibly while shaking his head back and forth almost imperceptibly. After a moment Singh appeared in the doorway of the study. Carrying a tray, he entered the room and approached the desk.

"I have placed a call to the lieutenant. He will be here shortly. Now you must prepare yourself for the day ahead."

Zarnak opened his eyes. How long it had been since he closed them he had no idea. He had planned to work through the night until he found what he needed and then act. He had not planned to sleep—an intolerable delay—sloppy.

Dangerous.

Nor had the doctor asked for a meal, or for Singh to telephone for Thorner. Since he would have wished for both these things to have been accomplished, however, he merely nodded, turning his attention to the tray.

"First," said the Hindu, "you have steak and lima beans in curry. You have a great struggle ahead of you, one which promises some amount of physical exertion—beef and beans will provide you the energy you need. Then, red peppers and yeen choy—it's a great deal like spinach. The greens will keep your system flowing properly."

"And the curry, and the peppers?" asked the doctor.

"I like curry and peppers," answered Singh as he filled the empty cup on the tray with tea. Zarnak smiled thinly and picked up the pair of chop sticks near his main dish. Snatching up a thin strip of spice-dripping beef and several beans, he brought them to his mouth and popped them in, thinking as he chewed.

If I am wrong in my theory, then I am not the man the old masters should have sent to this place. Following the notion with a healthy mouthful of yeen choy and pepper pieces, he chewed with relish, adding, But, if I am right, then I'm not certain how exactly I am supposed to survive.

The doctor slid the greens and pepper bits around in his mouth, sucking at the thick, delicious twin tastes of the mushroom and oyster sauces coating them. As he grabbed another load of beef and beans, however, a sudden thought invaded his mind.

Then again, who says I'm *supposed* to survive?

Somewhat cheered by his sober rational, Zarnak finished his meal rapidly as he finally began to piece together what he and Thorner would have to do.

* Allies Bicker *

"Guicet never asked for anything like this." The lieutenant stared into Zarnak's eyes, searching for some clue as to what kind of game the sallow-faced doctor was playing.

"Guicet," answered Zarnak with impatience, "never faced anything of the magnitude that we will face this morning. If, mind you, we are lucky enough to be able to reach the arrival site in time to affect a reversal."

Thorner's teeth and tongue worked the cigar in his mouth. An uncomfortable tightness choking at him, the lieutenant removed his derby, mopping at the sweat pooling under it as he answered, "Funny how the first day you show up in town suddenly the whole world's hanging in the balance. Must make you feel important."

"You are a fool," Zarnak snapped with an irritation he could not bring himself to control. "If you are not here to help me, please have the good grace to stand out of my way while I try and finish what must be done by myself."

"Hey," boomed Thorner. "Just who the hell do you think you're talking to?" The policeman managed to throw a restraining arm around his anger for a moment, but then suddenly, the big man found himself unable to contain himself any longer. His face filling with blood, he bellowed;

"You know, I've had enough of your piss-ass bullshit. You arrogant bastard—I'm not your mother or anything else that wants to lick your face! I'm the one who's fucking in charge around here! This is my investigation — *I* call the shots here! *Me* —" Thorner's finger banged against Zarnak's chest, the iron force of it threatening to shatter the doctor's ribs— "do you get it? Do you understand?"

"Perfectly," answered Zarnak quietly. "You feel threatened by that which you can not understand, and so you rage at the messenger because you do not understand the message ... much like a child ripping pages out of a Bible because they are unfamiliar with Latin."

Thorner's fingers curled, his arms throwing themselves skyward. Fists poised in the air, ready to piston down on Zarnak, the lieutenant bent himself forward through the horrific heat. But then, arms shaking, back frozen in position, head swinging from side to side, Thorner grappled his rage back into the dark corner wherein it usually lurked, throwing what chains over it he could.

Hating Zarnak, fearing the doctor's quiet assurance, the lieutenant spat, "You want my help—you want the city of New York to spend overtime money—you tell me what the hell is going on. I've got people to answer to."

"Hopefully people with fewer recent cave dwellers contributing to their racial memory's index," answered Zarnak calmly. "But, enough time has been wasted. The explanation you desire is simple. An ancient god is about to be brought to this island."

"What?"

"Do you remember the vacuum effect involved with the disturbance you asked me to investigate? The metal of the jitney automobile, raining upward and sideways? The soot-like residue of the cobblestones—ground down to powder, gouged from the material essence of the street and then exploded outward? Do you recall the curvature of the destruction, the circular scoop effect of the street, the smooth, limiting cuts across the metal of the jitney as it flowed upward—these confinements to the disturbance that destroyed the automobile and its passengers were caused by a globe in time, a doorway opening from some far beyond into our here and now."

Thorner half-closed one eye, working to concentrate his gaze even as he tried to consolidate his shattered thoughts.

"Someone opened a momentary gate to another dimension in this alleyway," Zarnak continued. "Most likely to eliminate the jitney's passenger. I have done extensive research since I saw you last—looking into what entities might possess the power to cause such destruction, which ones might be bound to this plane of existence at this time, what cycles are in communication ... well, not to stray too far afield, what I have discovered is that the time is right for one of the more prominent

Lemurian deities to establish a foothold in our world once more."

Thorner's mind reeled. He had seen many things with Professor Guicet—walls running with blood, plates floating in the air, spectral forms passing through objects ... and the worm, the terrible, terrible worm deep in the subway—the officer shuddered at the memories, suddenly understanding on a conscious level why he and Guicet had really gone to so many taverns together. Stumbling over his words, passion and pride suddenly replaced with duty and control, Thorner pushed his derby back on his head.

"You're sayin' ... some ancient god is tryin' to come set up shop here in Manhattan?"

"No, I'm saying that someone here is trying to bring something down on us all which I'm quite certain they do not understand and can not control."

"If they can bring it here," asked the lieutenant, "what makes you think they can't control it?"

"Any child can open a door," answered Zarnak, "allowing a tiger into its home. The simple truth is, Mr. Thorner, that none control Yama. They are controlled by him—as will be every man, woman and child scattered across the face of this world if we do not stop his arrival."

Thorner stared at the doctor once more. His eyes moved from Zarnak to the hole in the street to which they had returned, and then they fell to memory, seeing again the remains of an automobile so blasted and tortured it had taken nearly an hour's examination just to confirm that it had at one time been a vehicle at all. Finally, his teeth grinding into his cigar, the lieutenant asked;

"Awright, what'dya need us to do?"

The doctor did not hesitate to tell him.

* Closing In *

An hour later, Zarnak, Thorner, and the seven uniformed officers with them emerged from between the last buildings on the island's west side. Ahead of them lay the city's great shipping docks—hundreds of mighty merchant vessels berthed one after another, all unloading that which they had brought in, replacing it with new loads to take away.

With the police clearing the streets, the doctor had traced the path of the ruined cab back through the alleys of Chinatown to the spot where it had picked up its passenger. At that point, Zarnak had then begun the process of following the ethereal trail of Trevlin Fletcher back to its point of origin.

Every step made following the baking sun across the island filled the doctor with another sliver of fear. He could not avoid it. To trace Fletcher back to the point of his origin through his residual vibrations, Zarnak needed to feel what the man had felt. He had to collect the scant residue of the fleeing man's emotions, to allow each needle of terror to pierce his psychic skin and hang there, poisoning what courage or nerve he might possess with its craven stink.

Much in the manner of a bloodhound the doctor moved from point to point, gathering those scraps of scent still existent which Fletcher had left behind, propelling himself further and further until finally he was able to point toward the hundreds of ships moored along the island's coast.

"There!"

"'There' what?" asked Thorner.

"That ship, the merchant freighter, Congo Lady—that is our destiny." As Zarnak began to make his way across the street, the lieutenant stepped after him.

"So, what'da we do? What'da we need?"

"What we must do," answered the doctor, still walking forward, his speed increasing with each step, "is board that ship, find the high priest making the casting, and stop him."

"Huh, sounds easy enough," replied Thorner, suddenly—ludicrously—somehow feeling more at ease. The mood passed as Zarnak chuckled, shaking his head sadly. The big policeman inquired as to what the doctor found so humorous.

"My dear lieutenant," Zarnak answered, keeping up his brisk pace despite the weight of his bag, "you are, I suppose, a decent enough man, one struggling gamely to understand the circumstances into which you have been flung. I should make some attempt to take that into account, I suppose."

As Zarnak stopped in his tracks, uniformed policemen swarmed around him and Thorner in the unrelenting heat to divert the late morning traffic speeding around them both. As they did, their movements slowed by the staggering heat of the approaching midday sun, Zarnak continued.

"In the time of pre-history, a force named Yamath made itself known in an ancient kingdom we remember as Lemuria. He was called the Lord of Fire. To the Tibetans of our own time, he is known as Yama, the King of Devils." Pointing to the sun, Zarnak said, "Now think and tell me, has it ever been this hot here before, lieutenant?"

When the big policeman shook his head in response, the doctor told him, "No, I wouldn't have believed so. I'll tell you why it's so hot. Yama's presence is pushing its way through to this world. When the sun reaches its zenith, he shall be here. And at that point, all discussion will become superfluous."

"What?" questioned Thorner. "You mean noon? This thing you're talkin' about gets here at *noon*?"

"I could be wrong, lieutenant. I would dearly wish it so," admitted Zarnak. "But mistakes about such things are not normally a part of my repertory."

Not waiting for an answer, knowing from the sun's position in the sky that he had at most only a half an hour—most probably less—to stop what was coming, Anton Zarnak moved on, headed for the Congo Lady. To his credit, with only a moment's hesitation, the lieutenant moved into the doctor's wake, waving his men on behind him. The seven moved after their commander, mere inches of shadow trailing them.

* Confrontation *

The grotesque wooden face swung back and forth before the makeshift altar. The worship site had been formed out of packing crates and several old blankets now covered with heathen scribbling most men had never imagined, let alone witnessed. The dancing visage before it was a terrible thing containing three glaring eyes and wickedly fanged jaws, all of it painted in scarlet and black and gold. Stylized flames dripped from the face's twisted mouth.

Sub pat'kiaa, yef yef, gordic trum'el kuna. Yama hidie'ay, Yama gibgib'conna gibgib'conna ...

"What the Hell are those monkey's doin'?" Thorner whispered through the handkerchief he was holding over his nose and mouth, pointing at the masked high priest in the hold before them and those who appeared to be his followers.

How had they taken the ship, he wondered. Had they been passengers? That statue on their altar? What was it?

What does it matter? snarled a different voice within the lieutenant's head. Concentrate ...

The interior of the Congo Lady seemed forty or fifty degrees hotter than the outside world. The lieutenant and his men had already shed their ties. Several of the uniformed policemen felt themselves on the verge of collapse.

Yama hidie'ay, Yama gibgib'conna gibgib'conna ...

On their way down into the vessel's hold, the investigators had found no living beings. The entire ship's company had somehow vanished. Reaching the ship's bowels, however, any questions as to the crew's whereabouts were answered. The bodies of sailors were found hanging from the deck beams of the storage hold's ceiling, their ankles roped in chains and docking cable. The flooring was thick with the sticky slime of their blood, the atmosphere of the massive room pungent with the odor of their disembowelments.

"That is the high priest," whispered Zarnak with urgency, pointing at the leaping figure wearing the wooden mask. "And he is but seconds away from completing his summoning. Order your men to fire."

"What?" asked Thorner. "What're you sayin'?"

"I'm saying kill him, and do it quickly! Before it's too late!"

Sub pat'kiaa, yef yef, gordic trum'el kuna. Sub pat'kiaa, yef yef ...

Thorner listened to the heathen words spilling through the slits in the high priest's mask. His eyes took in the spinning, swinging bodies ornamenting the ceiling, his nostrils reminded him of his foe's determination, his feet moved uneasily in the binding scarlet carpet spread across the hold's flooring. It all seemed so foolish, no reason to order murder ... then he thought of the eighty-nine dead, swaying above him.

Yama hidie'ay, Yama gibgib'conna gibgib'conna ...

"Stop!" demanded Thorner. Rising up from behind the crate he had chosen for cover, the lieutenant aimed his service pistol at the high priest.

Yama gibgib'conna gibgib'conna bing shem!

"In the name of the law!"

The high priest focused on Thorner. Bringing his staff about, the capering butcher aimed his totem at the lieutenant and gave out a string of orders in his strange, clacking tongue. As one, the bloody collection of ritually painted, half-naked cultists turned and began moving on Thorner. Understanding the heathen's intent well enough, the big policeman gave orders of his own.

Instantly, his men revealed their positions and opened fire on the approaching cultists. Armed with only knives and bludgeons, the first line of the ragged band went down to a man, their murderous lives cut short by well-aimed lead. Behind them, however, the high priest unfurled the left sleeve of his robe with a snap. Instantly a wild spray of powder was released from within a careful fold of cloth, contact with the floor transforming it into a dense and putrid billow.

As the cultists retreated into the cloud, Zarnak and the officers poured forth toward the altar. The doctor sank to his knees, studying the scarlet runes crudely painted on the blanket draping the ever-so-carefully stacked crates. And then, Zarnak looked up as a distant rumbling began to echo throughout the hold.

"Oh, no."

The two words were all he could say. If only they had arrived even just two minutes earlier—just two insignificantly ever-lasting minutes—it might have been enough.

"What is it?" asked Thorner.

"We're too late," answered Zarnak, pointing at the altar. "Look!"

Rising out of the stone idol resting on the makeshift worship site, curling wisps of violet smoke billowed and sparked, plumes exploding outward in all directions.

"So, what'da we do now?" demanded the lieutenant.

"I don't know," answered Zarnak. Pulling a thick volume from his bag, the doctor began thumbing frantically through it, ripping many of its thin, worn pages. "It's possible there is a counter-spell, something that might redirect Yama's arrival—deflect it as it were ... but I don't know any by heart. I have to find it ... need time ... just a few minutes ..."

Always just a few minutes ...

Thorner turned from the distracted Zarnak. Above the altar, a burning grin began to take distinct form. As the temperature in the boiling hold expanded exponentially, the lieutenant forgot everything he believed, falling through the thin crust of learning down into the deep and coldly dark pools of his instinct. Desperately, self-preservation reached into the well-memory of his soul—

Every evil thing, his captain had said once, no matter what—you treat 'em all the same because deep down they are all the same. They're all a bunch of cheap punks. Each and every one of them.

And then, his reality made simple for him, Thorner blew forth a deep cloud of smoke from his cigar and bellowed—

"Hold it right there, Yama!"

who are you

The words sliced through the lieutenant's brain like daggers, leaving his sensibilities fractured and bleeding. Ignoring the pain being inflicted on his rationality, Thorner stepped beyond mere humanity, retreating into the armor of his office.

"I'm the guy you need to listen to." The big policeman filled the air around his head with another stunning festoon of smoke. "Which makes everything easy if you know what's good for you."

His mind numbing with panic, Zarnak found he could not turn the pages of the book in his hand. Holding the volume with his right hand, he slammed the fingers of his left against the floor, splattering the thick blood there as he snarled;

"Work—damn you—work!"

At the same time, Thorner blew out yet another cloud of smoke, sneering at the ever solidifying Yama, "All you gotta do is take it on the lam, Yam. I'm givin' you just ten seconds to remove your sorry ass to some other jurisdiction, or I'm gonna slam you to a place so dark you'll think you were born blind with your head up your mother's ass. You buy me, dickwad?"

you amuse me, small one

All around Thorner, his men were going slowly mad. At his feet, Zarnak continued to thumb through his book frantically. The lieutenant saw his men staring, blubbering, losing control of their bodily functions one after another. Most of them had already fled the room, stumbling blindly back out of the hold.

They were good men, he thought, but they hadn't seen the things he had seen, weren't as prepared ...

"That's it, Yama," barked the big officer. "It's time to put up or shut up."

Thorner crossed his arms across his chest defiantly. Smoke circling his derby, he could hear Zarnak muttering at his feet in some unknown tongue. Not daring to take his eyes from Yama's now-nearly solid form, the lieutenant demanded;

"What's it gonna be, asshole?"

In response, Yama's horrible laughter echoed through the hold, shaking the plates of the ceiling, sending the bodies of the mutilated sailors swinging wildly. The last of his men long gone, Thorner drew his weapon, aimed it at the center of the growing god-thing before him, and then threw back his head and screamed;

"In the goddamned name of the law!"

Zarnak leaped to his feet as the lieutenant suddenly spun around and fired three times, emptying half the chambers in his revolver not at Yama, but into the horrible deity's high priest as the man made a mad rush for the altar. Retaliating in the name of his fallen servant, the curling mass of ambrosian flesh and fire flashed black, a thousand strands of burning lightning blasting forth from its body.

The fierce bolts were drawn to the corpses hanging throughout the hold, to the slain cultists on the floor, to the officers staggering across the deck. To everywhere. Three passed through Thorner's body, knocking him to his knees. Next to him, Zarnak read the words he had finally discovered.

"Sub pat'kiaa sia, tel tel, gordic trum'el s'a. Yama kel'ay, Yama kel'ay, Yama gibgib' conna gibb'conna ..."

silence!

The doctor turned his head at an angle, arching his body to resist the heated wind blasting forth from Yama's attention. As Thorner staggered back to his feet, Zarnak shouted, "The high priest must not have finished the last invocation. That's why he rushed the altar! I can still reverse the gateway."

"What can I do?"

"Get out of here—get your men off the ship—you, too—go, go now!"

Zarnak whirled back toward the solidifying god-thing behind him and shouted, "Sub pat'kiaa sia, tel gordic trum'el s'a. Yama kel'ay, Yama gibgib' conna, gibgib' conna ..."

As the lieutenant hesitated, Zarnak snarled, "*Go!* And take the high priest's mask with you!"

Thorner ran toward the cultist's body while the doctor turned back toward Yama. He was a child, he knew, a babe with a gun at the end of an alley filled with wild dogs. Yes, he knew what to do—use the gun to shoot the dogs and clean the alley of his enemies. That was the theory.

You Will Cease!

The heat dried the sweat on Zarnak's brow. It boiled the tacky floor and walls, evaporating their coating of blood, eating at their paint. Once more Zarnak said the appointed words.

His mouth could not lubricate itself. He kept his eyes closed, with an arm thrown over them, to save his sense of sight. His once sweltering great coat, now dry and brittle, burst into flames. The doctor knew he could never have faced such a thing as the King of Devils if the god-thing had truly reached our world—but it had not. The last words, those that had to be spoken once Yama's presence was felt, those the great one-time master of Lemuria had been denied.

If I can just ... a part of Zarnak's mind prayed. If I can just ...

Yama erupted forth from his distant dimension once more, filling the hold with another savage burst of searing power. One of the violet shafts slammed against the doctor's right temple, knocking him down as it zig-zagged backward over his head, burning him across his skull to the nape of his neck.

"Sub pat'kiaa sia—"

silence!

Zarnak clawed weakly back to his knees. Then suddenly he flopped to his back, screaming as the inferno finally ate through his coat and peeled away several layers of flesh from his back.

"Tel tel—ahhhhh, ahggghhh—gordic trum'el s'a!"

you will Cease—NowCeaseNow!

"Yama kel'ay," screamed the doctor. Wailing in pain, his open tear ducts painfully dry, he sobbed, "Yama kel'ay, Yama gibgib' conna gibgib' conna ..."

But, even as a part of his mind realized he might possibly succeed, another realization opened, reminding him of what had happened before—to the jitney ...

A fleeing man had left the Congo Lady to spread the word of what was about to happen there. Zarnak had been able to read his intent from the pain he had bled into the streets. The sailor—his car and driver and himself—had been surrounded by a momentary gateway and consumed in a microscopic bit of the fire god's being. For a billionth of a second, the tiniest fraction of Yama had forced its way into our temporal stream and blasted everything within its reach.

At least, thought Zarnak with humble resignation, *I'm the only passenger on the Congo Lady.*

At the same time, he wondered abstractly if any of the vessel's twisted remains would be visible above the water line to mark his grave after the dimensional portal he was sharing with Yama snapped shut. Then, a sudden wild thought filled Zarnak's mind. Emboldened by hope, the doctor embraced mankind's most reckless insanity and spat;

"Yama kel'ay, Yama kel'ay—gibgib' conna gibb'conna gibgib!"

And then, he threw himself forward at the approaching god.

* Interlude *

O utside, the dazed and burned Thorner reeled in scrambling terror as the Congo Lady twisted in on itself, boiling in mid-air, falling into the harbor in an explosion of steam and screaming water. The terrible hiss of hot salt flooded the docks for a moment, then fell away against the breeze coming in off the ocean. As it did the lieutenant scanned the water with fearful diligence, but not a trace could he find of the merchant vessel he had just been aboard. Or half the dock next to it.

Still gripping the scarlet and gold and black mask of the high priest in his hands, Thorner stared at it dumbly for a second. Then, after a single wrenching moment, he laughed, loud and wildly, frightening the living and cursing the dead.

* Epilogue *

"I still can't believe you survived."

The lieutenant looked down at Zarnak's hacking body. Spitting out another lungful of water, the doctor thought to try and explain, but wondered at how he could. In the last instance, when he knew Yama was departing, being pulled back to his own dimension, the doctor had done the only thing he could think of and attempted to step into the fire god's realm.

Being within the gateway—enough of his essence pulled into it by Yama's desire to reach him—he could grasp at its fabric as the King of Devils had grasped at his. Of course, he could no more hold onto it any longer than Yama could his own, but he had hoped, if for that fraction of a millisecond, if the contact with it could render him insubstantial enough...

"Just lucky, I suppose," he said, seeing no reason to burden the big man further. Thorner had carried on when Zarnak himself had frozen. Even if the doctor was never to succumb to such weakness again, he would always owe each new opportunity to confront it to the lieutenant. Sensing Ram Singh's approach from behind the gathering crowd, not questioning his servant's ability to know his business—grateful for it—he said;

"You know, detective, unless I were to die very shortly, and you to live far in excess of the normal human allotment of years, there's very little doubt that I will not outlive you. In fact, I probably already have." Zarnak hacked again suddenly, a last mouthful of water finding its way out of his system. Wiping his mouth, afterward he added a few more words quietly.

"But, all things considered, I'm not at all certain that is the most satisfactory arrangement the Fates could have made when they planned the destinies that would shape the world."

As Zarnak touched at the still smoldering line Yama's touch had zig-zagged across his head, Singh said to Thorner, "Congratulations, lieutenant. That is probably as close to an apology or a giving of thanks that anyone is ever likely to get out of the good Dr. Zarnak."

The officer blinked, his mind already smoothing over several of the things he had seen, readjusting his world enough so that he could remain king of it. Cars full of police poured into the area then, the new arrivals rushing to the aid of Thorner's uniformed officers. As they did, the lieutenant suddenly held up the mask in his hand.

"Bu-hey," he asked. "What'd you make me grab this thing for?"

Taking the heavy wooden piece from Thorner in both hands, the doctor stared at it and smiled.

"Quite simple, Lieutenant," answered the doctor with a lie as he laughed at his audacious good fortune. "I wanted a souvenir for my office."

And then, Thorner threw back his head and laughed once more. It was a clean and happy sound this time, however, and it stepped on the last traces of the King of Devils as a dog would an ant. Breaking off the joyful noise finally, though, the big man took Zarnak's hand and shook it, asking;

"Have you ever had a 'gin and sin?'" When the doctor admitted he had not, Thorner smiled. "A little orange juice, some lemon, a dash of grenadine ... and a bathtub full of gin. You'll love 'em."

"Perhaps," said Zarnak, warmly humble at the feel of the sun on his grateful cheek, "I will. Perhaps I will."

Our second story is CJ's second Zarnak story, but our reason for running it here is it also contains H.P. Lovecraft's remarkably resilient character, Inspector Legrasse. Taking over the duty of continuing the inspector's adventures (something Lovecraft himself confined to only the middle section of his seminal story **Call of Cthulhu**), *CJ has written enough further tales to fill an entire book (**The Tales of Inspector Legrasse**, available from Mythos Books), along with the original novel **To Battle Beyond** (available from Marietta Publishing). His insights into both of these characters, as well as their creators, is nowhere more evident that in this story—*

To Cast Out Fear

"There is no fear in love; but perfect love casteth out fear."

— St. John

* The Meeting *

Dr. Anton Zarnak slammed away at the nail, determined to move it to his will. Striking it and the wall around it several more times each, he grasped the nail and pulled at it to prove that it would hold solid. When the test concluded positively he smiled and dropped the hammer without regard, his attention firmly focused on reaching for the wooden mask waiting for him on his desk.

It was a leering thing, a gaudy horror painted in scarlet, black and gold. Its three eyes glared upward as the doctor's fingers ensnared it, the stylized flames pouring from its fanged mouth and glared nostrils cold to their touch. Hanging the mask against the tortured wall behind his desk, Zarnak stood back to survey his handiwork.

"There," he said with smug satisfaction. "Now it's *my* office."

"Indeed, this is so," replied a tall Hindu standing in the doorway. "But you are still soaking wet from your plunge into the harbor. You must change your clothing and take a meal."

The speaker was Akbar Ram Singh. Several score years earlier he had been charged by the monks of A'alshirie, a cold land hidden deep within the Himalayas, to stand as servant to whomever they sent to be master of their watchport on the other side of the world. The day previous, they had sent him Dr. Anton Zarnak. Before the doctor could unpack his bag, however, he had been pulled into an investigation—one which had threatened to loosen a black and monstrous demon upon the world, plunging the entire galaxy into charred and burning ruin. The encounter had almost cost the doctor his life. He had survived, however, taking the mask of the horror's high priest as his souvenir—the first prize dragged back by him to Number Thirteen China Alley.

Cold and wet, tired, his clothing stuck to his skin, head still smarting fiercely from the effects of one of the fire devil's blasts, Zarnak stared at the captured mask with triumph. Although a part of his brain questioned whether or not he might survive another such confrontation to ever bring home a second trophy, all he said aloud was;

"It really does look good there, don't you think?"

"Yes, sahib," answered Singh, already sensing more about his new master than the doctor could have suspected. "You are a shred and insightful decorator. Now, if you might turn your attentions to the hot bath I have drawn and the dinner awaiting you, perhaps you might live to garner another such trophy."

And then it was that the knocking began. It was a politely discreet, uniform summons. But there was more to it—a feel of command, an understanding that the knocker expected immediate attention. Singh directed his master once more toward the joys of the steaming bath awaiting him. In A'alshirie, Zarnak had learned the secrets of speeding his heart rate to warm himself. He had also learned to ignore the cold, physical pain and hunger as well as techniques to dispel more esoteric cripplers such as depression, fear, anxiety and all of their sisters.

Even so, he mused, a hot bath did sound most wonderful. After all, considering what he had just been through, who deserved a spot of comfort more than himself? Zarnak was just stripping off his harbor-drenched shirt when the door to his office opened once more.

"I am sorry, master," said Ram Singh, "but it seems that perhaps an interruption is necessary, after all."

A man carrying a package no larger than a loaf of bread entered the room. He was tall and thick-boned, a hard man who held a dangerously cold fire burning within his dark eyes, eyes that were etching their estimation of Zarnak into some unknown ledger. As the master of 13 China

Alley moved forward, the stranger spoke.

"I have been informed by your man-servant that you are not actually he whom I came seeking."

"I assume that means you came looking for Dr. Guicet," answered Zarnak. When the stranger nodded, his wet and tired host told him, "I'm sorry to have to inform you that the doctor has ... shall we say, left the premises. Abruptly, yes. But, anyway—an action which has necessitated his being replaced ... by myself. I am Dr. Anton Zarnak. May I be of some assistance to you, sir?"

"I don't know," the stranger replied with an abrupt and candid honesty. "But if you can't, then a vast number of people—perhaps all the masses of the world—are in a great deal of danger."

"And you would know all this because ...?"

"Because for quite some time I have lived in nightmare, and now know the smell of it when it descends upon the land. I am John Raymond Legrasse, Dr. Zarnak—former inspector of police for the City of New Orleans—and I have learned what signs may be ignored and which must be acted upon. To be blunt, I have seem more than one such of these portents recently. One of them named your Dr. Guicet. And, if what killed him is that which I fear, perhaps I am already too late."

"Ah, my," answered Zarnak, finishing the peeling away of his still dripping shirt. "Well ... so much for my bath."

* The Black Statue*

After Singh had brought him a thick cotton robe, Zarnak took the chair behind his desk. The mask of Yama watching all that transpired below, the doctor narrowed his eyes, studying the tall, thick-boned man before him. Quietly pulling a long breath into his lungs, Zarnak probed the air between himself and his visitor. He could sense immediately that Legrasse had not come to him with anything but business most urgent. There was more, however.

A dark, rank odor clouded the ether around his guest, a sinister presence clawing at the man's soul, a thing that so far Legrasse had managed to resist. But, Zarnak could tell from the look swimming in the corners of the man's eyes that how much longer he could resist was anyone's guess. Fatigued to the depths of his own soul, the doctor nonetheless held out his hand and said;

"All right, let's see it."

Somewhat surprised, but understanding, Legrasse reached into the package he had brought with him, instructing his host at the same time, "For your own safety, sir, until I have told you the rest of my story, please do not touch the artifact you are about to see."

Then, carefully keeping a thick rag between his hand and the contents of the box, Legrasse produced the "it" in question. "It" was a statue—a diminutive figure between seven and eight inches in height, a relic of exquisitely artistic workmanship. It was also a thing whose utter strangeness caused Zarnak's left eyebrow to lift dramatically. The horror of the piece lashed out at the doctor with its customary force. It did not frighten the man, however, a fact Legrasse noted with relieved satisfaction as he carefully set the piece down on Zarnak's desk so the doctor might view it more clearly.

The statue represented a monster of vaguely anthropoid outline, but with an octopus-like head whose face was a mask of feelers, a scaly, rubbery-looking body, prodigious claws on hind and fore feet, and long, narrow wings behind. The creature had been depicted with a round and bloated corpulence. It squatted firmly on a squarish stand etched with hieroglyphics so foreign that even Zarnak did not recognize the majority of them. The tips of the creature's wings stroked the furthest most edge of its stand while the long, curved claws of its doubled-up, crouching hind legs gripped the front edge and extended a quarter of the way down toward the bottom of the pedestal. None of that was what its viewers found so disturbing about the piece, however.

Slouching forward over a scaly and rubbery chest, the figure's cephalopod head was bent forward so that the ends of its facial feelers brushed the backs of the huge fore paws which clasped the croucher's elevated knees. The awkwardly formed cranium was tilted at an odd direction, an angle which forced its audiences to turn their own heads this way and that to get a clear view at the statue's eyes. Once accomplished, such a view left most individuals shaken and sweating.

Tiny they were, cold and silent, without depth or expression. Indeed, no great care had been taken by the figure's unknown sculptor in creating its eyes. They were, actually, mere circular gouges in the stone, neither uniform nor detailed. But still, somehow they had the power to command those who grew too near to it, to fill their minds with disquieting notions and sounds they had not heard since they were children—alone in the dark.

"Quite a find," said Zarnak finally. "But tell me, what connection has this thing with the horrors you mentioned earlier?"

The doctor kept his eyes riveted to the statue, motioning Legrasse to take a seat at the same time. The thick-boned man did so, gratefully, then began to speak once more, his eyes locking on the doctor.

"This is not the first of these statues I've come across. Some weeks ago, before I knew anything of the world beyond the one into which I had been born, this horror's twin came into my possession. At first, I thought it was a herald of something groping its way toward us. Recently, however, things have begun to happen that lead me to believe that whatever it is has actually gained purchase on our doorstep."

"The figure in the statue?"

"It, or one of its fellows," answered Legrasse. "My assumption is that either will be bad enough."

The doctor stared at the horrid length of ebony stone for a last, long moment. He did not have to decide as to whether or not his guest was correct in his assumptions. There was no doubt in Zarnak's mind that the paltry few inches of carved rock before him did not merely represent some terrible evil, but that the thing itself was a danger both loathsome and cruel.

"Let me assure you that I concur," said Zarnak finally. "I wish I didn't. Quite honestly, I've been most severely taxed of recent and would be much happier if I could brand you a lunatic and have my servant show you to the door. But, since such is not the case, it's obviously best we get down to business. Would you mind if I took my meal while we spoke? Are you hungry yourself?"

Legrasse declined Zarnak's offer, but insisted that the doctor have his own meal. In seconds Singh returned with a tray containing bok choi soup, chopped yellow bean sprouts with beef and pepper along with a main course of chicken wings and sliced potatoes in a thick curry gravy. As the servant departed, Legrasse explained that as police inspector he knew the value of a full stomach during an investigation.

"Especially one of these investigations."

"Oh, I agree," added Zarnak as he lifted his soup bowl, Chinese style, to drink directly from its lip. Finishing his sip, he added, "but then, I've always been one to look after my stomach. I studied with an order of monks for ... a number of years. They were always in agreement with Moliere, what was it he said ... 'Il faut manger pour vivre et non pas vivre pour manger' ... 'one should eat to live, not live to eat.' Alas, they were never quite able to win me over."

Legrasse smiled, offering, "Well, as Dr. Johnson said, 'A man seldom thinks with more earnestness of anything than he does of his dinner.'"

Delighted to be caught off-guard by his guest's unsuspected erudition, Zarnak thumped his desk top, laughing hard, spilling a few drops of soup, dribbling several more from his lips. His smile broadening into something warmer, he called out to Ram Singh. As the Hindu entered the room, the doctor told him;

"Mr. Legrasse will be joining me for dinner." When the inspector made to protest, Zarnak asked him, "Please, my friend, if we are to go rushing off to our deaths, whose advice shall we follow on the way, Moliere's or the good Dr. Johnson's?"

Smiling back at Zarnak, understanding him completely, Legrasse nodded to Singh, adding, "And if I might, sir, a double helping of those delicious smelling potatoes and chicken wings."

Ram Singh let it be known that performing no other task could please him more greatly. Then, as the Hindu left the room, Zarnak pulled a meat-freed chicken bone from his mouth.

"Now, sir," he said, wiping his fingers with a linen napkin as he spoke, "while your plate is being warmed, tell me something of yourself, and about this horror that is racing toward us. And, if at all possible, could you try to make your story last long enough to take us through to coffee?"

* The Inspector's Story *

"So," said Zarnak, his brain struggling against the extra blood his stomach was pumping to it in an effort to slow his internal processes to the point where he might cease contemplating moving from his chair, "as Inspector of Police in New Orleans you came across a cult of devil worshipers who called down an insanity from the sky. You slaughtered most of the cult and called in the Navy to tackle the monster."

Pushing his plate away from himself, Zarnak stretched his arms out to his sides, pulling at the kinks forming in his shoulders. His left hand shooting back suddenly to cover a yawn, he stifled it, then added, "Quite a story."

"Yes," Legrasse agreed. "Since the whole affair began, I have witnessed a number of things I wish, quite honestly, I could convince myself were only constructs created by too liberal a dosing of bourbon and mash cherries."

"Why don't you?" asked Zarnak, his eyes narrowing slightly with cynical curiosity.

"Because, doctor, as often as I have desired to return to the simple occupation of police inspector—to dealing with creatures that, while no matter how evil or pathetic or revolting, are still simple human flesh and blood—I can not ignore that which has happened to me. To that which I have been thrust toward head long."

Legrasse paused for a moment, his eyes darting about the Spartan walls of Zarnak's office. Not looking at the doctor—not actually focusing on anything, really—he continued, his voice low and filled with the sad knowledge that wishes were only the blankets children throw over their futures to try and hide their horrible inevitability.

"As I told you, after my first encounter with the dark beyond, a great number of the cultists perished. Many of them, yes. But not all."

"No? And what happened to the rest?"

Legrasse made a sour face. "Some were executed, still more committed suicide. But one, one had an incredible experience—a stroke of fortune I am ill-disposed to assigned to any agency other than Providence. The man was being transported from the asylum to the inevitable gallows that awaited him. Along the way, the vehicle—on a day as clear as the fate of the ignorant—was struck by lightning generated from a cloudless sky. Selective of its target, the bolt touched only the cultist, an itinerate seaman by the name of Maurizio."

At that moment, Ram Singh entered the room with a tray supporting a bottle of port and two glasses. Twisting away the last tendril of dusty cobwebbing still clinging to the neck of the bottle, the Hindu removed the cork, offering the crystal-encased affair to Zarnak. The doctor sniffed absently at the bouquet saying that he would pour later, thanking Singh, not needing to dismiss the servant as the man immediately took his leave. Nodding, Zarnak signalled Legrasse to continue.

"The officers with him were amazed—that they had not been struck, that Maurizio lived, that lightning could have been produced on such a day. But, the most surprising thing was the effect the mysterious bolt had on their prisoner."

"Yes?" asked Zarnak, leaning forward with the beginnings of curiosity.

"The man became a changed person. You see, sir, before that moment Maurizio had proved to be of a low, mixed blood, mentally aberrant—a degraded and ignorant man who worshipped, as he so sadly put it, 'the Great Old Ones who lived ages before there were any men, who ...'"

"'Who came,'" interrupted Zarnak with a bored flourish, "'to our world out of the sky when mankind was but undreamed of.' Yes, forgive me, Legrasse, but I know all about the Old Ones and their sanctuaries inside the Earth and under the seas, where they wait to return to be masters of us all."

Taking up the bottle Singh had brought earlier, Zarnak held it over the glass closest to the ex-inspector of police. Legrasse nodded politely. As the doctor poured, he admitted, "I apologize for the show of nerves. My problem is that the cults of the Elder Gods never seem to die. They remain constant, hidden in distant wastes and dark places all across the face of our world. They imagine that someday great Cthulhu will rise from his dark house in R'lyeh under the waters, and again bring the planet under his sway. My particular edginess in this matter is that, like yourself, I have lived through one of these attempted liberations. The only difference is, mine ended perhaps an hour ago."

"And you're ready to charge forth once more ..." Legrasse marveled. "Fire in the belly, eh? I was, I must admit, feeling somewhat the fool for thinking of challenging the darkness again, but with such an example..."

"Don't be too in awe of my recuperative powers," admitted Zarnak with surprising humility. "I was trained for this work, for far more years than you could guess. And, still I almost failed—would have failed, if not, in fact, for the intervention of a police lieutenant. So please ... your story?"

"Yes, uh well, Maurizio. After his accident, he seemed a changed man. He wept freely, babbling about 'the veil being lifted from his eyes' and so forth. To draw to the point, let me say that the man was judged to be once more in possession of his faculties. He also immediately jumped at the chance to make up for his crimes which he claimed were all committed under a horrible fog."

"Fog?"

"He claimed he had acted as if under a spell—in a trance, as it were. Perhaps we who live in New Orleans take such things too much for granted, but ..."

"No, no," answered the doctor. "Now, it actually isn't usual for the elder cults to work with such—there've always been enough volunteers to swell their fetid ranks—but still ..." Zarnak contemplated what he had heard for a moment longer, then suddenly dismissed his doubts and instructed Legrasse to continue.

The inspector told him that Maurizio revealed many secrets of the cult. The seamen led the police to several warrens situated in the least reputable parts of New Orleans, odious centers of filth and depravity, all of them turning out to be connected to the city's sewer system. They were places that had obviously been in use until only a short time earlier, each offered up to the investigators all manner of clues to crimes committed on the premises—blood-soaked floors, furniture crafted from human bones, cushions and drapes fashioned from vulgar peels of human skin—barrels of revolting, sickening evidence of a hundred years' worth of monstrous depravities.

Legrasse, although no longer an inspector, was none-the-less invited along to lend whatever special expertise he might have to the investigation. After he and the police had rummaged through the debris of all the various lairs to which Maurizio could lead them, the seaman had taken them to one final site. Deep in the sewers, it was a large, even spacious, room that served as a main flow-way for the city's sewage. It was the last area known to him which had any relevance to the cultists. It was also to have been there that the blasphemous worshippers were to hold their next and, Maurizio had believed, final damnable ceremony.

"When I asked him what led him to believe that," Legrasse said, "he beckoned us forward toward the wall furthest from our position. We made our way carefully over the wet and treacherous stone flooring to find a breech in the wall, one disguised by an ingenious counterfeit section of brick."

Legrasse shifted uncomfortably in his seat, then said, "At this point Maurizio smiled. He told me that he could not explain what he was about to show me, but that I could find the answers I needed at Thirteen China Alley in New York City, from a Dr. Guicet. I made a note of the name and address. While I was busied writing, it happened."

Pointing toward the repellent figurine on Zarnak's desk, the inspector said, "Reaching inside the hidden chamber, Maurizio pulled forth ... that."

At this point Legrasse stopped speaking. He held his lips tightly, one against the other for a brief moment, obviously pausing to arrange his next words carefully. Zarnak sat back patiently, still feeling the effects of their meal, just beginning to feel the effects of the port. After only a few seconds, however, Legrasse began again.

"I must admit, up until that moment I had held some reservations about Maurizio. Perhaps I was just hanging on to the normal paranoia of a policeman, but I had felt all along that the seaman was, although certainly transformed from his former self, still not dealing top deck—holding something back, as it were. What happened next changed my mind."

To the untrained eye, Zarnak's mood seemed to show no change. The inspector noted several small things, however, unconscious, practically imperceptible fluctuations in the doctor—in his breathing, the focus of his eyes, et cetera—that allowed Legrasse to know that his host's interest had suddenly intensified greatly. Having no desire to disappoint him, Legrasse continued his tale.

"The man started to hand the statue over to us, when suddenly he began shaking. Froth appeared upon his lips, his eyes bulged, his longish hair flailing wildly. He tried to throw the statue from his hand, but it had burned itself to his palm. The smell of searing flesh filling the chamber, overwhelming the putrid aroma of the place. Two of the other officers on the scene, suspecting a seizure of some kind, tried to wrestle the seaman to the ground. A good-hearted gesture, but a terrible mistake."

"Why, what occurred—exactly?"

"Maurizio began to scream—if 'scream' is even the proper word. What to use in its place ... wail, perhaps? Shriek? Screech? I pause at this because, although the noises bursting forth from the man were certainly cries of pain, they were more than that. They were beyond the sounds a human throat can produce—beyond the shrill of birds, even. They were the vibrations of agony, and I will take their memory with me to the grave, as I will the sight of what happened next."

Stiffness assaulted Legrasse. He bowed his head slightly, not able to meet Zarnak's gaze, needing to cut himself off from even that slight human contact to be able to finish his story.

"The man's eyes exploded at that point. They had been bulging horribly, but then the expanded skin of them simply popped, blood and fluid shooting outward. His brain followed suit, boiling within his skull until a second later the room was filled with a burning shatter of blood and tissue. The two officers holding Maurizio down released him at that point, of course, but it was too late."

Zarnak sat silent, strong suspicions as to what came next shouting through his brain.

"A gaggle of thin, reed-like tendrils burst forth from the center of Maurizio's body. Lashing wildly, they adhered to whatever they came in contact with, slashing and choking. A number of us, we retreated as far as possible in the confined space, as quickly as we could over the slippery stones ... some of the others, however, were paralyzed, understandably panicked by the sight. Having more experience than the rest in such matters ... I was able to withdraw my revolver and begin firing. That ... that was all it took to snap the others out of their shock."

Legrasse went silent for a moment, his mind filled with the memory of himself and the officers with him blasting the transforming carcass— along with its two helpless captives. The inspector knew the pair stood no chance of surviving, that indeed they were dead already. Still he had wept as his finger closed again and again on his trigger. As he wept once more in Zarnak's office.

Tactfully ignoring the strength of Legrasse's emotion, the doctor nonetheless was somewhat startled by his guest's remorse. To Zarnak, Legrasse had acted properly. The men were lost. Any bullets that struck them not only assuredly had helped put them out of their misery, but may have actually been a blessing. The doctor wondered if he himself was even actually capable of experiencing such deep regrets over a situation in which he triumphed by doing the correct thing. Finally dismissing the question as a mere intellectual exercise, however, the doctor continued.

"So." he said simply, "with no other avenue open to you, you followed your only clue, which has led you here to me."

"Yes," agreed Legrasse. "And sir, now that I am here and you have heard my story, what do you think we should, or even *could* do next?"

"I would suppose," answered Zarnak, shifting his gaze once more to the statue in the middle of his desk, "considering what happened to the last person who touched this thing, that we should try to find someone who *can* put their hands on it."

* The Ebony Harlot *

"And that's all you want?"

The African woman sat in the chair next to Legrasse's, staring at the stone horror on Zarnak's desk. The doctor noted the woman's mocking tone, but he was not sure as to exactly what it was she was mocking. His other guest had no such uncertainties.

"Fear becomes your type," said the ex-inspector with a sneer, "doesn't it?"

"You so big the ugly ol' beyond don't put the fright in your bones, you reach into its heart and pull out some answers."

"Madame Sarna La Raniella," Zarnak interrupted. "Let us not allow ourselves to be sidetracked. I would extend this suggestion to you as well, Inspector Legrasse."

"Legrasse, is it?" said the black woman with apprehensive surprise. "Legrasse." The word hung in the air like an accusation, or a prayer. Madame La Raniella's dark eyes narrowed sharply. Her nostrils flaring, she shifted in her seat, turning to face the one-time policeman.

"Legrasse ... you far from home—'cept you got no home. You could root like a mushroom in de deep black shadows, but it wouldn't matter. You ain't got no place what will hold you to its breast now. No place that foolish. You a traveller, now. You walk de silver path. Dangerous for a stiff white man—your mind not flexible, can't bend really, can't stretch far enough."

"You listen to me, *Madame*," growled Legrasse. "You've heard of me—good. That means you know what I'll tolerate and what I'm capable of. As for your comments on my stiff, white man's mind, to date it's stretched admirably enough to keep me alive through everything your gruesome swamp friends and their Hellish playthings have been able to throw at me."

Pointing to the statue once more, he added, "And it's stretched far enough to bring me here with that horror tucked under my arm. Now, if you can help us determine what Dr. Zarnak's predecessor would have been able to tell us about it, then please, *Madame*, by all means, spin your own particular brand of voodoo. I promise to be most suitably impressed. But, if you have nothing more to offer than gibes and speeches, I assure you that we can acquire all we need of those on any corner from the soapbox socialists."

Madame La Raniella nodded her head, her full lips smiling in satisfaction. "They say you one tough patch of weeds, Legrasse. Maybe you won't get us all elected to de grave after all. Very well, let's review."

The woman dragged a small, but thick stone dish from her bag, as well as an opaque bottle. Pouring a thick dollop of a shimmering green syrup into the dish, she struck a match and lit the center of the resulting puddle. As it began to burn with a thin, mostly blue flame, she pulled back the light veil of her hat, then removed the wide brimmed affair altogether.

"You have seen de other side, both you two. Doctor, if you de good Guicet's replacement, that's enough for me. And Legrasse, as you say, the underworld is aswirl with tales of you amazing ability to alive remain. Meeting you now in person, I think this is maybe not being a fluke."

With a shrug bordering on the sensual, the woman knocked her shawl back from her shoulders. The colorfully embroidered black silk slid over the top of her chair, drifting to the floor, landing soundlessly. Waving her hand over the dish, she extinguished the growing flame, replacing it with a smoldering billow of exotically scented smoke. As its bluish tendrils drifted toward the statue next to it, La Raniella said softly;

"Legrasse, you had one o' dese before and blew it to Hell. Now another comes to you—looks the same, but de bite is different."

The woman stared at the statue as she rose from her seat. Stepping out of her shoes, she shoved them under her chair with small, casual movements, her eyes never leaving the nightmarish bit of stone.

"The first was a magnet ... call things to it. But you, my ugly little child ..." La Raniella's supple fingers reached out for the statue, turning only at the last second, drifting by mockingly as she whispered, "what kind o' thing be *you*?"

The belt holding the woman's skirt somehow came undone, allowing her to step out of it even as she bent her shoulders backward so that her jacket could slide to the floor as well. Her hands glided up the front of her blouse, undoing its buttons with a casual salaciousness that made Legrasse uncomfortable in particular. As she shrugged away that bit of cloth, her arms moving to some unheard rhythm, legs bending, hips swaying, the circle of her movement expanding with each rotation, the inspector bent his head toward Zarnak.

"Doctor, what in the name of Heaven ..."

"A powerful place, my friend," answered Zarnak. "But one that has no answers here. I believe Madame La Raniella is attempting to, as the sophisticates might say, create an *atmosphere*."

"You right about that, doctor," purred the black woman as she rocked from side to side. "De elder things ... dey know many hungers ... but dis hunger ... dey don't know. Dey don't understand. But you do, don't you, doctor?"

Before Zarnak could answer, La Raniella began to make her way around his over-sized desk. The mask of Yama leering down in approval, the woman released her undergarments one by one. Her motions were unlike anything either man expected, remarkably fluid, the silken scraps offering no resistance, falling to the floor like spring rain. Softly. Quietly. Their tender warmth unnoticed, the two men thought only on the storm to come.

"De elder things," whispered La Raniella from deep within her throat, "dey don't feel de lust for flesh, dey don't hear no blood pounding in der ears. Dey be cold things, swimming in blackness, their only interest in what dey can digest. Not like men ..."

The woman's toes dragged suggestively along Zarnak's thigh as she lifted her left foot over his right leg. In a husky whisper, she breathed steam into the doctor's ear.

"Not like you."

Legrasse pulled at his dampening collar, feeling the embarrassed moisture gathering within its fabric. As a police officer he had seen many and varied things in the dark underworld of New Orleans, but his badge had held power against them. Now, citizen Legrasse sat helplessly, watching the serpentine woman's limbs encircle Zarnak suggestively, listening to the overpowering beat of her bangles and bracelets as they rattled against each other. Listening to the growing throb of his own blood blasting through his veins. Smelling the growing passion within the office's ever shrinking boundaries.

"Can you feel me, doctor?" moaned the woman as she slid her legs and buttocks across Zarnak's chest. "Do your fingers tingle, dying to touch? Is your tongue drowning? Does it ache, begging to be released from your mouth like a hungry viper?"

Zarnak nodded involuntarily. On one level he knew the woman was merely performing a ritual, setting forth a deceptive smoke screen under the cover of which she might handle the artifact upon his desk in safety. On a deeper, more personal level, however, his objectivity was clouding terribly. For all the control he had been taught in A'alshirie, the techniques availed him naught if he declined to use them. And, such was the case at that moment.

The feel of Madame La Raniella against his body—the smooth, frictionless sheen of her skin, the pulsating warmth that rippled outward from her muscles, the dripping, animal call of her mesmerizing voice—all of that coupled with the years he had spent apart from the female species in general had combined to infect him with an irresistible madness.

Nor could it have been any other way. The witch woman's potent smoke filling the doctor's office, her burning words spinning within his mind, each movement of her body, every clang of her carefully arranged jewelry was designed to arouse and enslave. Watching Zarnak slowly succumbing to Madame La Raniella's spell, Legrasse had to admit that if the gyrating woman were sitting on his lap, that he would be faring no better. And then, the wet smell of the room telling the witch that she had done all she could in the way of preparations, the woman reached out and took up the statue before her.

"Now ... what be you, eh, little child? What way mama got to stroke you to make you hers?"

Legrasse stared, his fingers nervously twitching, inching their way slowly toward his concealed pistol. If the same scene were to be replayed that he had witnessed in the sewer, if the same blinding speed were to follow, when he was still so close ...

The former inspector undid his jacket's buttons, fighting the part of his brain urging him to throw off all his clothes. His eyes, straining to stay on the horrid figurine, drifting ever upward toward the magnificent breasts, the wet lips, the dark, bottomless eyes ...

Zarnak noticed the shift first—long before Legrasse, even before Madame La Raniella who was in firm contact with the conduit. Banishing his fever as best he could, the doctor narrowed his vision, then shook his head, catching his guest's attention. As Legrasse stared, wondering what Zarnak was up to, the melodic cadence of the woman's words suddenly shattered, replaced by a series of stumbling questions and observations.

"What's that? Who calls?" a fascinated horror tinged La Raniella's voice. "Cold the smell ... dark cold, old and wet ... green and great and wet and old ... what you want dis place? What you want, Guicet?"

A vortex of sound filtered through the stone and wood and plaster of the walls, a dread pulse slapping at the tender flesh filling the room, organizing itself into words in the same fashion that grease formed puddles.

Guicet is no more with you

"We know that ..." answered Zarnak. "Are you responsible for his demise?"

Demise—the word was chuckled—*We are responsible for all things*

"What do you want here?" snarled Legrasse with a desperate relief at finally having something else to concentrate upon. As the inspector unlimbered his sidearm, the voice continued leaking into Zarnak's office.

Most interesting, it sniffed. *You have blocked us. We can see you, but cannot touch you ... for the moment. Intriguing*

"Answer the question," snapped Zarnak. "What do you want here? Name yourself."

"No, no," cried Madame La Raniella. Her voice small and frightened, she warned, "it's reach is shortened only by that which it does not understand—you can not confront such a power, you fools! Not here—not unprepared."

Too late, small thing. They already have

Before any of the three could react, a stygian length of force, a thing not muscle nor skin nor flesh of any kind, but a roping coil of self-conscious power exploded forth from the statue on Zarnak's desk. The undescribable essence slammed into the ceiling, driving a vast and wicked hole through to the next floor without injuring itself in any fashion.

Legrasse jerked free his pistol, jammed the barrel against the side of the frightening intensity and then pulled the trigger. One shot was all he got. The collision of separate universes exploded with a violence none of the humans present had ever before contemplated. Legrasse's weapon did not explode—there was no time for such a simple reaction. The device was instead transformed into a pure state of excited atoms, the interaction of which hurled the inspector across the room. Legrasse collided with the wall, hitting it hard enough to leave an impression detailing half his body.

At the same time Zarnak and Madame La Raniella scrambled away from the unleashed fury slashing out from the center of the desktop, even as its voice crackled through the room once more.

Guicet gone ... a good start. Soon you shall join him

Legrasse struggled to his hands and knees. Above him, the ceiling exploded in sparks and fire. A rainbow of unexplainable colors shattered the room's natural light, distorting not only the look of everything, but its feel as well. With a breath the pulsating maelstrom expanded, shattering the desk beneath, filling the air with splinters of wood and metal.

So few there are to stand against us. And so easily toppled You are the last

Crawling back to his feet, Legrasse grabbed up the over-turned chair he had been sitting in moments earlier. Hurling it at the ever-growing vortex, he shouted to Zarnak.

"The witch's spell! You have—"

Human sound was pulverized as the wood and leather touched the nether dank spinning in the center of the room. Once more Legrasse was thrown from his feet, once more hitting the wall as if flung from a speeding train. Slamming into the already shattered divider face first, the inspector's nose was broken, his forehead laid open, his jaw dislocated. From across a trillion miles of time, the unnamed presence stopped to laugh.

It was a cruel sound—mocking and pitiless—every syllable of its mind-wrenching trill steeped in a cold and passionless malevolence that struck all who heard it with an awesome terror. Outside Number Thirteen China Alley, those few people who braved the ancient street's greasy cobblestones fell to their knees in mindless horror, grasping their heads, retching their dinners, screaming as they felt the fabric of their souls being plucked and shredded.

Lying on the floor, panting, entangled limb to limb with Madame La Raniella, Zarnak tried to clear his throbbing head. The unknown force dragging its way into his dimension through the conduit opened by the now disintegrated statue had to be stopped. But, numbing his brain against the panic it wished to experience, calming his breathing, Zarnak could see no way to stem the tide. Maybe if he could get to his books, if he had hours to investigate the proper texts, there were people he could consult ...

The witches' spell ... you have ...

But no, he could not conduct a proper investigation—not the clever and swaggering Anton Zarnak. Several hours earlier his arrogance had gifted him with a lightning blast that left a jagged scar across the top of his head. Now, it seemed he had pushed himself and those with him into a plain and solid corner from which there was no escape ...

The witches' spell ... you have ...

Legrasse was moaning something across the room, but the doctor could not make out his words. The inspector's jaw was broken, and there was so much noise, so much confusion—La Raniella, filling the air with terror, her mind drained of hope, the atmosphere one of dread and frenzy...

The witches' spell ... you have ...

And then, suddenly, Zarnak understood. Grasping the thrashing, terrified witch woman on the floor next to him, his hands gripping her head tightly, he forced her eyes to his. Locking his gaze on hers, the doctor caught her attention with a blinding flash of force. He pushed the radiant moment outward with desperate hope, plunging his heart into free fall as he blurted—

"I love you!"

Several of the colors flowing outward from the center of Zarnak's desk were suddenly stripped from the visible spectrum. The tendril of solidifying energy snapped sharply, its probing into the Earthly plane cut off as if it had run into a thick and daunting wall.

You will cease!

Lightning, black and pulsating, flashed from the blinded vortex, splashing cruelly against Zarnak's side, burning his arm and ribs, legs, head and shoulder. He did not feel it. Falling further and further into the dark fire that burned within Madame La Raniella's gaze, tears burst forth from his eyes as he cried out;

"I love you now and forever, with all my heart and all my being."

As he had been taught to slow his heart rate by the monks of A'alshirie, to maintain his breathing or to expel his fear, Anton Zarnak had been shown the secrets of controlling all human functions and sensitivities. Moving fearlessly into the depths of his emotional arsenal, he punched his way through La Raniella's spirits' protective doubts, imploring her with a truth that froze time and rationality.

"I love you, Sarna," he implored. "Now and forever—You are my universe, my focus. You are all that I have dreamed of, and every dream I shall ever have. You are my perfection."

Swimming through the madness all around them, Madame La Raniella strained to comprehend what was happening. Her eyes met Zarnak's even as the walls of the room began to snap and shatter. Plaster and ribbing board broke apart and began to swirl through the air, joining the splinters and nails and cracked shards of furniture spinning faster and faster around the exploding onslaught pouring into the room.

I will not be dismissed, ranted the assaulting storm of colors and decay. *I cannot be dismissed!*

"There is no one else for me," screamed Zarnak with passion. "Can not be anyone else for me. For now and all time, my beautiful Sarna ... you are my love!"

The chamber exploded, the shadows hissing, the air burning. Legrasse stared helplessly from the other side of the room. Crumpled in the corner, a pile of forgotten flesh, he could see that Zarnak had understood him. They had been so recklessly eager, allowing the witch woman to set up her veneer of temporary emotion to blind the thing clawing its way toward them, never stopping to consider in their careless rush that such a flimsy veil as desire was easily distracted and torn aside.

Zarnak had restored their fortification with love, however. Daring to reach into his heart with an honest hand, he had stolen the elder thing's glimpse of them by hiding them behind a shield the horror could not understand. He had had no previous feelings for the black woman, had never seen her before Ram Singh had summoned her through the use of Dr. Guicet's files. But that did not matter. Damning the consequences, Zarnak dared all, throwing himself headlong into passion.

But, thought Legrasse, although it can no longer see us, the invader is still secure in its purchase. To actually dislodge the beast is going to take something more ... but what?

Outside in China Alley, people crawled away from Number Thirteen, spilling out of their homes and the neighboring shops, screaming, bleeding, weeping. Above all of Chinatown, from the wharfs on upward toward the heart of the city, darkness filled the air, great purple and green shafts of burning light exploding from the sky, tearing free rooftops, blasting fire through the streets, melting brick and glass and pipe, filling the atmosphere with cinderized atoms.

Inside Number Thirteen, Zarnak pushed his lips against Madame La Raniella's face. He kissed her eyes, her nose, her mouth and neck. He kissed her cheeks, drying her tears with the heat of his ardor, then held his breath in cosmic joy as she whispered with painful understanding, "And I love you," before kissing him squarely back.

Again the barrier was reinforced, again the nightmare was denied. But still not repulsed. And then, Legrasse realized why. Staring at the naked black woman in the white man's arms, watching their souls meet in pure and happy joy, he found the chink in their armor against the elder horror clawing its way toward them.

My God, he realized in shameful understanding, it's me!

Not simply shoving aside his distaste, but hurling it away, smashing it, denying it, Legrasse refused the power to judge, reaching for a higher power, instead. Crawling to his feet, pushing himself against the swirl of wind and hail blasting through the mangled room, the inspector held his hands before his face to turn aside the worst of the flying debris as he stared at Zarnak and La Raniella.

"What?" he asked himself aloud, his broken jaw mangling words and thrashing him with pain. "Tell me what is wrong in what you see."

In the honest depths of his heart, beneath his upbringing and the bigotry with which it had gifted him, Legrasse could find nothing wrong. Through new eyes he saw only two people, suddenly in love, oblivious to all else, with the power to shut out the world.

And, with Legrasse's blessing added to the mix, the veil became a river flowing beyond the clawing hunger's needs. With a rush of sound and color, the doorway faded, the vortex ceased, and three people screamed as the ceiling buckled and collapsed upon them.

* Epilogue *

Several hours later, Ram Singh had finally managed to clear a pathway from the hall into the battered office. He was amazed to find the trio within all still alive. His master's guest had fared the worst. The inspector had suffered a number of broken bones. His head and hands, back and legs and arms had all been torn and slashed in a thousand places. Splinters of wood and glass and metal all lay lodged beneath his skin.

Madame La Raniella and Zarnak had suffered far less physical damage. Ironically, the hard wood mask of the fire demon which the doctor had hung on the wall only hours earlier had fallen over them when the final explosions had slammed them up against the wall. It had leaned over Zarnak and the woman, just managing to support the ceiling beam that had toppled toward them. Even the mask survived nearly intact, only a few miscellaneous bits of its paint being chipped away.

Ignoring the shredded remnants of La Raniella's clothing, Singh instead gave the woman a set of his own pants plus a shift along with an overcoat so that she might make her way home. Zarnak grappled with the pain in his heart, bowing his head slightly as he struggled to return to the world of a few hours previous.

"I, I would like to thank you, Madame La Raniella, for ... for all your assistance." Pointedly eyeing the gold band on the woman's left hand, he asked, "I assume ..."

The woman nodded. Tears filled her eyes. Wiping at her face, lamenting the pain within her own heart, she whispered;

"I'm sorry ... he's a good man ... I couldn't ... my son ..."

And then she turned and fled China Alley, running not so much from the malignant, consuming horror she had witnessed, but from the tender sensuality she had been forced to accept. As real as any love ever felt since the beginning of time, the aching mark of it was carved forever within her heart as it was Zarnak's. A never-ending memory of what could not exist, but had to be.

Ram Singh left at the doctor's command, hurrying to escort Madame La Raniella to her home. She had been summoned to perform a service. The witch woman had risen to the challenge, responding to it with far more of herself than she had ever dreamed she would be called upon to give. At the least, he felt, they owed her safe escort back to the world they had ever destroyed for her.

Besides, thought Zarnak, with Legrasse mercifully unconscious for the moment, best to be alone just now.

Pulling a small set of tweezers from his medical bag, the doctor lay it alongside the scalpel he had already found and laid out. Then, taking a bottle of bourbon he had brought from the kitchen, he poured a healthy portion of alcohol over both instruments.

Legrasse lie on the table where Ram Singh had stretched him out. Still bleeding from a hundred wounds, Zarnak knew the ex-inspector was in for days of terrible pain. His skin had been flayed. Digging all of the splinters out of his body would take hours—every minute of it promising to be mind-numbing torture. Zarnak stared at the one-time policeman, the unlettered street fighter who had somehow thrown aside a life-time of prejudice in an instant for the good of the human race.

"We both gave up things today," muttered the doctor, staring at his unconscious patient. "And we were both injured in the process."

Feeling the longing in his heart for his Sarna, remembering her eyes, the curve of her hip, the way the left side of her upper lip bent when she smiled, the surprising softness of her hair, Zarnak felt his hard-learned controls slipping away. His cheeks moist, chest heaving, he grabbed up the bottle next to him once more and drank until he gagged.

Then, wishing he could take Legrasse's simple agony of a thousand wounds as his own, gifting the inspector with his broken heart instead, Anton Zarnak bent to the task before him. Propped against the wall in the far corner, the mask of Yama sneered at his efforts and laughed at his tears.

This tale contains several elements that will be familiar to long-time CJ fans. First is the setting for the story's beginning, The Narkane, the tavern situated on the nexus of all universes. The second is the most popular character from his Teddy London supernatural detective series, Paul Morcey. This tale was meant to be a comedy. See if you can guess the spot where our author no longer thought the subject was amusing.

The Last Night of the Lazarus Brothers

"Glimmer?" I said the word, givin' it a tone meant to imply I knew what it meant normally, not what it probably meant now. "What the hell is Glimmer?"

Sittin' across from me at my table — well, really, just sorta occupyin' space more than sittin'—was an apparition I'd come to know pretty well over the past few years.

"Glimmer is the latest thing to hit town," answered the wraith. "Very powerful, very addictive, and as you might suspect, very illegal."

"Accordin' to the cops?"

"According to the cops," said the man sittin' with us who looked just like the wraith down to the permanent frown etched in his face, "According to your Aunt Lucille; according to everybody."

That was a mouthful of trouble, and the presence and his doppleganger pal doin' the yakkin' knew what they were talkin' about. The specter in question was the ghost of Lazarus—yeah, John 11:1-44, *that* Lazarus—and he knew exactly how very powerful, very addictive and very illegal this Glimmer crap was.

After all, he was the first immortal it'd killed.

But not yet.

Before thing get too complicated, I'll explain.

My name is Paul Morcey, and I'm a detective. I'm part of the one private investigations firm that can help you with problems that have more to do with phases of the moon and the alignment of the stars than with runnin' background checks or trailin' cheatin' spouses. Now, don't get me wrong, we got nuthin' against good honest work. Hey, I'm tellin' ya, give me a good, old-fashioned search-for-a-high-school-sweetheart job anytime. Cases like that don't tend to turn your hair white, or leave you with your spine pulled out through the back of your neck—you know? I guess it's just that when it comes time for the general population to hire up some protection against those thing that go bump, chew, swallow and burp in the night, we're about the best there is.

All of this comes by way of explainin' how I happen to be on a first name relationship with the Lazarus brothers. Of course, they're not really brothers. As you probably know, Lazarus's been walkin' the Earth ever since Jesus did his PR swing through Bethany and worked his whammy on him. Now, Laz himself says he doesn't understand why he's still mobile. After all, his first question to Jesus when he found himself back in the flesh was whether he was going to die again, and was told;

"'You must go the way of all men.'"

For more than two thousand years he's been waitin' to travel that All Man Highway, but so far he's still kickin'. The strange part is when he first met his ghost. You see, being a made man, supernaturally speakin', it was only a matter of time before he heard about the Narkane and stopped in, which is where he met his dearly-departed self. True to form, his first question to his shade was about dyin'.

When his spirit told him it didn't know how he'd died, or when, but just that he would, Lazarus decided the way of all men was either to accept the absurdities of life, or just go buggie. The Narkane, of course, is the only place the two ever run into each other, and since they're the only people either of them can talk to that know all the same places and people and events and the such that they do, they tend to hang out together a lot. Thus their nickname of the Lazarus brothers.

Anyway, jumpin' back a bit, I must admit I was intrigued by his mention of a new drug. Havin' no better topic at hand myself, I threw us forward into his by askin';

"So, what makes this Glimmer so unique?"

I thought this was an innocent enough question. I had no idea I was invitin' them to challenge me not to hurl. Anyway, with a sad smile on his face, the only kind he's ever been able to manage since findin' out he was goin' ta die again, Laz, he tells me;

"It's made from the bodies of fairies." In a blink I ran so far past "aghast" I couldn't even see the mile marker for it. Tilting my head, perhaps to make room, I squinted as I said;

"Run that horrible thought by me again."

"Yes, don't worry. You heard him correctly."

The ghost of Lazarus nodded after backin' up his better half, then took a moment to knock back a little of his Honolulu cocktail. It's odd, I know, but the disembodied can actually still drink liquor, and it'll effect them just as it did in real life, but—and here comes the real noggin' knuckler—only if it's a drink served with one of those little umbrellas. Even weirder, don't think you can get away with just slammin' a mini-parasol in a boilermaker and then chuggin' yer way to disembodied happiness. Don't work. If it's not a drink that traditionally takes a rainshield, then it's no-taste/big-waste for the spook in question.

What can I say? I don't make the rules in this universe, I just report on them. One tends to pick up a lot of fairly useless, area-specific information when hanging out in the Narkane. But then, for those not in the know, perhaps I should be bringin' you up to speed on that particular piece of real estate.

The Narkane is situated on one'a those nexuses where all possible dimensions lap over and intersect one another. Like mosta these places, on any other day you can watch Judge Crater tossin' one back with an Orc, a couple of Martians and the Buddha; the reanimated corpse of Ed Wood, Jr. hittin' on the bride of Frankenstein, and a poker game seatin' Doc Holliday, the man-eating cow, Santa Claus, a pair of right angles and a set of Siamese triplets, two of whom are Mormons and one who's an Orthodox Jew.

I'm Reform myself. After all, having come in one night when Jesus Christ was on stage, half in his cups, acting as emcee for the wet T-shirt contest (and you don't want a list of what was up on stage there with him), I sorta had to agree my Dad had gone the right way and stay the path myself. Even if that wasn't enough, Lazarus swears by him, so what can I tell ya?

Anyway, I apologize. Get a couple of Tom & Jerry's in me and I can lose focus faster than a program produced by Microsoft. Gettin' back to where I was, Lazarus' wraith was explainin' to me how they manufacture Glimmer. First off, he wasn't kiddin'. The punks makin' this stuff were actually takin' the bodies of dead fairies, dryin' them out, and then grindin' them down into a powder. Of course, the stuff is incredibly powerful. For one thing, it has to be cut with cocaine, one part to six, just to keep it from killin' humans.

"Who's talkin' Glimmer?"

The voice was tiny, but threatenin', the way atom bombs can cause trouble way outta proportion to their size. It belonged to one'a my favorite people, though, Rita Na'jarerr. Rita's a fairy, but understand me, that phrase is meant to be interpreted much like "Marilyn Monroe's a woman," or "money's a concept." Now yeah, I know, when you're in the Narkane there's no set reality by any means, but Rita was actually born in our own surroundin's. In other words, she's one of our world's fairies—and she's one of the coolest babes I know.

Unlike some dimensions, our fairies are a pretty loosely structured bunch. There are biker fairies in the hills of California, Civil War types in Virginia, pirate fairies in London, Viking fairies in Denmark—actually, there's a big bunch of Viking fairies in Brooklyn, too, which I never have been able to figure.

Anyway, fairies are all pretty much the same race, like humans. Their differences are basically only cultural. Of course, there've never been any fairy wars or nuthin'. It's not that they're so much smarter than us; I think it's more that with havin' us around to deal with, where would they find the time?

"Rita," I said, meanin' every word, "you look more beautiful every time I see ya."

"Wish I could say the same for you," she growled at me. I didn't mind. Especially since she flitted up from the bar and rolled herself in my ponytail, purrin';

"Although, I do love your hair."

Rita really is one of the most beautiful of God's creatures. There's plenty of folk what have the idea that all fairies are gorgeous. These are basically the same kinds of people who worship the royal family, or who still believe in socialism. Lemme tell ya, I've seen my share of mule ugly fairies, but Rita ain't one of 'em.

For one thing, she's tall—nearly eight inches, with legs that practically put Sailor Moon's to shame. She's got an hourglass figure with all the sand in the right places, and eyes so intense—one good look from her and you'll know exactly what your place is in the grand scheme of things. She keeps her wings shielded in silver, and has the muscle to make them take her to the lower stratosphere in under ten seconds. Without the extra weight, no one's certain how fast she might be.

Rita don't hang with any one tribe, either. She's a current rider, goin' wherever she feels like, doin' what she wants to at the moment. She's put grub in her sack workin' as everythin' from a spy to an enforcer, and her clients range the spectrum from the U.S. Senate to the Palenoch, and from King Arthur to Ringo Starr.

He'eh, Ringo—have her tell you that story some time. Anyway, wonderin' to what honor we owed her presence that night, I asked. She told me;

"You two are already on it—Glimmer. Some friends of mine have disappeared. Word is these days 'fairie' is just another way of saying 'payday' in this town. Someone's gone into deep manufacture, and things are getting ugly."

I must admit, I went cold. I guess those damn Tom & Jerry's really do slow me down. Up to that point I'd been thinkin' of these lowlifes robbin' fairy graves ... I hadn't swung over to the idea of anyone needin' a high so bad they would start killin' fairies to get it. It was insane; it was a cruelty I could barely imagine.

Ya gotta understand, fairies don't die like you or me. They live so long, that when their personal clock gets punched, they experience the pain of all those years in one long rush. And that wail o'agony, it gets reverberated throughout the universe. You ever suddenly feel a pang of fear, of guilt or terror, a run of needled spider-legs up your spine, the bite of the beast bleedin' joy and love and the feelin' of security outta ya until you find yourself cryin' and you don't know why? You ever did, you were there when a fairy died and you know what I'm talkin' about. You never did, consider yourself lucky.

Anyway, that's what had me so shook, to do that on purpose, to inflict that kinda torment on a livin' thing, and themselves, to be at the epicenter of that—be the cause of it, take the brunt of it—on purpose, just to make drugs ... well, anyway, I could see why Rita was so pissed.

"If it's so popular," I asked, "what's this shit do?"

"Not much for some, but humans," Lazarus spun his hands in the air, then pointed toward his head, whispering, "It gives them the sight."

And there it was in a nutshell. "The sight" is basically the ability to see the entire spectrum of realities. Understand, just because I've had some experiences some of you may not, that don't mean I've got the sight. That's hard come by, let me tell you. My boss, he's got it, but precious few others.

What it does, it allows you to see everything—ghosts, glistenin' fairy trails, all manner of shades and sentient shadows, images trapped in mirrors, the pink of night when the stars talk ta each other—there's no end to it. And all the other senses open up as well.

Suddenly you can hear fish bubblin' one to another, the song of the wind, the death cry of skin as it flakes off your body. And touch, taste and smell? I don't even wanta get started. Suffice it to say that it's not for everybody, but there's a lot of nutjobs out there that think havin' the sight is nigh on to bein' a god. Wonderin' what they were chargin' for godhood by the minute, I asked. Rita gave me the scoop.

"A gram goes for as low as $800 to over ten grand." When my eyes did the Slinky tango, she explained further.

"Quality depends on the fairy—male or female, for instance. Male fairy Glimmer enhances visuals better. Females enhance sound quality."

It made sense. Women are better listeners. There was a lot more. The age of the fairy at death, how long they'd been that way, whether they were winged, or one of the lower classes. It also seemed important as to whether or not they'd been sexually active, for how long, how many different partners, et cetera. Then again, even diet mattered.

"Word is this current ring is grabbing fairies, and then breeding them to specific tolerances. Feeding them certain things, forcing them to have sex, in and outside species ... you want the whole menu?"

I told her "no," and not just to be polite. It was more than disturbin' to think about, it was what they call soul-shreddin'. You hafta understand, thinkin' about somethin' connects you to it. A lotta people, they ain't really matured enough for this to happen. But, sensitivity's a real two way street—insight gained at the shatterin' of illusion.

This prof I know, he talks about everything bein' an illusion, and how the way things are perceived bein' up to the beliefs of the most powerful. Well, if that's the case, those things most powerful in this universe think it's a real nasty when a fairy dies, and even just the concept sickens anyone who can emote in the slightest. I shuddered so hard, my elbow sent the table wobblin', makin' everyone grab for their drinks. Rita asked a lot of questions. She admitted she was fishin', askin' who was in-dimension, what had been spotted and where, had anyone heard of humans ODing from unknown causes, et cetera. She had no leads, no ideas, and was feelin' the frustration.

"You just got back inta town," I told her. "These things take time."

"Thanks, Confucius," she snipped. "Now that you've imparted your great wisdom, I feel so much better."

Our food arrived then and everybody dug in. Havin' got there after we'd ordered, Rita said she'd "just pick." Now she's one gal who can really put it away, but since she's only eight inches tall, even her most impressive feedbag-donin' can't hit you for more than half a burger. With her there, we guys decided to just have a Chinese dinner. All the plates were put in the middle and everybody ate what they wanted. We four shared cottage cheese and fresh pineapple, one Pile O'Pork, a fried zucchini platter, an order of broccoli stuffin' with moonbeam-gravy, three Klondike bars and a half a hollowed-out watermelon full of vodka with fourteen parasols gaily twirlin' across its surface.

The next day I came into work with a worse hangover than the one I was sportin' the day after Aunt Lucille's funeral. It's not that I went crazy at the Narkane, but just sit in there drinkin' nuthin' but spring water ... believe me, the place has its affect. The air is so thoroughly polluted with intoxicants, narcotics, potion's forwarnin' vapors, magical dusts, et cetera, it honestly makes me wonder who even needs drugs? Of course, somethin' like Glimmer, for instance, it wasn't made for people who could spend an evening in the Narkane.

It was for the wannabes, bottomfeedin' molocks who'll do anything to live for a few minutes in a world from which, if they actually understood what they were askin' for, they would run screamin'. Even occasional views into the shadow aisles of reality can get a guy mutilated. A dust that gives people a way to side-step into the dreamplane—this was somethin' I had to believe was a really stupid idea—like NBC cancellin' Classic Trek, or trustin' elected officials.

Laz had said the hangover left by Glimmer was a real gutterslammer, a kick to the walnut bag if ever there was one. I wondered, slumped in the foyer couch, too zammed to limp to my office, if it could possibly be worse than how I felt then. Seein' my condition, Lisa, my other partner in the Agency, she took pity on me and volunteered to do a coffee run, gigglin' while she did so. The gigglin' did not help. She returned with my Mr. Beat cup topped off hot and extra sweet, the way she knows I love it. Then, doll that she is, she let me get a couple of sips in me before she said;

"Oh, and you have a client waiting for you in your office." When I asked who it was, she merely shook her head, sayin';

"Just when I think I might get a handle on what goes on around here, the sun comes up again, and ..."

Lisa let her words trail off, pointin' at the door to my office with an interested look in her eyes. Fillin' myself with the necessity of a Prometheus,

I pulled myself outta the corner of the couch and threw myself in the direction of my office. On the other side of my door, I found;

"Hey, long time no see."

I said the words sub-vocal—thought them, mostly. But that was okay. Ghosts pick up. While I walked as softly as I could to my desk, I whispered;

"What? What could you want?"

"I've been murdered."

I looked up. When he said what he did, I craned my head, forced it to focus. Knowin' I wouldn't like the answer, I still asked, wheezin' as I did so;

"Haven't ... haven't you ... been murdered before?"

"This time it took."

As I gasped for breath, I pulled a water bottle from my lower desk drawer. Opening it, I took a long pull to get my throat workin' and my jaw movin'. Then I splashed my face with it, pourin' what was left over my head, workin' as much as I could into my forehead and neck, lettin' the rest drip down inta my shirt. I wouldn't call myself refreshed, but I was awake enough to concentrate.

"Maybe you shouldn't go to the Narkane," suggested my would-be client.

"If I'm goin' to stay in this line of work, I gotta do the homework. Besides, I might as well have some fun—I mean, how long you think this gig's gonna last? Somethin's gonna have my number on it sooner or later. Every time I turn around, somethin' new is comin' at me."

I gasped then, the pain so sudden and so cripplin' I simply put up my hand and broke communication. Eyes closed, head loose on my shoulders, I felt around blind in my side drawer that held a bottle of all my various pain pills. After knockin' back a handful of who knew what with my coffee, I was just about pulled together when a knock came at the door. Lisa's hand pushed it open without waitin' for me to croak out a response. She knew what kind of shape I was in and I accepted the charity.

"I know you're with a client," her voice called to me, "but there's someone here who might be able to help."

I looked at Dead Laz the way he looked at me. He had come to me to announce someone had finally managed to kill him. Our eyes revealed our possession of the same bit of missin' information, mainly who could have anythin' to tell us before we even knew what was goin' on?

"I know what killed you, Laz."

A shadow formed in the middle of the light comin' into my office from the foyer. Rita buzzed in, tellin' us;

"You were killed with an overdose of Glimmer."

"And how the hell do you know that?" Half-angry, half-confused, Laz's ghost vibrated in a way I'd never seen him move before as he asked, "How the hell did you even know I was finally dead?"

"Mother Nature told me."

And at that moment, I felt the universe begin to collapse inward on me. Only fourteen months earlier in my life, I had been nothin' more than a fairly content maintenance man. It hadn't been all that long I'd been seein' things beyond me comprehension. And, the longer you keep doin' stuff like we do at the London Agency, the harder it is to reach that same inability to maintain your cool.

But suddenly, it was day one again, and all of it was spinnin' my mind like a piece of amusement park art. The ghost of an immortal wanted me to find his killer, someone who apparently had something to do with the Glimmer trade. I had a vengeful fairy who wanted me movin', a calliope-soaked brain filled with wop-wop, and an auto club road planner takin' me straight from my startin' place in safety to a face-to-face with an elemental so pure she made Mother Theresa look like Cruela Deville.

A cool rush of relaxation tidaled over me at that point, and I allowed all my tension to drift away on the wave. After all, I asked myself, what was the point in worrin'? There was no percentage in wastin' time with stuff like that.

Not when I already knew I was doomed.

I wrote my body an IOU and dragged myself back to the hallway. Stumblin' through the handful and a half of steps from the door to the elevator, I got myself inside, downstairs, outside and into a cab. It was a superhuman effort and in a just world I would've been awarded a medal. As it was, I gasped an address to the driver, and we were off.

The address had been given to me by Laz, or more correctly, he had given it to the driver, but it had taken me to do the translation. The driver couldn't see him anymore than he could see Rita. The spot where Lazarus lie dead was down in Chinatown, a good twenty minutes away at that time of day. I announced I should be left alone by the world until we got there. I was talkin' to Rita and Laz, but it didn't hurt for the driver to hear. Grabbin' for the chance to close my eyes the way hungry spiders grab for flies, I turned myself off to the universe, knowin' that even though I was doomed, I now had at least until we reached #11 Mott St. to figure my way out of it.

What you find at that address is a set of restaurants—a walk-up restaurant which is one of the finest in the city, and a walk-down one where they served tourists and greenhorns. Lazarus' body was in one of the booths upstairs, with Lieutenant Evan Delvecio and his main toe-tagger, one Sergeant Anton Thorner, along with a few street badges, tryin' to preserve a crime scene that didn't much look like one.

"Oh my stars and garters, if it isn't one of those wonderful detectives from the London Agency, here to show us poor lowly cops how to do our jobs."

The voice was Thorner's, but the attitude was that of every cop in the joint. Every major police force has someone that handles the "Twilight Zone" cases. Thorner's great-great grandfather, or somethin' like that, was the guy who first did it here in New York City. Delvecio does it now, but he's groomin' Thorner for his shield, which means I get to run into the pair of them every so often.

"Only until you learn to do them for yourselves," I told him. Hung over, I am never in a good mood.

"You two will start nut'in today—you got me?" The lieutenant was apparently not in the mood, which was okay by me, 'cause neither was I. Laz's body was sittin' in a booth, starin' out at the world. His left hand was holdin' a set of chopsticks, a prawn the size of a chicken leg firm in their clutches. It was like any other time I'd seen him there, except the butter and garlic sauce on the prawn had congealed, his eyes weren't movin', and neither was his chest.

Delvecio and I have a standard deal—we tell each other everything we know, we tell the truth, and we try to keep this city in one piece so people can keep enjoyin' it. Ours is a pretty rarified beat, if you know what I mean, and it don't pay to alienate what few people there are that can help you.

What "everything" came down to was that Lazarus had been found by his waiter about two hours earlier. When the initial cops to respond to the call checked Laz's wallet, they found a card orderin' them to call in Delvecio's squad. There's a lot of those cards floatin' around out there. Hell, I got one.

Anyway, Laz had been killed by an overdose of somethin' they couldn't identify. I told them what it was. They hadn't heard of Glimmer yet. Rita filled in Thorner on the details. That the kid could see her without squintin' impressed me. While they did that, Delvecio asked how it was we were so sure it was Glimmer what did Laz in. I told him the answer to that, too.

"Ma Nature?" When I only nodded, an action I made gently and with great care, the lieutenant asked how she knew. Of course, Mother Nature knows everything, and Delvecio knew that. What he was really askin' me was, why'd she give out with the info.

When asked, Rita claimed to be as puzzled as we were. As she told us;

"I have to admit, I didn't think about it. She summoned me; I went immediately—duhhh—and she said she'd heard I was looking into the Glimmer problem. She said I might be curious to know Lazarus had been murdered with it. So I went to find the wraith here," she pointed at Laz's brother, "and I found him with Morcey. He knew to come here, and here we are."

"I notice you said, 'Lazarus had been murdered' rather than that he had OD'd. Why's that?"

"Because, officer," snapped Rita, "that's what she said. I'm just quot..." The fairy's voice trailed off as she made the same connection the lieutenant had made.

"Perhaps," he said, "we should all go see the old lady to discover by what means she has made this monumental discovery, or more to the point with her, why she has chosen to share it with us in this most circuitous fashion."

"Let's go with facts, shall we?" Official heads turned in my direction, lettin' me know I musta been the one talkin'. Givin' out with a look of apology, I added, "Just whadda we know on our own?"

"Not a lot," Thorner admitted. "We recovered traces of a colored powder from the victim's fingers and nostrils. Found a packet of what appears to be the same in his pocket. Our boys are doing interviews with the help right ... in fact," he switched gears as a pair of plainclothes came outta the back;

"It looks like they're done."

Delvecio waved his men over. The didn't have much to report. The only thing they could get more than one staff member to agree on was that Laz had been joined at his table for a moment by a male Caucasian, glasses, large nose, long hair, past the shoulders, greasy, tangled, just beginnin' to go gray, a bit on the heavy side—

"No," said one of them as we tried to put it all together, "not heavy—not solid. Sloppy. A bit on the sloppy side. Like soft fat."

I knew what he meant. Delvecio knew *who*.

"When's the last time anybody saw the Lutheran?"

A vibe ran through the room that let us all know everyone agreed with the lieutenant's guess. Daryl Wittenberg, the Lutheran. He's not a religious fellow; his nickname just ties back to Martin Luther. You know, 1517, the Reformation ... well, maybe before your time. Anyway, convinced we were onto somethin', Delvecio put an APB out on the Lutheran. Then, just as he and his were gettin' set to release Laz's body to the coroner's crew, Rita asked Thorner;

"You said the powder you recovered was colored?" When he acknowledged her good hearin', she asked "what" color. He told her pink and green. That's when things got ugly.

Rita went pale at first, the warm orange of her goin' clammy, drainin' away until her flesh tone had thinned down to a weak lemon. The shine of her hair went pale, brittle, and all the strength in her frame just drizzled away for a moment—a short moment. Before we knew it, her wings started vibratin', first just flitterin', then crashin', howlin', 'til things on the table she was standin' on started blowin' away.

The noise that came out of her was a deep and rendin' screech, a nightmare stab at everyone's souls that peeled our spirits the way a paint scrapper shreds wallpaper, in tearin', gougin' strokes. When the plastic chop sticks started meltin' I caught hold of her, burnin' my hands as I shouted;

"Rita! Get holda yerself!"

It wasn't so much the words, but a human touchin' her that shocked her back to reality. Fairies ain't keen on contact with our kind, and the cold of my mortal flesh held enough terror to bring her outta her rage. Then, for a giant surprise, instead of pullin' away from me like I suspected, Rita flew up against me and threw her arms out, grasping my shoulders. Tears the size of grape seeds splashin' against my jacket, she wailed;

"Sally Jean—they killed him with Sally Jean."

No one else knew what she was talkin' about, but I did. Sally was an extremely young fairy, a baby really. Only a little older than I am. One night at the Narkane, a lowlife had gotten her head twisted and talked her into posin' for a series of skin shots, wings showin'. That was when Rita and I met. She came to the agency to recover the photos. With today's camera tricks, no one woulda been convinced fairies were real just from some photos, but printed they wouldn'ta done Sally no good in her own realm.

It was an easy job, but Rita's always been grateful. Sally Jean was a younglife she was watchin' over, teachin' the ropes. From the way her sobs were shakin' my whole body, it was pretty certain school was out for good.

Somehow her pain banished mine. My hangover was suddenly gone, replaced by an empty hole that was rapidly fillin' up with anger—an anger I could feel bein' matched ounce for ounce in the tiny form clingin' to my shoulder. Everythin' stayed quiet for another minute or so, then Delvecio interrupted things as tactfully as he could, sayin';

"If you two are interested, I just got a call back from downtown. We have a current residence on the Lutheran."

Rita somehow turned around and was suddenly hangin' in the air in front of the lieutenant at a speed none of us could follow. Her look was all he needed. Laz's spirit, Rita and I were all given space in the two squad cars that headed off for Brooklyn. Apparently the Lutheran had taken up in a loft in the former industrial area under the Manhattan bridge. A dump for decades after all the manufacturin' fled the city back in the 60s, it was now one of those highly desirable up-and-comin' neighborhoods—a single train stop away from Manhattan, but with Brooklyn rents.

From Chinatown we were on Pearl St. in less than ten minutes. Of course, sirens do have their way of improvin' traffic flow. Rita hit the front door with a bit of juice and the lock opened nicely. Did the same for the Lutheran's place. Bein' the impetuous types we are, we let ourselves in. Our boy wasn't home, but a few minutes expert explorin', and it was easy to see he'd left us plenty of indication as to where he might be.

One of the shields was left behind to take the Lutheran inta custody if he showed up. The rest of us headed for an address we had a bad feelin' was not gonna make anyone feel any less uncomfortable than they already did. Delvecio requested a SWAT team and was told they'd meet us there. Technically I shouldn't have been there. Of course, neither should Laz's wraith or Rita, either. But, those in Delvecio's unit knew the score. It woulda been useless for them to try and keep Rita or the spirit out.

Oh, don't get me wrong. Delvecio's people ain't no supernatural pygmies or nuthin'. They know ways to stop Other Than Human types, believe me. But, it woulda just been a waste of time that made bad blood all around. They knew Rita would behave herself if allowed to be on site, and besides, it wasn't as if she hadn't worked freelance for the NYPD once or twice over the past fifty years. I think she mighta even introduced Thorner's old man to his wife.

As for me, like I said, Delvecio's unit and the London Agency have an understandin'. Between Rita and Laz, I had a stake in this case, and they knew it. I'd be listed in their report as a freelance expert brought in to identify somethin' we found at Pearl St., soon as we found it.

The immediate problem we discovered upon arrival was that the place from where the Lutheran was dealin' took up half a city block. It was an old plant where God knows what was made until God knows when it shut down. Now it was big, dank and empty-lookin'. Somewhere inside somethin' rotten was goin' on—but where? The back end of the place abutted the East River. If we went in the wrong way, we could lose mosta the rats we were after—maybe all of them.

Thorner suggested lettin' Laz's spirit do a little recon. Since it was acres faster than callin' for heat or voice or motion detection equipment, everyone gave the idea a big thumbs up. Laz dissipated, drifted through the squad car door, then on into the building. While he was gone, the SWAT team arrived, stayin' outta sight a couple blocks away, waitin' for us to call them up.

After some ten, fifteen minutes, the wraith returned. He was lookin' thin and watery, and I knew his time was numbered. He'd been able to remain cohesive while his mortal self had still been alive. But, now that the actual him was finally dead, he was on his way to final breakdown. Gaspin', he floated back inside the car and reported that;

"They're in the basement. They've got hundreds of fairies in breeding cages. Great quantities of Glimmer already processed. The walls are all covered with some sort of dampening foam, the kind that is usually used for soundproofing. This stuff, though, is covered with very specific glyphs. It might be what they use to absorb the death pain."

Laz went over how many exits he had found, where they let out on the outside, how many people total were inside, what kind of security they had, how many were armed, the whole deal. While Thorner and I sat tight, keepin' an eye on as much of the place as we could, Delvecio and the others, includin' Laz, withdrew to where SWAT was waitin' and filled them in as well. They also put their assault plan together and got the place surrounded. Total time since we'd arrived—less than a half hour.

Now, for those of you who formed all your ideas of legal procedure from your televisions, understand that things work kinda different for this level of police work. Waitin' for search warrants could result with a zombie army bein' raised, or a doorway to some dark dimension bein' propped open, or Gods know what. Way too often those tryin' to take care of stuff like this have trouble enough gettin' on site in time. No one's worried about the niceties when the fate of the universe can be at stake.

Besides, even if something like this got to court, who would believe any of it? It's just another reason for the cooperation between the police and guys like me. I'd vouch for them, and they'd vouch for me that none of us was ever anywhere near some place someone thought they saw us.

Halfway through our sittin' around, Laz's wraith started to unravel. He wanted to stick around, wanted to see what happened, but he'd already been on the scene longer than he should—way longer, if you thought about it. There was no time for goodbyes; he simply faded. His atoms driftin' away from each other, he finally went the way of all men—uncomprehendin' as to why he couldn't have just a few more minutes.

Thorner and I didn't have much to say to each other after that. Neither did Rita. We weren't bein' anti-social; after what just happened, we were all just gettin' our heads in the right place for when the signal came to move in. With what we were headed into, the kinda people we were about to deal with, exactly what were we supposed to find to chatter about? Granted, we tried for a moment or two, just to be polite. But, ultimately it came down to silence with three sets of eyes starin' through it toward a shuttered and boarded up mill we knew was sittin' on top of a death chamber.

When Delvecio's signal came we were across the street in seconds, followin' two armored SWAT boys in through the front door. Rita roared past us, the wake of her passage pullin' so much air outta the hallway it was hard to breathe for a moment.

We met scattered resistance on our way to the basement, but nothin' that could stand up. All I could figure was these guys had to feel they'd paid off the right people because they weren't expectin' anythin' more than perhaps a rival gang tryin' to hit them. Their weapons were standard issue, nothin' fancy. They went down or gave up quicker than extras in a James Bond film. We were in the basement before we knew it.

In truth, there was barely anything for the cops or me to do. Rita practically took care of the whole show for us. She threw herself from point to point throughout the vast expanse of the basement, her speed a blur even those of us who knew where and how to look could barely follow.

Her blade in hand, she was takin' down everyone in sight fast and dirty. A quick slice across the throat and that was it. No finesse, no toyin' with them, nothin'. She just raced from body to body, droppin' them one after another. Delvecio and the SWAT team were perfectly happy to give her the floor. After all, they'd seen what was motivatin' her.

Everywhere you looked there were cages—cages filled with fairies—

most with their wings hobbled. The majority of them were restrained in a manner you could tell had been used to keep them from killin' themselves. They'd been starved, forced to have sex with all manner of partners, kept alive against their wills, raped by machines and beasts, who knew what else. And the hell of it ran deep. You could feel it in the room, in the air, in your soul. Even with rescue in sight, maybe even because of it—most of the survivors still wanted to die. There was a palpable shame bloating the atmosphere, a sickening self-loathing that forced tears outta almost every one of us.

Then, then it got worse.

Pushin' forward into the back end of the basement, we reached the last stop on the way to Glimmer. Spread out on a series of tables, we found the dryin' ovens where the dead were roasted and drained of their remainin' moisture, and the grinders, where vital, ageless creatures were reduced to ten minutes worth of enjoyment for some miserable piece of crap with more money than brains.

Drawin' closer, I looked into one of the ovens and my teeth ground against each other. The thing was runnin', heat was pourin' off it, and inside, through the window in its door you could see the bodies of two fairies, chopped apart and stuffed inside. The limbs looked like plant vines that'd lost their spark—twisted and brittle and devoid of moisture, crackin' open and beginnin' to flake.

I turned away, suddenly knowin' what those first troops who came across one of the Nazi concentration camps felt like. The disbelief, the inability to understand what they were lookin' at, and finally, the horror. I sometimes have a laugh at my boss's expense, jokin' about seein' things beyond me comprehension. Well, it was no joke that time. What they were doin', why they were doin' it, for a moment I couldn't believe it, couldn't accept what I was seein'. And then, the Lutheran came into view. Runnin' from some of our guys herdin' him from the opposite direction, he threw himself on his knees when he saw me, squawkin',

"Morcey—that fairy bitch, she's gone flippo-psycho. She's killing everybody in sight. You have to save me!"

A part of my mind actually giggled, wondering just what in the world could make him think I had to do anything like that. My Auto-Mag in hand, I walked forward toward him. I guess he caught the look in my eye because he tried to stand up, but usin' my gun as a club I knocked him back down to the floor. The idea of shootin' him did cross my mind, but I wasn't feelin' as merciful as Rita. I lifted my arm and I swung and cracked him in the skull, bouncin' his head off the concrete floor. As long as he kept movin', I kept swingin'. Eventually we both stopped.

Rita and I weren't the only ones, it seems, to have troubles with what they found underneath Pearl St. By the time we'd torn through the place, there were very few types left who could put a few words together. Those with the capacity to do so were hustled off for their own safety. A little diggin' around turned up bank account numbers, links to the sales force and the beginnin's of a clear trail back to the big bosses behind the idea of Glimmer. A few of the names surprised me; they were low-lifes, but ones I thought shoulda had a bit more class.

It was clear people were goin' down, and that the Glimmer trade was well on its way to bein' put outta business before it got started. The notion cheered a small part of me, but mosta my brain was simply too numb to get excited. I sat down starin' at the ovens and didn't move. Not when the cops finished takin' out what they wanted, not when they started surroundin' the buildin' in yellow tape.

"Hey, Marlowe," Thorner's idea of a joke. "Wanta go get a couple cold ones? On me. Take your mind off stuff."

It was a nice offer, but I shook my head. I didn't have it in me to move. He tried a couple more times, but Delvecio knew how I felt, gave the kid a whisper and sent him outside. To me he just said;

"I'm going to turn out the lights now."

I knew what me meant. I just nodded to him. He knew what I meant. When he cut the juice, Rita came into view. She'd been pretty much handlin' things about as good as me. She asked if I wanted her to stay with me, but I told her;

"Naww, that's okay. You, you're a high flier. That's where you belong. Me, I belong here in the darkness."

Her lips were tight when she stared at me, like she wanted to argue but knew I was right. She took off, leavin' me in the gloom, nuthin' breakin' it but a sliver of light from one of the covered-over windows gleamin' off one of the grinders. I stared at it for a long time, losin' myself in the view. Zack Goward, that professor I mentioned before, he says you can actually remove yourself from a place without leavin' it by concentratin' on somethin'. It's a Zen thing, and it's harder than it sounds.

But, on the other hand, it does work. Starin' at that hateful metal frame, pourin' all my focus into it, I could feel myself fallin' through time, existin' at all moments that the grinder had been there on that table.

I saw it assembled and bolted down. Saw the dried husks of once vibrant beings reduced to dust by its whirlin' teeth. I removed myself from the world and saw every moment of its evil existence. And finally, what I'd been waitin' for happened.

In the middle of the basement, a deep emerald flow fused with the darkness, then repelled it, pushed it back, consumed it. In its place a soft yellow glow sprang forth from everything, complimentin' the green, moldin' it into a female form that encompassed far more than just the human. Although it walked on two legs, that was only because I was the one perceivin' it, and so its appearance was filtered by my limited human perceptions. Even still, those legs motivated a body incorporatin' every form of life that reproduced itself. I can't explain what I saw any better, don't even know how I was able to see it as well as I did, but for the next few minutes of my life that night, the force of the world pulled itself together and spoke to me sayin';

"Who is that, there in the darkness?"

"Paul Morcey."

As I stopped concentratin' on the grinder and on the god presence before me, I came back inta reality enough so she could recognize me. They ain't kiddin' when they say you can't fool Mother Nature. It's her planet, after all.

"You surprised me," she said, the honeyed frost of her voice dangling between bein' impressed and irritated.

"I wanted to know why you did it."

Of course it was takin' a chance—don't bother knucklin' me with the obvious. Of course I shoulda known better—called in the big guns, done anythin' but face the realized force of creation by myself. But I was too angry to be sensible. I had to know the answer and I had to get it on my own. Like gettin' a kiss-off letter from the girl you adore, a goddamned piece of paper ain't good enough. You gotta hear the lips you love beyond reason tell you you're a piece of shit for yourself before you can believe they mean it.

"Did what?"

"This!" I shouted, pointin' all around me. I didn't care. She didn't deserve any more respect in my book. It might have been her world, but if this was the way she was gonna run it, I didn't care if I was a resident anymore. "All'a this! What the hell were you thinkin'? How could you?"

"When earthquakes swallow cities, people wail. When a single human child falls down a hole, the entire world of man gasps."

The swirling green busied itself at one of the tables. I stood from the floor where I'd been sittin', my body rebellin' from the amount of time I'd stayed in one position, knees and spine and everythin' screamin' at me, remindin' me of just how pitifully small and human I was in comparison to that which I was challengin'.

"But when I breathe life into a species, and man stamps it out, slaughters or poisons or hunts unto extinction one of my creations ... who mourns for them? Who becries my children?"

I didn't know where to go, what to say. Bein' in the presence of the cosmic balance, all my questions fled before they could be asked, all my answers shriveled against the logic of her will. A few environmentalists could not stand for our species. The fact that nature itself helped in the elimination process did not negate what she was sayin'.

"You ask me why I have done 'all of this,' I shall tell you. I have decided I shall slaughter a species, too."

There was no doubtin' who she was talkin' about. Pullin' a canister free from a hidden compartment in the side of the stand where she had stopped, she said;

"I will miss clever little monkeys like you, Paul Morcey, but perhaps next time ..."

The wistfulness in the autumn wind which was her voice tore at my heart. She was mournin' me, and the crumbs of regret she was feelin' at gettin' ready to murder me and everyone I knew, everyone in the world, actually touched me. Desperate to understand, to alter the future she was draggin' us toward, I blurted;

"So why not just boil the oceans? Why create Glimmer? Why kill Lazarus?"

The mouth that kissed all newborns smiled sadly at me. The sight of it threw me back in time; I relived the terror of leavin' my mother's womb, the bombardment of havin' my world shattered, and in that split second, I felt her touch again, felt those lips graze my uncomprehendin' forehead, heard them whisper to me that everythin' was gonna be wonderful. Chokin' on tears I simply could not stop, I listened as she explained;

"Poor Lazarus. He understood life. After being condemned to never knowing its end, he embraced it so. He became a strict vegetarian, in a world which knew no such concept. For thousands of years now, he killed not so much as a flea."

"And you murdered him."

"There was need."

And then, it all fell into place. An idea so large I could barely understand the edges of it, I began to stumble forward into the horrible explanation, expandin' my ability to comprehend as I dragged the pieces I could see one toward the other.

"He was just a test, wasn't he? You're not plannin' on doin' humans in with Glimmer. You want it for somethin' else."

"I have it."

The canister she had pulled from its hiding place under her arm, Mother Nature began to move toward the exit. In desperation, I called out after her.

"This whole thing, you lead us here, turned in the whole operation to throw everyone off the track—make us think we solved the case. You got Laz interested in Glimmer 'cause he was always tryin' to find a way to stop livin'. But, so what? What did you stand ta gain ..."

And then, the whole terrible thing fell together in my head. When the god presence turned back toward me, a monstrous fear began to chill my body, lettin' me know I was right.

"I had to know the Glimmer would kill an immortal," she confirmed, knowin' all that was in my mind, the way she knew all minds.

"It is all ready. Jesus is always somewhere in the world, sustaining his flock. The universe's weak link, he gives it understanding of mankind through the prism of good works and simple mischief. Such a simple thing to bring him low, it will be. And already, I have an eager crowd of Allah's followers ready to take credit for his demise. And credit they will deserve—"

It was true. As she rolled across the concrete, her free hand reachin' for me, all she had planned flooded my brain. The Glimmer promised to waitin' terrorist hands, Jesus' location revealed at the right time, DNA from the Shroud of Turin matched to the body, the flames of manufactured conflict fanned—all of it, the oceans of blood, mountains of death, I saw it all unfold, the iron timeline she was creatin' hammered into place one murderous blow at a time.

"But," I tried to counter, "you had to kill fairies to do it. That makes you just as bad as what you're tryin' to stop."

The emerald god presence wavered for a fate-hingin' moment, then she looked at me sadly, her eyes reflectin' eternity as she said;

"One fallen moment for a permanent improvement. Mankind savaged back to the stone age. Time will forgive me."

"Maybe so," a voice sounded in our minds alone, "but I don't."

The words reached us like the sound of a gunshot, ringin' in the ears of the bullet's target a moment after the lead had already struck home. I'd had told Rita to go high, that I'd stay low. She had. And she had waited patiently, somewhere in the lower stratosphere, until Mother Nature had returned to the scene of the crime. Waitin' until I had her as off-balance as possible, Rita had then flown in with all her considerable speed and, with creation distracted, she had smashed her way inside the god presence.

Of course, the impact killed her instantly. It was what she'd been hopin' for.

With Mother Nature thinkin' about the fact she'd killed hundreds of her favorite creatures to work her terrible plan, Rita had shattered herself against the god presence's consciousness, throwin' her deathcry against all of nature. I braced myself for the shock of it, but nuthin' came my way. Like the cycle of lightning, fire and regrowth, the natural order absorbed all the thousands of years of agony Rita had thrown against it.

As I watched, the green visage went pale. Thousands of faces, mammal and insect and crustacean and everything in between, they all flashed before me, every species passin' judgment on the life force that had created them. One by one, they all shuddered in disbelief.

Around the form of Mother Nature, lights exploded, sparks burnin' the air from floor ta ceilin'. Dust began swirlin' around the figure, white and black streaks of energy intermixin' with wind and pain, envelopin' it, shieldin' it, dissolvin' it—I didn't know what.

I wanted to run, wanted to scream, but couldn't do nuthin'. I was transfixed, glued to the spot by a need more powerful than self-preservation. I had to know the outcome, had to see the coffin nailed shut on this one. The simple stuff that made up Paul Morcey didn't matter—not if this all wasn't punished.

What I wanted didn't matter, though. Before I knew what was happenin', I felt hands pullin' at me, draggin' me back toward the exit. I screamed, and struggled best I could, but I was done in. Exhausted to begin with, drained by drawin' Nature to the spot, maybe even succumbin' to common sense, I found I couldn't resist.

Thorner and Delvecio pulled me up the stairs and outside to safety just seconds before the buildin' began to collapse in on itself. Just like Rita, I'd thrown them a hint of what I was gonna do. I couldn't just tell them anything directly—couldn't risk alertin' Mother Nature to the possibility of their interference.

When it was all over, some two city blocks were gone, swallowed in a volcanic pit of black magma that burned for three days and then hardened over into a dark glass they say throws off compasses and kills satellite transmission in the area. What's gonna finally happen, none of us knows, but we're thinkin' we bought Jesus and the whole human race a reprieve.

That night, however, we had little idea what was up. I filled in Delvecio and his prize student on what had happened while the fire trucks poured into the area. They thanked me for what I'd done, wanted to take me out drinkin' to help me put it all outta my mind, but I couldn't think of anything but Lazarus and Rita. It didn't leave me in much of a mood for antics.

"Ahhh, com'on," Thorner said to me one last time, "nothing fancy. Let me just take you out for a round of Tom & Jerries."

"Thanks," I told him, meanin' it. "But I'll be okay. I'll be doin' some drinkin' tonight, I promise you that. I'm just not in the mood for a Tom & Jerry right now."

"You ain't drinking Tom & Jerries," Delvecio said with a whistle, "what the hell you plan on drinking?"

"I don't know," I told him, walkin' away. "I think I'll have somethin' with an umbrella in it."

The characters you are about to meet have only appeared several times, but CJ promises there will be more to come. His Arkham-based detective squad was a natural for this volume, mainly because they represent a strong return by the author to the idea of men looking into the supernatural having to learn to think outside the box. This was the first appearance of the Nardi Agency. We're quite certain it will not be the last.

The Idea of Fear

"We are terrified by the idea of being terrified."
— Nietzsche

He looked the house over from the street. Dark and old and tall and musty, like every other dilapidated dump in town, he knew. They were all the same, all creaking, all spongy—alive with mosses and spores and gas leaks—all filled with a thousand crinkling noises. The man stared out the window of his car and despaired dragging himself out onto the sidewalk.

Some detective, he thought. You sure aren't going to give Phil Marlowe a run for his money anytime soon in this town.

Franklin Nardi had left New York City after its police force had used up his strongest, bravest days. Many envied the life—work a job for a mere twenty years and retire with benefits beyond the dreams of most. With only the slightest of salaries on top of such a retirement package, it was said, a man could support a family in style.

Yeah, he thought, taking another long drag on his cigarette, and all it takes to earn those fine benefits is walking out the door with a target on your back. Every day. Every stinking, miserable day. For twenty goddamned years.

Frankie Nardi had no family. He did not lose them tragically, except in the sense that it was tragic they had never existed at all. Nardi did not by nature enjoy the company of women. He had witnessed the eternal grinding down of his father and his uncles, all men to be proud of, except when they ventured into the presence of women and their guts turned to cheese. He listened to them complain, watched them live their lives afraid to speak, afraid to contradict, afraid of what they might do to these women they loved if they ever stopped reining themselves in.

The detective was not afraid of women. He went out with them and played their games to the extent those rounds gave him what he wanted—flesh and momentary contact free from the rock-heavy drag of commitment.

"Ahhh, fuck," he snorted. He took another long look at his assignment for the night and then crushed his smoke out on the roof of his car, adding, "no one ever said life was easy."

Window up, bags grabbed from the back seat, car locked, up to the front door. Nardi assessed the ring of keys he had been given and with his usual skill picked the correct one on the first try. Throwing open the old door he threw his bags inside and surveyed his home for the evening. With a crunch of muscles he stretched his arms out, flexing his back and shoulders unconsciously. Even though he expected nothing more than a night's sleep, he was still a man who did his job.

After twenty years of not blinking, of watching over his shoulder, behind his back, of sizing up each and every human being that came near him, figuring their angle, investigating their souls in the split-second before contact, moving to Arkham was supposed to have been a breeze. The town was known for importing New York's finest. One supposed the New English hamlet would have preferred Bostonian coppers, but as the mayor of Arkham had put it to Nardi when he asked;

"This town has enough drunks with their hands out. We need real men. Manhattan is the attitude that goes over well here when people want protection."

It was true. New Yorkers took charge. Taking charge of his life, Nardi had left the city he simply could not stand any more and turned his back on it for trees and fields and runaway dogs. His idea was to open his own detective/security agency in Arkham with three other New York cops—one that had retired a year earlier, Tony Balnco, and two others, Sammy Galtoni and Mark Berkenwald, who were right behind him on the escape track. They had all agreed instantly—the one already retired fastest of all. In three months they were the fastest growing business in the city of Arkham, Massachusetts.

And why not? People cheated on their spouses in New England same as anywhere else. They stole from their bosses, needed background checks, wanted to find lost property or people from their pasts, required security like everyone else. Nardi had seen Bloods selling crack behind the playground at Allan Halsey Memorial High School the same way he had behind the playground at Thomas Jefferson High in Brooklyn, and every other high school throughout the five boroughs. There was no "safe" America anymore. The green was going to hell in all the same ways as the concrete—just a little slower, that was all.

Which is what had made Arkham perfect for Nardi and his pals. For five years they had built their business and life was good for them. They held the security contracts for nearly three/fifths of the businesses in town. They were the first contact point on the speed dial list of four/fifths of the town's lawyers. They had all the work they needed; which was what angered Nardi when Berkenwald took a job like the one he was stuck with that night.

"So?" he asked the house absently. "Let's make with the spooky noises. Let's get this over with."

In New York Nardi had found plenty of opportunities to placate the wealthy. Those with money were always finding some new way to waste it. Years ago the slugs bleeding cash could not move into a new property without calling in a *fung shui* master to make certain it was properly positioned in the universe. Now, in Arkham, the chic move was to have your home desensitized by a supernatural security team.

"What a crock of shit," muttered Nardi.

Berkenwald, getting wind of the new chump rage, had let it be known to only a few, close personal friends, mind you, that the agency had been called in to clear a few major hauntings back in New York. Hinted at terrible moments, let it be known they simply did not do that sort of work anymore. Too stressful. The hideous terrors that awaited the uninitiated...

The suckers had begun throwing money at the agency immediately. Any new bride or social matron who heard a noise she did not like, felt a draft that seemed a little too frigid, awoke in a cold sweat, et cetera, knew what to do—buy some peace of mind.

But Berkenwald had booked more work for them that week than they could cover. And thus Frankie Nardi, himself, the owner of the company, who should have been working on his model railroad set-up in his basement at that very moment, and dreaming of a date with his hammock for the next day, was instead stuck doing a point-by-point sweep of some ancient rathole for ghosts.

Ghosts, for Christ's sake.

"Does it get any stupider than this? I don't think I want to know if it does."

"Don't tell me you want the world to smarten up, Nardi," a voice said from behind the detective. "That would lose you a lot of business."

"I'm retired, remember?" He threw the line over his shoulder to the woman coming in the doorway. "The more business I have the less I like it."

"I think you're just afraid to run into the Headless Horseman or one of his pals. Something like that would be hard work," she said with a bite in her voice as she dropped her bags heavily on the floor, "and we all know you're afraid of that."

"Yeah, nothin' with tits is a feminist when there's heavy-liftin' to do."

The woman was Madame Renee, her profession, medium. Born Brenda Goff, she had cultivated her over-whelmingly Middle Eastern looks until a nose too big and brows too bushy had begun to work in her favor. As her love of all things covered in, filled with, or simply made from sugar had stolen her figure, she had made her shape a badge and transformed herself once more. Dancers had a short shelf-life, she had told herself when she had traded her tights for a beaded curtain and a crystal ball. Fortune-tellers could work from a wheelchair.

"Sweet as ever, ain't ya?"

"Oh, don't crawl up my ass; I've got all the shit I can handle today, and this job is half of it."

"You're not a happy man, are you, Frank?"

Madame Renee reached out to touch the detective on the cheek but he ducked the contact, his glower showing open hostility. "Look, "he told her curtly, "we're here to de-ghost this dump, and as stupid as I feel about this nonsense, a job is still a job. Mark told me you've got the checklist, so, if you do, then let's get to it. The faster we prove the Ghostly Trio isn't hiding up the chimney, the faster we get to go home."

With a shrug, the madame sighed and pulled out the official Nardi Security Occult Clearance Form from the large carpet bag she seemed to always keep with her. Without trying again to lighten the mood, she simply started calling off routines and posing questions while Nardi poked, prodded, and peeled back this and that part of the old house. Between them they searched every room for cold spots, listened carefully to each wall with their stethoscopes, made certain a mirror would reflect light in every room, and tested the air on every floor to make certain no unwanted chemicals, smells, gases or aromas were present.

They set up motion detectors in every passageway and sound-trigger tape recorders in every room. Powder was sprinkled around doorways and across table tops and mantlepieces to record the motion of any invisible forces. Hairs were secured across the doors of cupboards and the drawers of dressers with nothing more than a finger smear of saliva. If anything with the slightest physical presence moved within the old house outside the living room where Madame Renee and Nardi would be camped out for the night, it would be known.

The madame, of course, had her own bag of tricks to perform. She rolled her bones, did an open reading with the tarot deck she had made herself, and set herself to staring into the crystal shard she used for focus to reach out beyond herself to bind herself with the house's aura—searching for unwanted visitors. After that, as Nardi went room by room, setting his machines and traps, she pulled back into herself, and then opened her own aura to the building and to all and any that might be within it. Reaching deep within herself, she peeled back the layers of modern life, of concern over her daughter's college expenses, moved past the aches and pains a body some one hundred and sixty pounds past its medically approved weight-for-its-height felt constantly, dug down inward until she had found the pure essence of her inner being and revealed it completely and utterly.

By the end of the night the pair were utterly exhausted—Nardi from covering the old place attic to basement as well as every room of the three floors in between, Renee from having thrown herself open past all boundaries. She had poured her soul and heart into every bit of wire and plaster and mahogany the old home had to offer, placing herself out before it, helpless and beckoning, and had received nothing for her efforts.

This fact confused her greatly.

"What are you talkin' about?" asked Nardi. The detective desperately wanted to fall back into the recliner he had chosen as his bed and shut his eyes, but a job was a job and so he coaxed the woman further.

"Com'on, spill it."

Renee propped herself up on the couch with one of her massively fleshy elbows. Staring at Nardi, knowing he did not believe in anything they were doing, she struggled to find a way to voice her concern. Finally, she simply told him what was on her mind.

"Listen, I don't want to go around and around with you on this, so I'll just say it. I did several readings of the house before we got started—future glances, stability predictions—that kind of stuff. It's the low end of what I do for one of these things. Then I fired off the big guns, really put myself out there, bared my soul, big irresistible hunk of ectoplasm for anything nasty in the area and ... I didn't get a bite."

"Disappointed?"

"No, you Italian shit. If you had a soul that could be touched by anything you'd know I was more than earning my fee here. If this was a spirit shanty, I would've paid a price, believe me."

"Then I don't get it," answered the detective honestly, stifling a yawn. "What's the problem?"

"The problem is that something should have come for me." When Nardi said nothing, she continued, explaining, "those early readings I did, they said this place is, I don't know, that something's going to happen here. Something ... nasty, maybe, I don't know. I couldn't get a good sense of it. I didn't worry about it, because I figured I'd find something later that would point the way to the truth. But, the more we checked the place out the cleaner it seemed to get."

"And this is bad?"

"No; it's just confusing." Taking a tiny bit of pity on his temporary partner, and also knowing that placating her would allow him to get some sleep, he said;

"Look, we're just here to do a job. If we don't turn up anything more, then that's what we tell the too-rich pair of country club snots who bought this museum. We give 'em the bad with the good, tip our hats, and we leave."

"I know," Renee answered. "It's just that I met the wife. She's young. She's in love. She's," the sizable woman paused for a moment, then found the word for which she was looking.

"She's nice. I don't want to just take their money. Not this time. Am I making any sense to you?"

Franklin Nardi did not like to reveal much about himself, especially to women. But, he was not heartless, and he let Madame Renee know that he did indeed understand her concern. He also told her that, tired as they were, if there was anything in this house waiting to play with their minds, this was the time they would do it.

"We both came extra tired. That's the deal. Our systems are as weakened as they can get without us bein' sick or something. We're as vulnerable as can be. If nothing bites our asses tonight, and we don't find any reactions in the morning, will you be happy?"

"Heavens," the large woman answered. "I've heard concern in the voice of Franklin Nardi. Why, I'm happy already."

The detective simply reached over and turned off the lights as Madame Renee chuckled softly.

Despite his fatigue, from a long evening on top of a long day on top of a week where he had already worked two double shifts, Frankie Nardi could not sleep. Renee's words had stayed with him. As much as he was willing to trade quips with the woman, he respected her as a professional. To him, her tarot readings and the such were the hard evidence of her line of work. Opening herself up to her surroundings was subjective.

If her hard evidence told her one thing, and her subjective evidence told her another, he was wondering exactly what was wrong.
Did she just do a bad reading? Three different types? All wrong? Was that possible?

Nardi drummed the fingers of his left hand against the handrest of his recliner. Wide awake, he worried more and more over the problem before him. Although he did not like the de-ghosting part of his agency's business, it was not because he did not believe in the supernatural. No NYC cop lasted twenty years without hearing about the Zarnak files, the Thorner case loads, old Tommy Malone ...

"Damnit."

The whispered word hung in the living room air accusingly. Franklin Nardi was a good detective. He had been a good cop. He did not leave a job unfinished. All stones on his beat were turned over. His tongue pressed against his teeth, face a tight mask of skin and tension, he threw his jacket off himself and got up out of his chair.

"All right, house," he said, getting down on his knees. "You want something juicy, I got juicy for you."

Renee had done this kind of thing a hundred times. A thousand. Maybe that was where the problem was. Maybe whatever her readings had picked up wanted more than a few bites out of a pro who could reject their spectral advances. Maybe she had found something lurking in a corner that wanted to taste real fear.

Fine, he sneered within his head. Com'on, I gotta bellyful of it for you.

So saying, Nardi closed his eyes and began pulling off his clothing. A man who never went to the office without a tie and jacket, who did not like the beach, who showered strictly by himself, the detective peeled away his layers of protection and sat naked on the floor. Then, slowly, he began to peel away those mental walls he had built over the decades as well.

It was hard work for Nardi, mainly because like most people, he did not know where to begin, where the boundary lines were drawn. As he fumbled, the back of his mind whispered;

It's like George Carlin said, everyone driving slower than you is a moron, and anyone driving faster is an asshole.

The detective knew what he was trying to tell himself. With the courage he had used to knock in the door of a known gun dealer, that he had used when he had charged straight into a hail of gunfire thrown at him by both sides of a gang war, he looked into his soul and tried to figure out why he had never had a serious relationship.

What was it about women that he dreaded so? He had watched his father and others all his young years. So there were fights? So what? People fight. So families split up. His hadn't. Some women cheated, but so did some men. His mother and father had been faithful. Everyone in his family had been as far as he knew. There were plenty of ugly rumors about who stole what from who, and who didn't bathe, and who drank too much, his one uncle—the one who stayed a confirmed bachelor until he died, left all his money to the church, all those video tapes they found, Lassie, Wonder Years, The Andy Griffith Show, anything with a young boy in the cast—he had heard it all, knew it all.

So what's your problem, Nardi?

The detective could feel the sweat flowing from his body. He thought of women he could have made a life with, remembered their faces, their bodies, the way they smelled in spring, the sound of their laughs, and he shuddered as one by one he remembered shoving them away from himself. Until it became easy. Until it became routine.

He thought of women with whom he had slept, those he had used as rough fun, for sex and satisfaction and nothing more. And he thought of others. His mind brought him pictures of dozens of girls, some he had slept with, others he had played around with, those he had merely kissed, and even women he had simply dreamed about.

And then he remembered Anna.

Anna, with her perfect hair. Anna, with the shoulders so straight, body so taut, legs so long, whose lips tasted of happiness and whose eyes could see into his lungs, could watch the oxygen in them reach his blood stream and rocket to his brain. Anna, who had laid beside him the night he got his acceptance papers to the Academy, who had surrendered herself to him, allowing him his ultimate conquest on his day of triumph, when he was a king who could not be denied.

Anna, who had been so shocked when he had rejected her when she told him she was pregnant. Anna, who he had sent to have an abortion. Anna, who he had ordered to murder his son, and then had blamed her for his death.

Anna, who had spit on his shadow and told him to rot in Hell, and who had found herself another.

Nardi sank to the floor and sputtered, tears pouring from his eyes, spittle bubbling on the carpeting. Afraid to face responsibility, afraid to be father to a thing like himself, he had instead poisoned his own life and then spent twenty years trying to throw it away. His gentle sobs turned into wails of despair, so violent a noise that he never even noticed when Madame Renee rose from the couch and covered him with her blanket.

The next morning Nardi and Renee spoke at length. He explained what he had tried to do, and what the results had been. At first he thought he would be embarrassed, but he was too empty, too drained of anger and shame to care. For the first time in over a quarter of a century, he felt like a whole person and did not mind talking about it.

"So," he asked, shoveling in a large spoon of corn flakes, "where does this leave us?"

"I think it comes down to what you said last night. We went through the entire place this morning—not a tripped wire, not a bit of powder out of place ..." when the detective corrected her, Renee laughed, "all right, so we have to tell the blushing bride her pantry has mice—and small mice at that. But that's it. I'll offer to come back and do another reading after they move in, but that's it. This place is clean."

Madame Renee stared at the detective and marveled at what he had done. To throw himself open to such psychic damage, to be able to face his deepest fears, unaided, unprotected—this was a man, she told herself. A Hell of a man.

"It has to be clean," she added.

And so, the two packed their machines and clothing and bits and pieces and piled them into their vehicles. Making certain he had both reactivated the security system and locked the front door, Nardi took one last look at the old house, then said;

"Well, no one can say the Nardi Security Team doesn't earn it's pay."

Renee made a surprisingly graceful bow of acknowledgement to his statement, then headed for her car. Nardi turned back to the house, tipped his baseball cap to its weathered roof, and then headed for his own.

And, inside the house, the foul presence which had spent the entire time of Nardi and Renee's visit suffering in exquisite anguish, allowed itself to burst forth once more from its thousand different hiding places. It was an elder, jaundiced thing, and its hate bounded from the walls as it unfolded itself.

The fat cow, she had been so easy to resist it was a thing of amusement to the cursed soul, a humor so gay it crippled the violent spirit. But the man, all that marvelous, seething, ever-so-fresh pain ...

That had been hard to ignore. Agonizingly hard. Oh, for just a tiny tongueful of his snivelling grief, the merest pin prick of his pain ...

But that would have alerted the pair of interlopers, set them upon it, forced it to fight back, wasted time, lost it the prize.

No, it purred, remembering the bride soon to be thrust into the bowels of its domain, the smell of her innocence, the drooling wonderfulness of her softness, the flesh to be touched, the love to be poisoned ...

What did they think it was, some inconsequential? Some mere nothing of mere human memory? Fools.

The thing which pulsed with the old house exploded with laughter. It had been sorely tempted, but it had won its prize. It had been afraid for a moment, the detective had almost snared it with the delicious aroma of his fear.

Almost.

But it knew a thing or two itself, about the idea of fear, and it had conquered its own.

Now, it mused, bring me something else to conquer.

The house laughed, and the trees shuddered, but there was no one there to hear.

Yet.

Of course, no collection of supernatural investigators would be complete without the team of Blakely and Boles. These most unlikely heroes are college professors forced by monetary considerations to work together. This wouldn't be such a bad deal for them except for one thing — they despise one another. Still, it's your friends you get to pick, not your family or co-workers. With that in mind, we now present the tale wherein these two polar opposites began to attempt to get along, the fan-favorite—

Memories

> *"A memory is what is left when something happens and does not completely unhappen."*
> — Edward de Bono

Darkness blurred, the ebony reaches of it strained by a fizzing annoyance, a calling more felt than heard. Languid purple sounds slithered through the gentle shroud, unbalanced, straining, pushing aside the burden of shadow, burrowing toward the future—trying to finally remember itself in some complete sense before all was forgotten.

But one more, the still forming thought reminded itself, *but one more needed.*

And with that single realization, the retreating darkness was further dissolved, one more shade of it diminished, by the will of ego and the acid of patience.

DUKE UNIVERSITY, DURHAM, NC

The thrashing reptile let out a hideous roar, a long bark of hot air and frightened anger that echoed down the pristine, off-white corridor. The wrinkled gray dewlap beneath its throat fanned with indignation, its sparse and ragged crest fringes snapping sharply as it threw its head too and fro. The beast snapped its maw several times, biting at the air with curdling frustration, then roared again.

"I second the motion," said the man pushing the creature's rubber-wheeled cage. "Where the hell is everyone?"

The man ran his hand through his rough, dark brown hair, letting the doors to the Science Hall swing shut behind him. He was tall and lean, a well-muscled fellow with dark eyes and a heavy jaw. His mouth was drawn in a thin line, set hard with disappointment. His eyes scanning down the off-running corridor to his left, then the one to his right, he called out;

"Hey, famous explorer with his Nobel ticket here—hello?" The hallways maintained their deserted posture, even as the caged beast barked angrily against the silence.

"Christ," announced the man with understandable frustration. "Can't anyone hear little Edgar, here? Has curiosity completely died in this world?"

When no response came to his queries, frustration forced him to one final attempt.

"Where *is* everybody?"

Finally a young man's head emerged from a room close by. Recognition prompted him to call out.

"Professor Blakely, you're back."

"Glad someone around here notices the little things." The rangy, broad-shouldered man did not bother keeping the annoyance he was feeling out of his voice. "Where is everyone?"

"Auditorium C," answered the student. "Doctor Boles is giving a demonstration."

Did the young man have a twinkle of mischief in his eye? Was, Blakely wondered, the little son'va bitch mocking him? The doctor of Crypto-zoology could not decide if the amusement he detected in the student was actual or imagined. Then, Blakely caught hold of his temper.

Sure, he thought, Boles figured out exactly when you were going to arrive and scheduled one of his little smoke and mirror productions just so he could steal Edgar's and my thunder. Even though even *I* didn't know when I was going to get back and even though *he* didn't know about Edgar.

The large man calmed down. Yes, he admitted, it was true. The rivalry into which he and Boles had entered was fast becoming a point of amusement for the entire campus. Ever since they had been forced to work together by a staggeringly generous endowment, both those members of the faculty made jealous by the endowment and the student body in general had enjoyed watching the pair's attempts to upstage one another. Neither of them had gone to any outrageous extremes, of course, nothing undignified—not yet, anyway.

"Still," Blakely mused under his breath, "I would like to know what that little ferret's up to now."

So saying, the professor wheeled Edgar to his new, if but temporary home in the biology lab, and then headed off across campus for Auditorium C. There, he found his colleague seated at a small table, not on stage but down directly in front of the orchestra seating. He could not make out the man's face from such a distance, but Blakely could discern his counterpart's general form—the small shoulders, whipping black hair, slight frame, thinly oval face, and of course, his trademark wire-rimmed glasses, still sliding too far down his nose.

Okay, sneered Blakely within his head, go ahead and wow me, professor.

The crypto-zoologist noted that the auditorium was packed, and not just with students. He spotted more than a few faculty members, as well as the curious from Durham, and even local journalists. None of them noted Blakely's arrival in the auditorium. All their attention was focused on Boles.

At the table far down in front, Boles sat across from a young woman, a student with whom Blakely was not familiar. Boles was facing the audience but his attention was focused on the student, or more correctly, on the over-sized deck of cards she was manipulating. As Blakely settled into a seat, she spoke, loud enough for all to hear.

"Okay, Dr. Boles, that's thirty-eight out of thirty-eight. You think you can keep going?" Fraternity noises and other encouraging expressions of gusto thundered from around the auditorium. Boles put up a hand to quiet the room.

"I appreciate the enthusiasm, everyone ..."

"You kin do it, professor ..."

Boles smiled at the lone voice. "Thank you, Mr. Purcell. Your faith is appreciated, but it will not change your current grade." A knowing brace of laughter punctuated the quip.

"So," said the girl across the table from Boles, holding up a random card from her deck so that only she could see its face, "wavy lines, a circle, a rectangle ... can you guess number thirty-nine?"

Boles reacted as if he was ready to keep going, touching the tips of his fingers together, lowering his head, closing his eyes slightly. But then, he suddenly shifted his position—agitated—moving his head to one side as if listening to a faraway noise. After a few seconds, he responded.

"I'm sorry," he said with what seemed like honest fluster, "but I don't think I can. Suddenly there seems to be a blockage, as if a vast negative presence has joined us."

"Maybe professor Blakley's back in town."

A large wave of mirth rolled across the audience at Purcell's suggestion. Then, a sharp-eyed student sitting far to the back of the room shouted out;

"Chalk up number thirty-nine for Dr. Boles. Blakely *is* back."

Heads turned. Fingers pointed. Some students laughed all the harder. Many were amazed. A few frightened. Blakely scowled, his original good humor of the day shattered. In the front of the room, Dr. Hugo Boles seemed almost reluctant to respond to the growing applauds that wildfired its way throughout the auditorium. Finally, as it began to turn into a standing ovation, he acquiesced and rose as well, taking a short bow.

The next day found Blakely in the office of the school Chancellor, Mr. Gordon S. Pimms. Few would guess that the "S" stood for "Stonewall," for Pimms was a rotund and balding man of short stature who perspired far too freely for a man of academic importance. Although the political correctness of the times kept him from announcing his being named for the great general very often any more, still he realized the importance of the connection to many of the older alumni, and thus still maintained the initial on his business cards and office door.

"So, Hugo," he said to Blakely, hoping to find some small trace of good humor in the professor for once, "how's it feel to be back in the States?"

"For my part, being nine thousand miles from the sideshow antics of William Herbert Boles and his nightmare theater were a blessed relief. A jungle thick with buzzers who take a quart of blood every time they fillet you was sheer heaven compared to being coupled with his royal highness, the grand poobah of weird."

"Hugo, you're just caught up. Why don't you let me ..."

"No," Blakely snapped, "don't veer me off, Gordon. I'm collar hot and I think I deserve to be. Look at what happened to me yesterday. I arrive here with the find of the century ..."

"You know, I still don't really understand what it is you found," admitted Pimms. "They said it was an old lizard ...?"

"Euuuugghhh," groaned Blakely. Leaning forward, he held his temper back as he lectured, "Here's the brief, so you can dazzle the alumni. There are four branches to the reptile family, and the oldest is the Rhynchocephalia, which has only one member genus, Sphenodon, which has only one species, the ratty little tuataras, and you can only find those dusty losers on a few islands off New Zealand where they keep body and soul together living in abandoned bird nests. With the discovery of Edgar, I just doubled the Rhynchocephalian species count. He *is* the quintessential reptile morphotype. I mean, back in '56, when Romer wrote *Osteology of the Reptiles*, his constant anatomical point of reference was *Sphenodon*. Every major book since then has had to do the same. But, not any more. From here on in they'll be coming to us!"

Pimms began to grasp the importance of Blakely's find, at least in terms his outlook could appreciate. Not only would it bring additional prestige to the university, but its discovery fit the criteria of the lavish endowment the school had received to further both professor Blakely and Boles' work, and that meant far more to the chancellor than mere prestige. Gaining his slight understanding of the importance of the discovery, however, did not bring to Pimms an understanding of what had Blakely so upset. Questioning that brought the balding man his answer.

"But did anyone come yesterday? A new species found, a creature that dates back directly well over 200 million years? Why bother? Who cares?" Blakley panted, his voice growing louder and more agitated. "What's the point when we've got that trained frog Boles doing card tricks in Auditorium C?"

"My, my, and this used to be such a genteel office," came a voice from behind the two men. "Now they'll let just anyone inside."

Pimms welcomed the arrival of Dr. William Boles. Blakely pushed himself backwards into the overstuffed leather of his high-backed chair, retreating into its padding. Boles moved into the chancellor's office and took a twin seat next to his colleague. Turning to Blakely, he asked;

"So, what's this about some parasite you've brought back to the campus?"

"Bite me, ghost boy."

"Gentlemen," snapped Pimms, his good humor draining out of his system, "you two are becoming impossible. But, in many ways that is what I like best about you."

Blakely blinked, stared at Pimms for a moment, then let his eyes dart sideways toward Boles. His colleague merely continued to gaze forward, maybe looking at the Chancellor, perhaps at something behind him, or at nothing at all.

"I've taken the liberty of cancelling your classes for the next two weeks, William," Pimms said to Boles. Turning his head to Blakely, he added, "since technically you're still on leave, I've contacted Human Resources and told them to extend it for the same period."

"What's up, Gordie?"

"A Mr. Gary Railsbach has purchased some property he wishes to turn into a wildlife preserve. The only problem, it seems it's either haunted or plagued by monsters. I told him our world-famous team of investigators would be to his rescue shortly."

Blakely blinked hard, swallowed air with noise, then opened his eyes, flashing angry bolts at the Chancellor. Boles merely raised one eyebrow and gave a short smile.

WA'CHENKA VILLAGE, at the ALTAMAHA RIVER, GA

"Why stay in Townsend, he says," fumed Dr. Boles, staring out the window of Blakely's Explorer at the collapsing remains of what had once been known as the Wa'Chenka Village, a tourist attraction of the fifties which had not merely fallen on hard times, but indeed which had plummeted to them.

"Pretty hard to meet our contact," responded Blakely, aiming a thumb at the woman crossing the litter strewn parking lot toward them, "if we don't go where we say we will."

"Apparently," answered Boles slowly, cleaning his glasses at the same time, "you're willing to endure fairly much anything, if it has female body parts attached to it."

Blakely almost answered, then decided there was no point to it. Their contact was most of the way to his car. It made little sense to him to force her to knock on the window before they acknowledged her presence. Besides, he told himself as he opened his door with relief, ten hours trapped in the same vehicle with Boles was about his limit.

"Hello," started the approaching woman, "are you Dr. Blakely?"

"What gave me away?"

"I have to admit," she answered coyly, her eyes giving his body an approving stare, "it was hinted to me that the Blakley half of 'Blakely & Boles' would be the more interesting. If that's him still in the car, then he must be something of a demi-god. Not to be forward, or anything."

"Now, aren't you sweet," responded the professor with an appreciative smile, suddenly feeling better about things. "Whatever it is you're selling, why not throw a case in my trunk while I get my wallet."

"Touche," replied the woman. Extending her hand, she offered, "I'm Kate Skyler. I'm the representative from Friends of Wild Life you're supposed to be meeting here." Blakely took the proffered hand, approving of the rough feel to the fingers, incongruous with the rest of Skyler's appearance.

"Hugo Blakely, at your service." At the sound of his passenger door opening he added, "and this is my esteemed colleague, Dr. W.H. Boles."

"There wouldn't be a clean bathroom somewhere on these premises, would there, young lady?"

Skyler smiled. Pointing toward the endless stand of trees behind the dilapidated buildings at the edge of the parking lot, she offered, "the forest is a beautiful place, Dr. Boles."

The professor stiffened noticeably. Both Blakely and the young woman did their best not to laugh. Resigning himself, Boles moved off toward the woods beyond while the others talked.

"So," Blakely began, "here's what we have—supposedly there's a creature, that may or may not be tangible, on the loose in this little attraction of yours. That was enough to get our Chancellor to send us down to do a preliminary scouting of the site. Now why don't you add the reams of facts we're obviously missing."

"Glad to," she responded. "First off, the Wa'Chenka Village isn't an attraction anymore. Our organization bought this place so that we can turn it into a wildlife refuge."

"You *bought* it?" Blakely was clearly taken aback. "But, you're environmentalists, correct?"

"Yes. Not all Earth-Firsters believe the government should be involved in everything, though. We bought the land when it came on the market, and we've got plans that will not only make it a functional refuge, but should also turn a profit."

"Sounds intriguing," said Blakely honestly. "So where are the creatures? And what exactly do you want done about them?"

While Skyler answered the doctor's questions, his partner made his way back into the forest, looking for a spot suitably secluded to relieve himself. Coming to a particularly dense section of pines, he undid his zipper and began urinating when he felt a motion behind him.

Not far away, not moving, thought the professor. Reaching out with his senses, he told himself, quiet, patient, but solid.

Boles found beads of sweat breaking out all across his head. What was behind him, he wondered. Why was it watching him? What was it waiting for? When he was finished urinating, would it lose interest and wander off, or might it attack?

As the stream he was releasing began to break up into spurts, Boles went through his options. He could enumerate only two—turn and confront who or whatever was behind him or run for the car.

It stands to reason, he told himself, that anything truly interested in mayhem most likely could overtake me long before I can reach any form of safety. Indeed, I think it's safe to assume such would have happened already.

That thought in mind, the doctor finished his business, did up his trousers, then turned, saying;

"Hello, whoever you are. Pardon me if I don't offer to shake hands..."

Boles turned to find himself staring into the eyes of the oldest human being he had ever encountered. The man was obviously a Native American, possibly one of the Wa'Chenka the site's faded and cracked front gate had promised.

"Name's Na'kiraw," the man spoke in a raspy, tired voice.

"Any particular reason you snuck up on me without announcing yourself?"

"Not polite to interrupt a man when he's taking care of business. Besides, wondered if I could still do it."

Boles smiled. He liked the old man's attitude. As the pair walked back toward the buildings, Na'kiraw answered as many questions as he could. The Wa'Chenka Village had been a tourist attraction of no small repute decades earlier. The site was actually the tribe's reservation—in truth, the holiest of their holy places. Hard times had forced them to the practical, however. Erecting signs to lure tourists onto their land, the Wa'Chenka had put on shows, demonstrating ritual dances, archery marksmanship, native crafts, anything that might bring in a dollar.

"Got good at the showmanship after a while," the old man said with pride. "The best were the weddings. Any time we had enough tourists to make it worth our while, we'd tell them they could attend an actual tribal wedding. We'd just grab any two of us who weren't busy and they'd play the couple. Charge by the head, shame them into springing for gifts, good business—you know?"

"Seems as if you had it all worked out."

"We did," the man's face went soft with memory for a moment. "I remember one summer I got married twelve times. The groom always wore an emerald green robe, thousand hummingbird feathers. Very beautiful."

"Sounds like you enjoyed it, somewhat, anyway—yes?"

"It wasn't bad," agreed the old man. "Didn't get to keep the gifts, but I enjoyed the honeymoons."

"You put Mickey Rooney to shame," answered Boles. "So, what happened to this place?"

"Fuckin' Disney," answered Na'kiraw matter-of-factly. "There used to be roadside attractions all up and down I-95. Dinosaur villages, Santa Claus Lands, slave plantation re-enactments—all gone now. All dried up. Nobody had time for us—any of us. We Wa'Chenka, we were always a small tribe. Back in '74, '75, when there was just nobody stopping anymore, the influenza hit. By the time we got any real help, a lot of the tribe was dead. Big mess."

Boles and Na'kiraw reached the main building at that point, joining Blakley and Skyler as they came out the front entrance. It was quickly made obvious that Skyler and Na'kiraw knew each other. The old man explained.

"Skyler's group didn't want the Wa'Chenka lands to revert to the government. They bought it from me ..."

"It's a *lease*, remember?" Skyler corrected. "A custodianship set up in the tribe's name. The Wa'Chenka still have complete access to their lands in perpetuity ..."

"Which," the old man cut her off, "since I'm the last of the Wa'Chenka, means it will all be theirs to do with what they want fairly soon."

"But," returned Skyler, slightly flustered, "you knew that. I mean..."

Na'kiraw waved the woman's comments off, coughing as he did so. The racking noise went on for an embarrassingly long time. Hacking up a great glob of phlegm, he spat it out, tasting blood as he did so. Covering his mouth with the back of a hand, he lowered himself slowly into a chair carved from a twisted tree trunk that rested against the front of the building. "I know, don't get in a tizzy. I know. But, I also know I'll be dead soon and the Wa'Chenka will just be a memory."

Na'kiraw settled into the chair, moving his legs and back slowly as if he were squirming his way into cushions. It seemed obvious the old man was soaking what warmth he could from the wood, positioning himself in the late noon sun to gather more. The conversation between the four of them shrank to three as Na'kiraw made it clear he was more interested in napping than anything else they might have to say. As the trio wandered away from the front of the building, Blakley muttered in frustration.

"Damn, kind of an unlucky break there."

"Why?" asked Skyler.

"We've got some kind of new creature running around here. Pops there lives out here—right? He has to know more about it that anyone else."

"You'd think that, wouldn't you?" When both men turned to Skyler, the woman told them, "believe it or not, Na'kiraw hasn't seen the creatures. Or at least, he claims he hasn't seen them. I tend to believe him, though."

"Well then," asked Boles, "who is it that's been making these sightings?"

"That," she admitted with a trifle of embarrassment, "would be me."

While it was true that Na'kiraw had so far claimed to have had no encounters with the creatures, not only had Skyler seen the various beasts, but so also had numerous members of her organization. As the trio sat at a nearby restaurant, the environmentalist told Blakley and Boles all she knew. As she spoke, her head continued to dart back and forth, giving the obvious feeling she did not want their conversation to be overheard.

"If you'll forgive my asking, Ms. Skyler," interrupted Boles, "is there some reason for you to be nervous over telling us about this?"

"Sorry, but I don't want people thinking I'm a nut case," she replied. "I do have to live here."

"True enough," agreed Blakley. "But you're not the only person who has seen these creatures—correct?"

"No, but ..." the hesitation in her voice choked along for a moment, then fell into silence.

"But," Boles guessed politely, "all of the others who have witnessed anything have all been members of Friends of Wild Life—yes?" Skyler nodded. Blakley pursed his lips.

"Which means," ventured the crypto-zoologist, "people might be, or maybe already *are* thinking that your organization is up to something." The woman nodded sharply, her head down, teeth biting at her lower lip.

The waiter chose that moment to return, setting up a standing tray next to their booth. Clearing their soup and salad plates, he passed around their platters, making the usual tip-boosting chatter as he did so. In seconds, he had Blakely's crisp, double-battered chicken and potato wedge basket out with its sides of applesauce and corn-on-the-cob, Skyler's broiled snapper with rice, with her sides of butter beans and spinach, and Boles house salad and side of Melba toast and sliced lemons. The threesome made pleasant chatter until the fellow left, then got back down to business, eating as they did so.

The thing the professors most wanted to get from Skyler was a description of the creatures she and her group had been sighting. Hesitation returned to the woman's voice. Boles asked what the problem was.

"The problem," she answered, absently twirling her fork in her spinach, "is that there is no one description of a thing. It's *things* we've been seeing. All shape and size of them."

Neither man said anything immediately. Blakley held a still steaming chicken breast gingerly between the thumb and forefinger of both hands. Boles gnawed at a large piece of raw broccoli, his eyes looking somewhere far away. Blakely responded to the woman's comment first.

"Can you give us a 'for-instance?' Is there *anything* general to the descriptions people have been seeing?" When Skyler fumbled, not knowing what to say, the professor tried a different approach.

"Not to worry; no problem. Forget everyone else who saw the thing, things, whatever, for the moment. Just tell us whatever it was *you* saw."

Kate stared at Blakley, her eyes unblinking, her face unreadable. The crypto-zoologist pursed his lips, moving them first to the left, then the right. Still the woman said nothing, the uneasy look on her face growing more agitated. Understanding what was happening, Boles touched his napkin to his lips.

"Might I suggest the delay in your answering," he said, breaking the mounting awkwardness, "is because you simply don't know which thing to describe first?"

Skyler nodded, her hands starting to shake. As the two men watched, her hands grew more and more agitated, tiny flecks of spinach literally shaking off her fork. Boles reached across the table, his fingers gently sliding the utensil out from between her fingers.

"I'm sorry," the woman said, her voice a ragged whisper. "I knew I was going to make a mess of this."

She looked up, her eyes moistening, mouth forming a pitiful, small puckered line that seemed to get smaller with each passing moment.

"I asked that *any* of the others meet with you," she told the professors. "I knew I couldn't do this. They all begged off ..."

"Hiding behind a woman ..." growled Blakely.

"Letting the boss do her job," corrected Boles.

"You're right," Skyler confirmed. "Can't fault them for not wanting to ... not ... it's the remembering that's ... it's ..."

And then, Kate Skyler began weeping uncontrollably, long and loud moans of pitiful anguish which defied her ability to control. Blakley reached over to take her hand, offering consoling words, whispering reminders about where she lived and whom she might not want to think of her as a nutcase. Skyler simply laughed at his efforts, her fingers absently closing and unclosing. When they descended to her plate and started to tear her fish apart, the agitated digits flinging bits of oily snapper flesh about, Boles smiled. Squeezing the last bit of flavor out of one of his lemon slices, he moved it carefully, making certain to fill every crevice of a particularly good looking slice of tomato. Finally things seemed to him as if they might be leading somewhere.

WA'CHENKA VILLAGE, at the ALTAMAHA RIVER, GA

"Why have we come back here?"

"I told you, Dr. Blakley," answered Boles in a reedy sneer, "as usual, no one is going to be able to help us. We need to see these things for ourselves."

Blakely thought to reply, then stifled the impulse. Boles felt Skyler had been unable to answer because she was simply too frightened to respond coherently. The para-psychologist explained he had seen such behavior all too often in the past, where individuals experiencing hauntings could not describe events they had witnessed; even families whose members had suffered through visitations together sometimes simply could not relate what they had seen. Even over time, as the intruding forces battered away at their lives, often two people confronted by something beyond their ken would relate the details of the event so completely differently it was hard to believe they had been in the same place. Or that they were not lying.

Whichever was correct, however, Blakley did not want to argue the point. It did not matter if Boles' theory was correct as to why they had no concrete description with which to work. What mattered was they had no description—period. The more he had questioned Skyler, the more hysterical she had become. Eventually the crypto-zoologist had relented when she excused herself, allowing her to flee the restaurant.

"All right," snapped Blakely. "So what's your idea? We just go out and walk around all night until one of us stumbles across something that we can't describe?"

"And people say you have no grasp of the obvious," answered the para-psychologist with a bubbly glee. "It is truly a pleasure working with someone who, no matter how much education or how many worldly experiences they might acquire, can still manage to maintain a distinctly pedestrian manner."

"Bite me, Boles."

"Note how easily the subject switches to alliteration ...."

Blakely made a menacing motion with his fist that startled Boles enough to make him break off his chatter. The crypto-zoologist made to speak, then thought the better of it. What could he say? What would be worth the breath?

Deciding he had wasted enough oxygen on Boles for one day, knowing he did not want to hear even another syllable in the man's smug tone, Blakely stalked off into the night. Boles sighed, realizing he had pushed his colleague too far once more. He did not feel guilty at the realization, he merely enjoyed taunting Blakely so that whenever he finally succeeded in driving the larger man over the edge, it was always a let down.

You should have been able to make that last another twenty minutes, he chided himself. Smiling ruefully, he admitted that was a possibility, but that he had been having too much fun to contain himself. Removing his glasses, he cleaned their lenses absently with his handkerchief, then slid them back in place. When he did, he found his view remarkably changed.

As the para-psychologist stood frozen in place, a trio of forms moved out of the deep forest toward his position. They were all different from one another, but familiar to Boles in certain general ways. One of them was remarkably cat-like. Though it seemed coated with scales rather than fur, and was absent a tail, still, something of the feline permeated it. The thing was predominantly green, a shining, reflective shimmer highlighting its reptilian skin.

"B-Blakely ..." Boles' voice was scarcely more than a whisper. He did not mean it to be so, but he could not make it any louder.

The second was more like a badger, squat and low to the ground, with great sabre-toothed fangs curling over its lower lip. The thing walked with a rolling gait, its bullet of a head turning from side to side as its unblinking eyes scoured all directions ahead of it. Behind it, the third thing came, a bulbous, misshapen creature, one covered in long, red feathers. Great, apple-sized eyes protruded from its body in six spots, all of them staring at Boles.

"Blakely ..." The word hissed from the para-psychologist's lips, the sound of it so low even he could barely hear it. Boles shuddered, naked fear beginning to etch itself across his consciousness. He tried to ignore the terror, control the trembling in his legs, the shaking in his hands, but he could not. The trio of things had obviously seen him, had their attention focused on him. One by one they opened their maws, stretching their jaws to their fullest, flashing teeth and fangs and appetites that were not bound to mere hunger. Frothing drool foaming over their lips, the trio began to advance toward Boles.

They're coming for you, his mind whispered, terror frosting the words, the painful cold of them eating at him. What do you want? Why are you not moving? Run you idiot—run!

He did. Boles spun about wildly, screaming as he did so. His arms wavering wildly at his sides, he bolted off in the first direction he could find that did not lead him to the creatures. Not thinking, not capable of thought, Boles' voice strained and cracked as he shrieked, then suddenly was cut off as he crashed headlong into a tree at full force.

The para-psychologist rebounded from the hearty locust over two yards, his feet not touching the ground as he traveled. He did himself far more damage than he did the tree, hitting the ground after his brief flight with a bone-jarring force that left him gasping for breath. His arms scrabbled weakly, trying to lift him up, to drag him away, to turn him over, to somehow propel him along before the approaching things could reach him. Mercifully, he blanked out before anything more could happen, his screaming mind shutting down even as the three figures drew closer.

"Don't move," the voice was not a sound Boles wished to hear. Hands worked on him, loosening clothing, brushing at his face. He struggled to open his eyes, a part of him wishing the insane trio of things had done him in rather than leaving him to a worse fate than death.

"Where are they?" he groaned sadly. His eyes blinking, he made to sit up, but Blakely held him down with one solid arm.

"I said 'don't move,' and I meant it," growled the crypto-zoologist. "You've got thorns in your face and you're covered with blood. Now just keep still."

"Where are they?"

"'They' being...?"

"They being the three twisted nightmares that sent me screaming into the night."

Blakely laughed. It was a short burst, a noise more sympathetic than cruel, but the sound of it made Boles go stiff. The crypto-zoologist pried loose a particularly long thorn, fresh scarlet pumping free at its removal, running over the black crusts already streaking Boles' face. As Blakley worked, his partner described the trio of things he witnessed. He gave over what details he could, surprised at his recall.

"Why so surprised," asked Blakely with honest interest. "You are a trained observer, for Christ's sake."

"So is Ms. Skyler," Boles reminded. "And don't point out that I'm more accustomed to things odd and terrible than she—I went a'whimpering just as she did."

"What I find more curious is the details you're giving me. I could do sketches from all you're remembering."

"And that's a bad thing?" snapped Boles.

"No, just curious."

"How so?"

"Where are you getting all these details from? It was pitch black, and you didn't have your flashlight."

Boles shook slightly, a small tremor that snapped his body rigid for an instant. His eyes narrowing, the question resounded within his mind.

"I did see those things ..."

"I didn't say you didn't," answered Blakley. "And I'm not arguing with you. I just asked *how* you saw them. As soon as you think about it, I'm sure you'll see why."

Boles thought for a moment, then sat up weakly. Turning toward Blakely, his mouth open as if to answer, he slowed, then closed it again, his lips drawing into a thin line. He ran his tongue along the inside of his front teeth, then made a small 'tsking' sound, answering softly.

"I, I don't know."

"Yeah," answered Blakely, looking around himself and off through the trees, "that makes two of us."

The next morning found the two professors investigating the area where Boles had experienced his confrontation. Blakley had made a particular addition to his wardrobe, now wearing a holstered Sig Saur 9mm on his hip. The pair entered the forest following the markings the crypto-zoologist had made as they exited the night before which allowed him to return to the spot where he had discovered Boles without any difficulty. Back-tracking, they were able to discover the spot where Boles had first spotted the creatures with equal ease.

"All right," said Blakley. "That's the end of your tracks. Now where do we find theirs?" Boles pointed. When he started to walk in the same direction, his partner told him to stay where he was.

"Let me do the moving," Blakley instructed. "You just let me know when I'm in the same spot they were. You could wander all over looking for the spot, but our chances are better you'll be able to tell when I've found it a lot faster—line of sight and all that. You just tell me when I'm there."

In but a handful of seconds the pair found the tracks of the creatures. Blakely was able to separate out three distinct sets, finding evidence in the loamy forest floor that generally supported Boles' descriptions. But, when the crypto-zoologist tried to backtrace the tracks to their point of origin, or to follow them to wherever the beasts went after Boles ran into the tree, he found himself with nowhere to go.

"What do you mean?" asked Boles.

"I mean there aren't any more tracks. Oh, the things you saw, you saw 'em. They were standing right where you said they were. And they chased you along, just like you said. But ..." Blakley rubbed at his mouth, the fingers of his hand spreading across his face. "It's as if ... it's ... it's almost as if when you weren't looking at them, the damn things weren't there."

Boles stared dumbly.

"Hey, I'm not wrong about this. The ground's the same all across here. There's no rock ridges they could've jumped, no surface clay. Nothing. They just start, and then they just stop. Period."

Blakley waited for his partner to say something. Too trusting of the crypto-zoologist's skills to argue with his conclusions, however, Boles found he had nothing to say. Oddly enough, it was Blakley that made the next suggestion.

"You know, I'm beginning to wonder if this isn't more one of your cases than it is mine."

"Explain yourself."

"Sure. Since we came down here looking for 'creatures,' I was working under the assumption that this one was going to be more my line." Boles nodded in quiet agreement, expressing that he had been thinking the same way himself. "But now, I'm beginning to wonder. I mean, no one is seeing the same creature as the next guy, you see three different ones all on your own at the same time. People can barely think about seeing these things without getting spastic, which you say is common in para-normal cases. Then, this whole thing with the footprints, as if there was nothing there unless you were looking at it ..."

"Are you saying I imagined what I saw?" snapped Boles.

"Possibly," acknowledged Blakely. Then, pointing at the impressions scattered across the ground before them, he added, "But, just because you imagined them doesn't mean they weren't there."

The two men went quiet. Each looked around him off into the trees. What they were hoping to see, they did not know. As the quiet of the wood curled menacingly around them, Blakely hurled it back with a question.

"So, what do you think? Is this some kind of a haunting?"

"I don't know," answered Boles honestly. Sitting down on the ground so as to be able to concentrate better, he said, "there are few of the signs of a traditional haunting. Of any kind of haunting, actually. To have this much activity in an area so open and empty ... no, the spirit world needs human energy to work with. But, there's no one here."

"There's Na'kiraw," suggested Blakely.

"Well, yes," agreed Boles. "But he's close to booking passage on the first cruise ship headed across the Styx, and hauntings are almost always accompanied by young people."

"Really?"

"Oh, yes. Most often girls, most often around the age of emergent puberty. Lots of psychic energy in the air for spirits to play with."

"Huummph," answered Blakley sourly. "Not quite the case here. Na'kiraw's about ..."

The crypto-zoologist broke off as he noted that Boles had slipped into a trance. The para-psychologist was a licensed FBI field psychic and Blakely had come to respect his talent, erratic as it was. Sometimes the moments of vision came upon Boles without warning; sometimes he induced them on his own. Whichever one this was, the crypto-zoologist was determined to let him get all he could out of it.

Blakely started to walk over toward Boles—slowly, quietly—when the para-psychologist stood up suddenly and instantly started running back the way they had come. When Blakely shouted after him as to what he was doing, he was given no more answer than to "hurry up and follow." Blakely caught up to his partner in the parking lot.

"What's going on?" snapped Blakley. "What did you see?"

"It wasn't a vision," explained Boles, panting, gasping for breath. "It was more of a calling. We've got to get to Na'kiraw right away—now. He's dying."

Boles began to stumble off in the direction of the elder Indian's home. Blakley followed along, not bothering with any more questions. He might dislike the para-psychologist, but he did respect the man's abilities. The two rounded the teetering row of long abandoned gift shops and all the rest, heading for the modest home the Native American had made for himself years ago. As they approached the place, both men called out, but no answers were forthcoming. As they arrived at the door, Boles said;

"Break it in."

"What?" responded Blakley, more than a little taken aback.

"There's no time to waste. Break it down."

Slightly amused, Blakley reached out instead and simply turned the doorknob. The door slid quietly open. The crypto-zoologist smiled as Boles shoved past him, hurrying inside without a word. Blakely's smile soon faded, however, as he stepped in behind him. They had found Na'kiraw.

The old man was stretched out on his couch, breathing in raspy, heavy gasps. He was covered with a thin blanket despite the heat, his one arm clawing at the air above his head. His eyes closed, Na'kiraw muttered some inaudible phrase over and over. It was not the old man, however, nor the terrible sound of his breathing that captured the professors' attention. Indeed, to all intents and purposes, the pair forgot about him almost the instant they saw him.

All about the room stirred an incredible assortment of unknown creatures. The things Boles had seen the night before were there—the shining, reptilian feline, the sabre-toothed bullet-headed beast, the bulbous one covered in red feathers. And more. Dozens more.

There were bat-like things hanging from the rafters, some all fang and claw and smelling of death. Some were curled on the floor in fearsome heaps, legged serpents with fold of skin tucked against their bodies appearing to be wings. A vast and powerful bear-like thing sat in the back corner, dragging its claws along the floor absently, sending large curls of wood peeling upward with every stroke.

Eyes green and orange and yellow stared at the two professors. Jaws opened and closed, tongues of all shapes and sizes and weights curled around fangs of every description. Blakely's hand unconsciously unfastened the strap of his holster. When he realized what he had done, he began giggling, his mind highly amused at the comedy of his action. Boles' eyes darted from thing to thing as he whispered;

"I swear, I believe this proves Von Juntz's doctoral thesis, one part of it—"

"What are you babbling about?" demanded Blakely.

"Von Juntz, 'The Origin and Influence of Semantic Magical Texts.' Can't you hear Na'kiraw? He's chanting. He's causing this."

"But why?" asked the crypto-zoologist, his hand still on his weapon. "What is he causing? How is he causing it? What's going on?"

"When Von Juntz was in school in the early 1800s, there were all sorts of random magicks lose in the world—unexplained events, creatures—"

"Sure," agreed Blakely, "that's when sightings of Bigfoot began. So...?"

"Von Juntz offered one hypothesis for creatures like Yetis, or the Loch Ness Monster, things people continually see, but can never find. He said they were race memories of destroyed cultures, left behind as reminders, or avengers, of peoples who were wiped from the face of the earth.

"His theory was that the life energy of the last remaining member of a people could be used to create such a thing. A memory of them. Of how they felt, how they wanted to be remembered."

Blakely looked about the room again. A number of fanged mouths seemed a great deal closer than they had been a moment earlier.

"Yeah, well exactly how does this guy want to be remembered?"

"I think we'll have to ask him that question."

Boles moved a foot forward slightly, testing whether or not they might be able to reach Na'kiraw. Blakely watched stunned, allowing the para-psychologist to move off several feet before thinking to follow him. The two moved in inches, quietly, slowly, steadily. All across the way, hate-filled, unblinking eyes monitored their progress, always seeming ready to pounce at any moment. Dust snowed down from the rafters, the agitation of the things hanging there sending down the decades of build-up. Low hisses and deep growls challenged their every movement.

"Na'kiraw," whispered Boles, kneeling beside the couch, "can you hear me?" When there was no answer, the para-psychologist asked again;

"Can you hear me?"

Again there came no response. The old man simply lay on his couch, clutching his blanket, muttering his never-ending mantra. Back behind them, the professors realized that various of the things had blocked the way to the door. Others were sliding across the heavily curtained windows.

"Na'kiraw," snapped Blakely, out of patience and almost out of courage, "wake up!"

The command was shared by a vicious slap across the Indian's face. Growls sprang from every corner, but nothing stirred as the old man's eyes blinked open. Before Na'kiraw could react to what was happening, Blakely asked;

"Is there anything we can get you? Do you have pills? Should we call an ambulance? Can we—" Na'kiraw held up a silencing hand.

"Too late. My time. Too tired, don't care anymore."

"Na'kiraw," asked Boles, his voice tense and desperate. "Can you see the things here in the room with us? Do you know what is happening?"

The old man blinked, straining to see. Sweat poured down his forehead and into his eyes, clinging to his moving lashes. With a smile, he answered in a tired voice.

"The children of the Wa'Chenka. Come ... come to take my place. Our place."

"But," blurted Blakely, "you said you didn't see anything."

"True. Never saw them. Came when I was sleeping. Dreaming. The darkness ... reaching for me ... telling me to choose ..."

Boles held the old man's hand at the wrist. His pulse was fading fast. Around them in the room, an agitated growling began to rumble. The light piercing the windows flickered, phasing out as the darkness blurred, reaching for them. From beyond, an ebony voice called out in vibrations more felt than heard. Languid purple sounds slithered through the gathering shroud, advancing, clamoring, shrieking—

One of the solidifying things, an apeish beast with four arms, brushed against the green scaled cat. A reptilian claw tore down the ape's side, thick black ooze spurting from the parallel wounds. The ape pounded back in raging anger, but the cat had bounded away. Others in the crowd bit and swiped and snorted at one another. An arc of blood splattered down from the ceiling, splashing against Bole's head, sloshing down over his forehead as he said;

"Choose? Choose what? One of these things? Why? What for?"

"To be our memory. To remind people that the Wa'Chenka ever existed."

Blakely pulled his weapon as the disturbances around them grew more intense. Boles bent close to Na'kiraw, struggling to catch his every word over the growing din of the creatures all about them.

"Tribal elders, coming ... demanding a choice. Many voices, scream for revenge. Death to the white man. Death to the pillager. Death to the yellow hair ..."

"What he saying?" demanded Blakely as he used his 9mm to warn off those things showing interest in himself and Boles.

"He's rambling. Not talking to us anymore. He's talking to himself. Dreaming, I think. He's only verbalizing because we're here intruding on his subconscious."

A set of shelves crashed down from the wall, spilling the old man's collected treasures. The things that knocked them down smashed the personal items into rubble as they tore and smashed at each other in unthinking combat.

"Elders coming," Na'kiraw repeated. "Elders coming ..."

A fox-like beast tore the throat from the red feathered creature with the terrible eyes. Acrid smoke filtered from the wounds, bleeding across the floor. The long feathers dropped from the body one by one, floating in the thickening smoke.

"Elders ... elders here."

As if commanded, several ghostly figures passed through the front walls of the old building. Short, many of them seemed, but weathered of face and taunt of muscle. They came in what looked like pounded leather clothing, most of them adorned with shells and beads and feathers. Old were their eyes. Gnarled were their hands. Stern were their expressions. As the two professors watched, the figures walked silently across the room, moving toward Na'kiraw. One by one, they came up to his resting place, and then they walked into him, sinking inside his flesh, disappearing within his soul.

They came by the dozens, the scores, the hundreds. Every chief and shaman of the Wa'Chenka from the first prehistoric days when they had ceased being random creatures and become men instead. Rude were some of them in stance and form, but they walked erect and their eyes shone with purpose.

As the last of them merged with the dying Na'kiraw, the beasts in the room continued to battle one another, tearing off limbs, gouging eyes, ripping hair out by its roots, biting, clawing, slashing. Blood of all kinds flowed. Brains were bashed, bodies were pulped—but nothing died. Not truly alive, the mashed remains continued to struggle. Severed appendages dragged themselves along, grasping blindly. Ruined bodies forced themselves toward one another, fleshy mallets battering one another senselessly as the ghostsouls invading the old man demand he choose a champion.

Blakely and Boles unconsciously shoved themselves up against
Na'kiraw's couch, straining to get as close to the old man and as far from
the children of the Wa'Chenka as possible. And then, when they were
practically lying across his body, the old Indian sat bolt upright, his arms
flinging upward.

"The choice is made!"

The words leapt from his body, echoing through the rafters,
reverberating through the old shack even as its owner fell dead to his
cushions. The creatures and pieces of creatures gave out a great hiss in
unison, and then began to burst into flames.

"Jesus Christ a'mighty!" shouted Blakely. "Now what do we do?"

Boles had no answer for his partner. The flames spread to all the walls
and ceilings in an instant trapping the two professors in the center of the
room. On the outside, purple smoke leaked from every crack and opening.
Flames ate their way through moments later and the entire building
was quickly covered, the torch mouth of it reaching for the clouds. The
blazing ceiling caved in soon after. The fire spread to the other buildings
quickly. Long before the fire trucks could arrive, the Wa'Chenka Village
was reduced to cinders.

DUKE UNIVERSITY, DURHAM, NC

"Yes, yes, and then what happened?"

"We came home to see you, Stonewall. That's our job, isn't it?"

"Yes, no, I mean," Mr. Gordon S. Pimms went red, flustered in his
excitement. "But how did you escape the burning building?"

"We didn't," answered Boles in an almost bored tone. "The roof
caved in on us. Everything burned. Poof."

"But, but, butbutbutbut—"

"Ladies and gentlemen," said Blakely, "the world's first hot air-
powered motorboat."

"Now see here, Hugo ..."

Blakely let loose a short laugh. Boles merely smiled quietly. The
school chancellor ranted for a while longer, but both professors stuck to
their story, refusing to tell him anything else—though both remembered
what happened quite clearly. When the ceiling had collapsed, the only
remaining beast, the one chosen by Na'kiraw, despite most of his
ancestors' wishes, flew above the two men and began beating its wings
furiously. As it did, it created a dome of air over the professors, enough to
sustain them while the fire raged. As they clung to the old man's corpse,

sweating from the heat, they heard his disappearing voice in their heads.

"The Wa'Chenka were never great warriors. Many argue for revenge, but revenge against who? Against what? Fearsome should not be our memory. Small we were, fast we were, clever, but unnoticed. Beautiful, but rarely seen."

Finally leaving Pimms' office, the pair waved at the flustered chancellor as his polished mahogany door closed behind them. As they headed quickly for the hall, making to escape before Pimms thought to come after them, Blakely said;

"Well, duty's done and all that. What'dya say, Boles, want to go get a drink?" The para-psychologist's eyes went wide for a moment as he considered his colleague. Before he could answer, Blakely added;

"I was just thinking, maybe the two of us had better start trying to get along before we get into something ... I don't know, something where a little more teamwork might work better than the way we've been doing things so far."

"I'd really like to say something sarcastic," admitted Boles, "but the simple truth is I think you're right. It's a thought that occurred to me as I watched the ceiling caving in on us."

"I know what you mean," answered Blakely, his tone quieter than normal. Chastised. "Com'on, I've got a bottle of Jack Daniels' in my office—"

"Green label, I hope?"

"Yeah, that would be appropriate, wouldn't it? Sure, the good stuff, why not?"

As the two walked down the hallway, Boles ventured a comment bordering on the friendly.

"Heavens, who would have thought it? We're almost Humphrey Bogart and Claude Rains at this point."

"Yeah, it could be the beginning of a beautiful friendship at that. And if it isn't, I've still got the pictures I took of you layin' all sprawled in the forest with your face full of thorns and ..."

"You what?"

Boles sputtered at his colleague. Blakely laughed. The two men kept walking toward their liquid reward, however, and far away in the deep wood, a hummingbird—one not fearsome but fast, clever but unnoticed, beautiful, but rarely seen, chirped in approval. Beating its emerald green wings, it flitted off deeper into the forest, searching for the perfect spot where it could sun itself.

The following story stars Jhong, the deadly martial artist from the Teddy London series. One of the world's greatest warriors, his entire body is a deadly weapon. In his varied adventures, he has battled vampires and werewolves, and even Hercules, always coming out triumphant. But, what happens when such an individual goes up against a god, and suddenly brawn is of little use? Or, in other words, how does a warrior combat—

The Dungeon
of Self

"We are all serving a life-sentence in the dungeon of self."
— Cyril Connolly

They had waited for the worst of the afternoon heat to dissipate. Once that had passed, the Captain of Police had taken the old man to the spot outside of town where it had happened. The place was everything he had expected.

The site was over thirty miles into the depths of the great desert. It was a blasted terrain of weary rock and drifting sand. Some defiant shocks of scrub stood here and there, but mostly it was a lifeless, acrid place—drainingly hot—suffocating and quiet.

"What do you think?"

Jhong turned toward the officer who had just spoken. The questioner was a soft man, not particularly tall or strong. He was not a heroic figure, just a sack of bones and meat stuffed into a uniform to perform duties for payment. Because of this, the older man decided to tell him the truth.

"It is a demon."

The policeman stared blankly, not knowing how to respond. His mind reeled at the thought.

Demon. He had fought within his brain for days—knowing something beyond human ken was at work—refusing to believe it. Now he had a word he had to face or refuse. Demon.

The Captain did not know what to make of the older, Oriental man kneeling on the ground before him. After all, he had been hoping to avoid the entire affair. It was out in the desert. Outside his jurisdiction. Something he had been doing his best to ignore.

Now this intruder had showed up—asking questions, stirring up interest. Just another part of the problem the Captain desperately wished would simply go away. He knew it was not going to, though.

For some eighteen weeks people had been dying out in the desert. Over thirty bodies had been discovered in various places—in the brush and in the open, hanging from cliff walls, half buried in the sand. Where they had been deposited had varied greatly. Their condition, however, was always the same.

"What do you mean—demon?"

The bodies were void of life. Blood and bile, all the internal juices were gone—sucked away—evaporated without a trace. A pregnant woman had been found drained even of her milk, her womb a brittle sack filled with dust. One man, well known for his corpulence, was found crisp and shriveled, his flaking skin hanging in billowing folds. The smell of fried fat still clung to everything for yards around.

All the victims were found thus—their flesh like dried leather, and their faces terrified masks of unbelieving fear.

"I mean that your killer is not a man—that there is some sort of unnatural thing loose in your desert."

The policeman jerked his head a fraction of an inch in one direction, then the opposite one. His eyes twitched. His mouth tried to speak. He could not respond, however. He was too afraid.

He had seen all of the other bodies. Some he had only examined when they were brought into the city. Some he had seen where they were discovered. All of them had cried out to him, their terrible condition screaming that something was not right—that there was nothing normal or ordinary or even human in their deaths.

And then, of course, there were the tracks.

"You have thought this yourself," said Jhong, reading the other man's attitude as he rose from the ground.

The policeman nodded. He had purposely driven the old man out to the site of the latest murder himself—alone. He had left behind the officers under his command because they were all young men—modern, sophisticated—too intelligent to believe what their captain had begun to suspect. To fear.

Although he had tried to keep a cap on the inevitable stories, not wanting to disrupt the tourist season, the policeman had known whispers were leaking away out from his control. When the man identifying himself as Jhong Feng had arrived at headquarters, the captain had at first thought him a reporter.

"What are you going to do?"

"I will remain here until this thing returns," answered the older man. "Then I will dispatch it."

The Captain stared again. Shame and anger raged within him. Relief cooled his nerves, pushing him back toward his official vehicle, urging him to run while he had the chance. His pride howled hotly in the background, however, demanding he at least make a show of having a spine.

"What do you mean ... 'dispatch it?'"

"I am no stranger to such occurrences," offered Jhong. Studying the fading tracks surrounding the spot where the last body had been found, he said, "this is what I do. Whenever the veil that separates us from the ghost realms is pulled aside, I go where I am needed. To do what must be done."

The captain looked at Jhong, at the single small bag he carried slung over his shoulder. It was obvious the older man had few supplies with him, certainly not enough to survive a night in the desert. Not in the desert where so many had died.

"How can you be certain this, this ... demon, as you called it, shall return?"

"The tracks. The photographs you showed me taken at the other sites all displayed the same peculiar never-ending circle of footsteps. But, in those pictures, there were two sets of tracks—one going clockwise, the other counter-clockwise."

"Yes," said the policeman. "So?"

"There is only one set of tracks here," answered Jhong. "In the photos, the erosion of one direction made it obvious time elapsed between the making of the two sets. My guess is, whatever is doing this will return. Tonight. I will meet it."

"Why?" asked the captain fearfully. "Why would it do such a thing?"

Jhong shrugged.

"A ritual of some sort, perhaps?" he theorized absently. "Why does it circle its victims? Why one way and then the other? Why wait to make the second circle? Why does it kill at all?" The older man turned back to the captain.

"Every action produces questions. By remaining here tonight I hope to discover some answers."

"So, that's why you do this," asked the policeman. "Curiosity? You're some sort of scientist?"

"No," answered Jhong plainly. "I do this because I can. Because others cannot." Noting the position of the rapidly setting sun, he added,

"All these murders took place after sundown, to the best of your knowledge, did they not? Perhaps you should depart now, Captain. If you would be so kind as to return in the morning, I would not mind avoiding the walk back to the city."

The policeman wanted to protest. It was his duty—not some stranger's—to stay there and meet whatever might be returning to the scene of the crime. It was his responsibility. It was what he was paid to do.

No, a voice whispered within his head. *You are paid to maintain the peace. That is all. You check the locks on the stores and you chase vagrants away from businesses. You are a lackey, a sanitation engineer—not a hero.*

The Captain nodded in quiet defeat, then slunk back to his official vehicle. He watched the older man in his review mirror as he headed back to town, praying that the morning would hold more for him than yet another dead body.

Jhong waited quietly, alone in the gathering darkness. He did not attempt to built a fire. He had no need of either the light or heat it might provide. The old warrior had trained for years for exactly the kind of moment ahead of him that night.

He had begun his training after studying the ancient prophecies—anticipating becoming humanity's savior. He was not the chosen one, however. That mantle had passed to another. At first Jhong had been resentful of this fact. Later, once he met the man whose place he had tried to take, he acknowledged that fate had chosen wisely.

Perhaps he would have succeeded in the other's place, he thought. Then again, perhaps not.

The answer no longer seemed to be of any real importance. Although the line had been held and the universe spared by someone else, there still lurked a great army of dangerous, unholy things just beyond the veil—all of them waiting for their chance to strike at humanity. There was still much work to do. He had not trained in vain. His pride, unlike the captain's, could still be soothed.

"And you believe this."

The voice crawled over the sand out of the darkness, the barest hint of it stinging Jhong's ears. The warrior sat cross-legged within the circle of tracks, directly on the spot where the last victim had been found. He did not stand, did not jerk his head from side to side. Did not even open his eyes. There was no need.

"You were cheated, Jhong Feng," the voice assured him. "You worked for years for your chance, and it was snatched from your grasp by one unworthy."

The whisper was closer—deeper—behind him this time. Its point of origin still indicated the speaker was some distance off, though, so Jhong maintained his meditative pose, the only movement the shallow but rhythmic rise and fall of his chest.

"You were to be the one to turn back the flood of nightmare. You were the one who was to wear the mantle of hero. Now, another holds your glory, and you chase but specs of evil instead."

"I am here chasing you," the elder answered softly. "If but a spec you are, then my task is that much easier."

A rush of approving applauds came from out of the darkness.

"Very good, old man," sneered the voice. "I had been expecting that frightened bag of pus, the good Captain of Police. But you promise, oh, so much, much more. Perhaps tonight will not be so boring as all the others have been."

The warrior opened his eyes as footsteps neared his position. Whatever was approaching, he could tell by the sound of the sand being displaced that it used bipedal locomotion. He was also certain it was no larger than an average man. This was good news.

Jhong carried few weapons, none of them modern in design. He was a martial artist—his body his most important weapon. If that which was almost upon him weighed no more than a man and stood no taller than a man, he reasoned, then hopefully it would be no more difficult to defeat than a man. As prepared as he could be, Jhong rose to meet his adversary.

A tall, slim figure came toward him out of the darkness. It held the shape of a much younger man, finely muscled and limber of movement.

Its face, however, was another matter. The eyes glowed slightly. They held a sinisterly regal manner, the look of an ancient pharaoh, or a fallen archangel. And yet, Jhong could not help but note the shining orbs also held an equal measure of capricious humor.

The form was dressed in hand-woven robes, colorful silks girdled with spun gold encrusted with gems. Its head was sheathed in an intricate metal crown which, although surprisingly unadorned, glowed with an inherent light. Jhong regretted a moment of surprise, but he could not help himself. Oddly enough, he had not expected to see something so ordinary.

The thing swept apart its human arms, saying, "This is not what you expected?"

"Evil is all I expected," countered Jhong. "My surprise is at seeing it clad in such an ordinary skin."

"It has been said that I possess a thousand different forms," mused the shining figure, "as if human reckoning could put a tally to all that I am."

"And what are you?" asked Jhong.

"I am the messenger and the soul of the Outer Gods. I dwell in a cavern at the center of this world. My name is Nyarlathotep, and I am the end of all things." The Egyptian veneer of the figure faded, replaced by that of a hairless man with dead black skin and cloven feet.

"Men have worshipped my various aspects in every corner of this globe throughout your recorded history and long before." During the scant seconds it took the thing to speak, its aspect shifted repeatedly. Jhong saw a winged sphinx with a featureless head bearing a triple crown transform into a four-armed dwarf that stood upon three pulsating tentacles. This faded into a two-headed bat which in turn became a swarm of monstrously huge locusts.

"Why, one form even you might know."

The spitting horde faded then, congealing into a figure hidden from sight by a shimmering black fan. Jhong's eyes widened as he recognized the creature before him. Although he knew it as a legend only, he was certain that behind the fan was a monstrously obese woman, a thing festooned with five mouths and horrible ropes of tentacles. How the fan hid the terrible shape, he did not know, but he was certain he looked upon the terror described to him by his great grandmother decades ago in his native China.

"But," said the thing as the air swirled around it once more, "when all masks are stripped away, each of us has but one face. This is mine."

The corpulent form folded inward on itself, rising upward at the same time. Enormous it grew, wretchedly gnarled and clawed appendages springing from its trunk. Again it stood on three legs, but these bent and twisted around each other at the waist in a fashion so grotesque it was beyond Jhong's ability to comprehend how they operated. This was not the most bizarre aspect of the form, however.

Atop its shoulders, taking the place of both neck and head, a great, lashing blood-red tentacle tongued its way up out of the creature. A yawning gash of a maw, split from the top of its chest up through the tentacle, moved to form sounds although not in the manner of a human mouth.

Jhong did not speak, but instead began to assess the possible vulnerable spots within the creature's latest form. Slowly, he dug the toes of his right foot into the sand. Muscles throughout his body went limp—others tensed. His arms moved fluidly, hands positioning themselves automatically. Civilization relaxed within his mind, animal instincts flowing through his nerves—sharpening his edge.

"You're a stubborn man, Jhong Feng," sneered Nyarlathotep, listening to the warrior's thoughts. Then, the creature added with a gagging chortle, "But, haven't you always been?"

Suddenly, Jhong was no longer in the desert, but somehow found himself in China, in a jade palace hung with silk tapestries and appointed with the finest furnishings. The warrior did not move, throwing his senses outward into the room. The light hitting his eyes was real. The reverberation of his heartbeat from the walls bespoke the proper distance, the feel of it brought with it a shimmer of glazed terra cotta. The smell was of teak and ginger and steaming tea.

""You were not a happy man when last you strode this place, were you, Master Feng?"

Jhong shut his eyes, refusing the images all about him. Sending his senses throughout his body, he strained his nerves to find the flaw in the hallucination all about him.

"You did not like anyone then, including yourself."

And then, the warrior felt the toes of his right foot—still buried in the sand. Instantly he swerved to the left. His right foot flattened, supporting his weight. His left flew forward, slamming into Nyarlathotep's chest. The blow was one of Herculean intensity. If connecting with a tractor door it would have removed it from its hinges. The great creature did not fall from the impact, but it did teeter. The dream world fell to pieces.

"Clever, Master Feng."

Jhong made to follow up his blow, his limbs moving even before Nyarlathotep's words began to ring within his head. His left heel crashed against what appeared might be one of the towering god's knees. The warrior swerved his heel on contact, digging into the joint, seeking to do the maximum amount of damage. Then, Jhong flipped back away from the god. While still in mid-air his hand snaked into his bag, pulling out three shurikens. His fingers had them spaced cleanly before he landed.

The warrior spun as he neared the ground, his wrist snapping, sending the trio of throwing stars flying before he actually touched the ground. All of them dug into the massive tentacle head, tearing flesh, finding blood, embedding themselves deeply enough to sending rippling pain throughout the massive body.

"Well done," said Nyarlathotep, as if unaffected by the weapons. "Now what?"

Jhong stared at the outer god, wondering what he could do next. Further physical attack seemed useless. Indeed, he had grown to wonder if he could inflict any lasting hurt on the thing before him. The warrior had expected trouble, of course. The murders in the desert had beckoned him with the lure of some terrible beast which he could pit himself against—another devil-thing he might bring low with nothing more than skill and courage and a few sharp edges.

"Didn't work out that way," asked the god. "Did it?"

The warrior did not answered.

"My reach to this plane is limited for the time being. So I've been testing the waters, so to speak, here in the desert. Finding juicy little bugs. Do you know why?"

When Jhong did not respond, Nyarlathotep smiled, then faster than the speed of thought, the creature manipulated their surroundings, returning them to the jade palace which the god had manifested earlier.

Jhong marveled at the illusion's accuracy for a moment, then he thought, Of course they're correct. This thing has searched my mind to find this scene. If the smell of teak and ginger and steaming tea is what I remember, then that is what we will smell, whether it is correct or not.

"Impressive, Jhong Feng. Humanity has come far in the few short decades since last I was here."

"And why have you returned," asked the warrior. "Just to hunt for juicy little bugs?"

Nyarlathotep stretched out its gnarled appendages as it paced along the perimeter of the room, wringing its fingers violently. As it moved along, its ugly whisper filled Jhong's brain.

"In an eon before," it hissed, "the great Old Ones strode the Earth and ruled the million heavens from its fragile shores. Vast were their powers and never-ending their reach. But, the time came for them to rest and so they retired to their castles and caverns, awaiting the moment when the stars would align and beckon them back once more."

Jhong stared at the walls of his former home. So long ago had it been when he had left everything behind to go out into the world. He had not thought about it for years—about the life he abandoned when he believed he was to become humanity's savior—that which he had turned his back upon to wander the globe, battling grotesque nightmares like the one whispering to him at that moment.

"That time of alignment is coming, Jhong Feng. That is why I am here. The outer and elder gods are bound away from this world for the tiny brief now. But every day leaves the walls between our realities the slightest bit more sheer. Even now, whenever certain rituals are observed, we may can wander here once more."

Half of Jhong's mind remained riveted on the god as it strolled about the edges of the image it had created. The other half, however, could not help but stare into that image and remember his past. The warrior did not want to be bitter. He did not desire to give in to the pettiness he had spent so long trying to grow past. But still, to see it once more—all he had given up ... for nothing ...

"And that is why I am here," said Nyarlathotep, "to spin my web and draw flies to it. Every time some fool reaches for the false treasures I have set out, another soul becomes mine. Each soul gathered giving me more substance within this world."

Jhong forgot his memories for the moment, concentrating on the creature's tale. He puzzled over why it had bothered to erect the image of his former home. What, he wondered, was its plan? If all it wanted to do was kill him, why waste so much time?

"The more of you I destroy, the more the story spreads, the more terror is created. The more fear of me in this world, the greater my power grows."

The warrior listened to the thing as it moved past him once more. "What do you think will happen when pictures of what has happened here are broadcast to every corner of this globe—once fear of me spreads exponentially from mere scores to billions? What exactly do you think will be the reaction to the knowledge that I am moving across the land?"

Jhong blinked, trying to comprehend everything Nyarlathotep had told him. His mind seemed dazed, however—fractured. He could not concentrate fully. Too many conflicting pieces of the puzzle vied for his attention. One after another, they all shouted within his brain.

Should have never left home/have to watch this monster/lost everything in the past/gave it all up for nothing/why does he show me my old home?/what about all those he killed?/isn't that why you came here?/why did I come here—why?

The warrior's training bristled, sending warning alarms shrieking throughout his mind and nerves. They only added to his confusion, however.

What good being prepared, he mused, if one doesn't know what they are prepared for?

The god made yet another journey around the room. And then, its purpose suddenly became clear to its victim.

Spinning its web, thought the elder. Setting out false treasures.

Jhong's mind raced back to other things that had come from the same nether regions as the one before him. Unlike the simple terrors he so often came across—trifles such as vampires and werewolves—these things were creatures bound more by mathematics than magic.

Circles of footprints, he realized suddenly. Circles!

With a speed born of ten thousand hours of relentless practice, the elder threw himself forward with all his strength. He slammed into Nyarlathotep with a frightful force, toppling the god onto its side. Air crashed out of the thing's lungs. The image of the Chinese mansion faded, returning the combatants to the desert.

Ignoring the change, Jhong remained on the offensive. Instantly he flipped up onto his feet, his left driving down hard on the shouldered tentacle while his right slammed against the things ribs—once, twice—twice more.

The god made to stand, but Jhong fell sideways, swinging his left leg hard, knocking two of the monster's twisted limbs out from under it. Again the thing crashed against the ground, its hideous scream echoing across the desert.

This thing attacks through its victims' weaknesses, thought Jhong as his assault continued. For me it chose pride.

Nyarlathotep lashed out with its main tentacle, snapping the air near

Jhong's head. The warrior dodged, pulling his knife from its sheath beneath his shirt with one quick, short motion. He slashed with the speed of a panther, dragging the blade several feet down the great, howling tongue.

It reads their minds, find their lost memories, and then uses them to mesmerize until it completes its ritual geometry.

The god dug its legs into the sand. Jhong raced forward at the horror, his knife hand extended as if intending to stab his enemy. Nyarlathotep extended its twisted limbs to catch the warrior, only to be surprised when Jhong flipped upward over its head, slicing its back open as he came down behind it. The god spun around, its fists slamming the ground where Jhong had landed. It was too late. The warrior had already dodged off into the darkness.

It sums us up from our worst parts, thought Jhong. *Trapping us with one ill-considered moment from our pasts. One failure all it takes to damn us forever.*

Turning slowly, Nyarlathotep called upon the reserves it had built up from the souls it had drained, preparing for its next assault. "Your performance has been most impressive. But it will not save you."

Due to the barriers erected against its kind in the distant past, the god's connection to the Earthly plane was not firm. Nyarlathotep had to cast lures for its victims. Each one captured made its hold stronger. The thing had not worried overly about confrontations with humans. Even with its power the merest shade of what it should be, still with the ability to know its enemies' deepest secrets and intents, it knew it had nothing to fear.

That, of course, was before it had met Jhong, before it discovered some humans did not need to think before they acted—that their instinct was sufficient to win them through.

"You have dragged me back to my merest shell, Jhong Feng," snarled the god. "But your moment of triumph ends—now!"

Nyarlathotep shot its twisted appendages forward with unimaginable speed. The gnarled lengths of leathery flesh entwined around Jhong and dragged him forward until his face was but inches from his foe's. The warrior struggled, knowing he could not escape, finally realizing that his pride had rendered him powerless against the god. Nyarlathotep dropped its massive tentacle lower, whipping Jhong across the face over and over.

Suddenly he knew why the priests whispered for their flocks to think pure thoughts. Thoughts were energy—energy that could not be destroyed—only collected and then manipulated by those who know the secret of its harvesting.

Again the tentacle slammed against the warrior's face. Blood broke free from his lips and nose. His left eye began to swell and close. Soon his bones would begin to break. Then he would die, and with his soul would Nyarlathotep begin again. Death after death would follow, more and more until the god-thing had won through, opening a doorway from its world into the warriors' own. The god shook Jhong violently at that point, answering his thoughts.

"Yes!" It bellowed. "Then shall I throw open the doors behind me. Great Q'talu will follow as I bring forth his palace from the ocean's deep. Tulzscha's flame will split your sun, Glaaki and ebony Bugg-Shash will swallow your peoples, Cyaegha will crumble your mountains, even forgotten Gol-Goroth will swarm forward with all the hosts of the outer realms, dining upon the essence of this dimension as we have so many tens of millions of others."

With a snarling laugh, Nyarlathotep hurled Jhong across the sand, bouncing him off an outcropping of rock. The warrior's shoulder and forehead were torn open from the contact, blood gushing forth. Ignoring the pain as best he could, struggling to see, the elder's hand slipped into his bag pulling forth his roped fighting sticks.

"Sticks," the god howled with glee. "You think to fight me with sticks? Don't you understand it yet, human? I offered you a chance to reject your past, and you failed. You cannot resist me now! I win!"

Jhong struggled to his feet. Terror crept through his system. He knew the god was right. Ever since the split second when he had wondered why he had left his old life, a part of him had felt trapped, pinned down—damned. For the first time in years, the warrior was uncertain as to what to do. And then, as Nyarlathotep stepped across the sand to claim its prize, the first bullets tore through its enormous body.

"NOOOOOOOOOOOOOO!"

The Captain of Police had somehow braved the night and his own terrors to return to the scene of the last murder. He had thought to return to the city, to drown his foolhardy desire to be a man once more with the cleansing grace of alcohol—as he did most nights. Then, with the glaring yellow of the city's lights just coming into sight, he had turned his vehicle around and headed back out into the desert.

"Kill you!"

The god tore across the sand, charging into the machine gun fire. The fat, balding officer stammered at the sight of the terrible beast closing on him, tears streaking his face and spittle foaming from between his clattering teeth. His terror left him screaming, but his trigger finger held tight and round after round tore through the leather skin of the nightmare figure. And then, despite the massive damage the captain's heavy weapon had caused Nyarlathotep's temporary form, the god closed on the officer, sweeping him up in its gnarled hands.

"Coward," whispered Nyarlathotep, confusion shuddering through the thing's cold voice. "You were a coward. I was so sure."

The thing laughed pitifully, and then suddenly it dropped the Captain, its once more intangible body again barred by the mystic barriers it had struggled so long to overcome. The officer fell to his knees, his hands shaking violently.

Moving slowly, Jhong staggered to the man's side. The Captain turned, crying, "I had to. I had to."

"I know," said the warrior with heart-felt sympathy. "I know."

The men hugged each other then, fear and relief dragging them toward each other's reassuring humanity. Their wounds scraped one against the other, mingling their blood. If there was any pain in the action, neither one of them noticed.

When the two finally stood and looked around themselves, the clean moonlight showed no trace of the horror they had faced except for the litter of the officer's shell casings. Nodding to himself with surprising satisfaction, the Captain of Police asked,

"Did, did we beat it?"

"You beat it," replied Jhong. "Or, more exactly, you beat yourself. For most of us, the greatest monster of all."

"Thanks," answered the Captain, smiling. "What say you to a small nip? I have a bottle of Macallan in my jeep."

Jhong nodded. The two men walked through the darkness toward the distant vehicle in silence. Once there, the Captain found his bottle, uncorked it, then offered it to his companion as he asked,

"I really did ... did see that ... that thing, didn't I?"

Jhong took a long swig of the sherry-casked scotch, then passed the bottle back to his host, assuring the policeman. "Yes—you did."

A familiar tendril of fear curled around the officer's spine for a moment, but he brushed it aside, adding, "And I shot it in the ass, didn't I?"

"Yes," Jhong laughed as the Captain took his own long drink. "That you did, my friend. That you did."

The two drained the bottle before they had gone two miles. Many songs did they sing before the morning sun dawned.

*Our last Anton Zarnak entry for this volume is the latest one created by CJ. Knowing he would not be doing any more tales of this character for the Carter estate, he wanted to seriously consider the question of how ordinary mortals can do combat with the gods. In **The Dungeon of Self**, CJ explored what a warrior might do when faced with a fairly powerful dimension-spanning entity. But, with a character like Zarnak, who actually does have a fair amount of mystical training, how else can one up the stakes, than to have him faced with not **a** god, but the source of all life and power itself?*

The Questioning of the Azathothian Priest

Recorded by Dr. Anton Zarnak

The judge's pupils rolled, slamming against the upper lids of his eyes with a martyr's force. He groaned loudly, not with sound, but with the twisting of his body, hissing his pain throughout his chambers. Already knowing the dread answer, still he asked;

"You can't be serious."

"I've never come before you, your honor, when I wasn't serious."

The speaker was a middle-aged man, tall and rough-shaven, regulation length dark wet curls slopping across his head. It was August in New York City, and the weather was draining the life from the planet. Captain Thorner did not like the city when it reached this stage of unmoving heat. He had only felt it once before. He did not care for it then, either.

"A man's been *shot*, Captain," the judge moaned. "Murdered. And you want me to dismiss it."

"It's been known to happen."

"And that *man* was known to be in the hands of the city's police department at the time," the judge said, his words set at a distinct tone, as if anyone needed any reminding. "The man was being questioned by police while his lawyer waited in the next room."

The judge closed his eyes for a moment, his left hand to his face. Rubbing at his eyes, more for distraction than anything else, he mused, "It's not bad enough the city fathers look like fools, not ready in any way—Canal Street just buckles—an earthquake, an earthquake in New York City ... and now you saddle us with this, this ..."

"I'm aware of what it looks like—"

"Oh, you are? Then tell me, Captain," demanded the judge, his voice trembling with a rage bordering on the religious, "what am I suppose to tell that boy's mother?"

"Your honor," interrupted the only other person present. "Before you tell anyone anything, I propose you set aside your biases and read the report."

Silence fell across the room in ripples, fat rolling ones, like layers of caramel folding into a pan. It emanated from the judge, the strength of it sniffing for lies or half truths, deception of any kind.

"And why would I believe *anything* you have to say, Dr. Zarnak?"

The other man stared at the judge. His visage made him seem a youth, but though his face was unlined, his eyes whispered of uncounted years. He was tall, slender and saturnine, with a fine-boned visage as sallow as antique ivory. His hair was thick and black as night, save for a dramatic silver streak that began at his right temple and zigzagged backward to the base of his skull.

"Because I am a man of honor and I know of things that you cannot imagine."

The sallow mouth moved precisely, spitting words cold and crisp, "You pray that what they say about me isn't true. But, in your locked away heart of hearts, you know it is, and you fear that all your power is just some worthless speck, a puff of nonsense in a mad world."

"Anton," said the captain softly, his fingers brushing the doctor's arm, auras joining for the moment of contact needed for true conversation ...

The single word worked. Zarnak reeled in his anger—resumed his mask. He could always count on Thorner to remind him not to dwell on any single stupidity in the world around him. It was always those kinds of moments that killed Zarnak's kind, those ridiculous instances of emotion where logical and calm reason were sacrificed in an insane attempt to beat another at his own game. Ego. Mages could not afford such luxuries. Going where he should have in the first place, he set a vibration in his voice that would make the judge more ... open to suggestion.

"Your honor," a pause was added to allow the moment of respect-given to balance the weight of the coming request, "for everyone's sake, just read the report."

Judge Tyler Reis's head snapped back a quarter of an inch, the sides of it tightening visibly at the ears. His emotions jumbled, his subconscious pushed him along the path of least resistance while his momentarily scrambled consciousness pulled itself together.

Reis looked down at the document that was suddenly in his hand with shock. It was political suicide to touch a case like this. An honest man, but a careful one, he wanted no part of the nightmare he could see headed for whichever member of the judiciary signed off on this one. Why had he accepted it? He had told himself he would stay out ...

It did not matter. Reis shrugged with resignation. He had allowed them to make contact, to force his hand. His breath filled with the chill of long dreaded fear, the defeat in it so palpable that it pained him to listen to it. Sitting back in his chair, he decided to just get it over with. Folding back the cover sheet, just a title page containing certain city-significant numbers, he started with the first paragraph.

My name is Dr. Anton Zarnak. In my capacity as a trained psychiatrist, I was brought in by Capt. Mark Thorner to assist in the interrogation of one Tidril Belbin. The following is a transcription of that account, with commentary by myself at the appropriate junctures.

To begin: I arrived at the station shortly before 9:00 PM, the time scheduled for interrogation. I studied the prisoner beforehand through the standard two-way glass. It served no purpose. Despite the relative newness of these stations, subject knew he was being observed. Moreover, he assumed a stance designed to indicate that he could see through the glass as well, and that he was studying those on the other side.

I note this here since I would expect others to as well, and I wish to strongly point out certain aspects of this interrogation as uniformly disturbing to those in attendance. On more than one occasion during the preliminary observation, Belbin made references which made no sense unless taken in context with what was happening on the other side of the wall, down to and including the rejoinder "Gods bless you" when patrolman Daniels sneezed, and then said "Thank you" to Belbin as he wiped his nose.

Seeing the futility of continuing the "unsuspected observation" we moved inside to confront the suspect. While he was questioned by Captain Thorner I put together the following portfolio on the man.

Belbin could best be described as benevolently arrogant. I see him as a potentially dangerous individual simply because he absolutely believes that existence is futile. If he were to choose to retire from the folly of said futility, he would end his life in a millisecond. I believe if the idea were to come into his head on its own, he might possibly die then and there.

If he were to decide to feel pity toward others, though, he could become the most dangerous of random killers the world has ever seen. There are no simple terms to label such an individual. He is powerful—within his own mind—to the point of invincibility.

Further: On the question of Rationality: Belbin is the most rational of creatures. He is highly intelligent, ruthlessly logical and exactingly precise.

On the question of Sanity: Belbin would be insane if his belief in himself were misplaced. Since it is not, he must be thought of as—

"Sane?"

Reis slammed the document against his desk.

"I won't stand for this, Zarnak. Who do you ... oh, I won't go there again. But, damn you. How am I supposed to explain this to anyone else?"

"You're not, Tyler," said the Captain softly. "You're supposed to understand what actually happened, and then figure out how to explain it all. Any way you can."

"But, what are you asking me to accept here? For God's sake, Thorner, I mean ... yes ... what you've brought me in the past—" images flashed through Reis' mind—dozens of sailors, slaughtered for their blood, tornadoes caused by "things," as the Captain had called them, "personalities, angels—well, demons really. But, incredibly powerful, Godlike,"—The winged bodies that had been brought in, burned and slashed—that ape thing ...

"This is ..."

Reis went silent. He knew someone had to read the report. Someone official had to sign off on one of the most terrible murders in the city's colorful history. During the war, people were easier to distract when the insanity hit and Zarnak prowled the streets. But now, with the monster Hitler and the miserable reptile Tojo off the front pages, the newspapers were always looking for some new creature to bleat about to the rest of the sheep.

Tidril Belbin could be that monster.

Judge Tyler Reis turned back to the report. He skimmed over the rest of Zarnak's opening remarks. They mostly concerned things with which the judge was already all too familiar—the circumstances of Belbin's arrest, the young women's bodies found, the mindless carving, blood paintings, the charnel pits. Indeed, what was in the report was old news—there was still information coming in, new discoveries, new terrors to hide being unearthed in Belbin's mansion ...

Freak palace is more like it, Reis thought, remembering the horrible, horrible photos. Monster—goddamned monster ...

"It's not a good enough word, anymore," the judge muttered under his breath.

"What isn't?" asked Thorner.

"Monster."

Thorner moved his eyes in a noncommittal gesture. He added his shoulders to the motion. Zarnak sat impassively. Waiting. The judge skimmed the rest of the regular formula of the report, finally getting to page 8, the statement. Its statement. Belbin's words. His justification, his attempt at self-exoneration, absolution, legitimacy ...

Reis shut down his indignation and his horror and got down to business by reading;

Explanatory Excerpt 1:

Here within Belbin explains himself in relationship to his deity.

Bel: "You must understand, I am a priest of Azathoth. I do what is expected."

Tho: "Meaning you're thinking of yourself as a member of the clergy? You're thinking this gives you some kind of special rights?"

Bel: [amused] "Meaning, Captain Thorner, friend of Anton Zarnak, that as a priest of Azathoth, I need not really worry about such as you."

Tho: "Really. When you want to leave, you'll what? Snap your fingers? Snap. Like that? And this Assholethoth, he'll just come and save you?"

Bel: "Hardly. Azathoth pays his followers no mind. Nor does he need to. After all, I am powerful enough to destroy you all with but a moment's concentration. In other words, I have only accompanied you here because it pleases me to do so."

Tho: "You're a tough guy, is that what you're saying?"

Bel: "I am all-powerful, Captain."

Tho: "You? You're the one who's all-powerful. Not this god you shill for?"

Tho: "Azathoth simply is what is. At the center of all time and space, all existence and dreams, all that can be and will be, there exists Azathoth.

"Greatest of them all.

"What you must realize, of course, is that we do not exist as he exists—we but exist somewhere within the deep and violent crevices of his mind. All of us, Captain Thorner, friend to Anton Zarnak, you and all you know and all you do not know. Azathoth creates fate and destiny, love and chaos. His dreams are our substance. His nightmares, our calamities. He is the absolute, true, pure and only lord of existence."

Tho: "Well, if you won't mind the asking, why would it please such a powerful nabob as yourself to consort with us lowly types?"

Bel: "Please, Captain, what more could I ask for? I plan on placing the city under my control. I've decided mastery of one small planet is something Azathoth can be directed toward. Please understand, his unconscious whims are our reality. There are those of us who have begun to unlock his secrets. Once I've finished my work here, it will be safe for me to proceed with my overall plan."

Tho: "Your work here? And what business do you think you have here outside of answering for your crimes?"

Bel: "[smiling] Captain Thorner, friend of Anton Zarnak, you two individuals are really the only people who could stop me, if, of course, you knew to what extent my powers reach. But by coming here quietly, I am able to have you both together in one place, not yet prepared to think of me as a menace worthy of your full powers. You consider me nothing more than a simple madman, a psychopath. Your thoughts at present are to do no more than evaluate me."

Tho: "And what are you here for?"

Bel: "I've come to eliminate the two of you."

Reis fanned himself with the report. Though the horrible heat had begun to subside, still it sent the sweat running down his face—neck, chest, everywhere. The fanning turned the rivulets into icy fingers, chilling his body. As he closed his eyes for a moment, a shudder ran through him. His voice a whisper, he asked;

"Why does he say he came to eliminate you? You two? Why would he want to?"

"It's all in the re—"

"Just tell me," snapped the judge.

"Belbin thought it was within his reach to take over the world," answered Thorner matter-of-factly. "He felt Anton was the only mystic close at hand who could counteract his abilities. He also claimed to be somewhat worried about me because I was the one member of the force who had consistently been able to deal with things beyond the normal mortal ken. Working as a team, he saw us as, at the least, a formidable nuisance. His plan, therefore, was to get us both in the same place and destroy us."

"And why didn't his plan work?"

"We destroyed him first." Zarnak's cool words brought a rising bile into the judge's throat.

"Yes, that's why we're here in the first place—because you allowed this pathetic lunatic to be ..."

"Your honor," Zarnak said the title drily, flirting with the idea of finding it humorous, "every minute you spend arguing with us allows this affair to drag on longer—the main thing I believe you wish to avoid. Again I recommend that you ... read the report."

Once more the doctor set that particular vibration in his voice that bent the judge toward cooperation. Once more the judge turned back to the report. He picked up where he had left off, amazed at the self-assurance of Belbin. Wondering if it came from his faith, Reis skipped to:

Explanatory Excerpt 14:

Here within Belbin explains Azathoth itself.

Tho: "So when you offered these sacrifices to this ... Azathoth..."

Bel: "Offer sacrifices ... [amused, distant] ... I do not offer sacrifices to anyone or anything, Captain."

Tho: "But the women you ... murdered ... why did you do it? Weren't they ... don't you offer sacrifices to this thing of yours?"

Bel: "You are so hopelessly mundane, Captain Thorner, friend of Anton Zarnak, so wonderfully low.

"Azathoth does not accept sacrifice. He does not bestow gifts. A priest of Azathoth is an explorer. A miner. Those who flock to the mindless one do so to gain insights, notions on how best to manipulate the universe."

Tho: "You want to explain yourself?"

Bel: "Through drugs and dreams, I have found my way through the layers of reality and deception on down through to the center of existence. There lies Azathoth, steaming and whirling, mad beyond reason, not maybe even living—not actually alive in the sense that we understand it.

"He is perhaps more of a, a reaction, a contradiction. There is no way to know if awake Azathoth would actually be conscious. If he ever does awaken, of course, we will all blink out of existence. Instantly. If he ever remembers us, the planets we stride, the voids in between, we will snap back into existence. And if he remembers us as fiddler crabs, then we will snap back into existence and fiddle our lives out on the bottom of the sea.

"Dr. Zarnak knows this. I have seen him, skulking the high planes, gazing on great Azathoth, watching from afar, afraid to approach closer. I am not afraid.

"I have learned the dreams Azathoth enjoys. I live them to give myself a scent he finds pleasing. I curl within the folds of his immeseness, each time bringing away knowledge and more.

"Azathoth is power. He is power that I mine for myself."

Reis set the report down as his phone clanged on his desk. He took the call, not caring what it might be about. Anything that turned his attention away if for even a moment from the Belbin insanity was welcome. The questions on what to do with the new quake victims that were being found proved all too easy to handle.

Before he knew it, the judge was finished with the caller. His mouth dry, neck sweating, he cradled the receiver back on its perch.

I'm getting too old for this, Reis thought sadly. He was, consciously, thinking on his appointment to manage the disaster relief coordination. Subconsciously, however, he was thinking of Belbin. Just too goddamned old.

He breezed over part of the suspect's statement where he confessed to the murders. "Confessed," of course, was not exactly the right word. That implied resistance on Belbin's part, a certain amount of coercion to gain the admission. The priest had needed no prompting to list his dark crimes. He laid out what he had done, to whom he had done it, how often, to what degree, with the thoroughness of a surgeon and the dull precision of a certified public accountant.

The lists of atrocities went on for pages. Kidnapping the victims, drugging them, incarceration, mutilation. All of it was there on the page, Belbin's words recorded in court approved detail, how he had skinned the girls alive, taken tongs to their fingernails, burned out their eyes, used razors on their tongues, on their fingers, their underarms, their ears and breasts and abdomens ...

Reis read Belbin's descriptions of the things he had already read about in police reports: the bathtub filled with blood, the bloody fingerprints everywhere, the walls and ceiling of the old main room, painted with blood, festooned with organs, the four poster bed in the center of it all, draped with intestines utilized as curtains ...

Reis looked up from the report for a long moment. His mind whirled, desperate to find an escape route. He found nothing. He knew Zarnak had somehow tricked him into picking up the report, into accepting the resolving of the Belbin mess.

If only the madman hadn't been appointed an attorney, thought the judge. Hell, he hadn't even wanted one. But, on no, procedure is all, and so now we have this gadfly buzzing, and the police asking for a cover-up, and this, this ... he shook the report in his hand with violence ... and we have *this* to explain it all away.

With a dry and weary sigh, Judge Reis returned to the report, turning to:

Explanatory Excerpt 23:

Here within Belbin explains his power.

Tho: "So you think of yourself as what, exactly? Some kind of demon? Or God? What?"

Bel: "I am but a man, like yourself, Captain. I have simply armed myself, as you have armed yourself. My weapons are merely more powerful than yours. As mankind has learned to plunge daggers into the hearts of atoms to split them open, so too have I absorbed the knowledge of this power from great Azathoth. Indeed, to wipe this city from the face of the planet would be simplicity itself."

Tho: "Then why don't you?"

Bel: "As I told you, Captain Thorner, friend of Anton Zarnak, I like this city. It will serve well as my capitol. [highly amused] But I will obliterate some other municipality if you so desire.

Tho: "Yeah, well, maybe later. Right now, why don't you tell me exactly how you're going to eliminate Dr. Zarnak and myself."

Bel: "I have no specific preference. Is there some way you wished to die, Captain? I might be able to oblige you."

Tho: "Oh, well that's swell of you. But perhaps you could just outline any way that comes to mind, strictly for illumination, you see. After all, to us, the way we see it, you're a prisoner. You have no weapons, your hands are cuffed, your legs are shackled ... it seems like eliminating people should be a bit out of your reach right now."

Bel: "You view the world through such a narrow window, Captain Thorner, friend of Anton Zarnak. But why not? The simplest way to dispose of you both will simply be to think you out of existence. First, though not necessary, I would most likely seek to remove your restraints."

[at this point Belbin stared at his handcuffs. One by one the links began to disappear. There was a sound akin to escaping steam accompanied by small flashes of light as each one slipped out of existence]

Bel: "At this point, it is all a matter of whim, really. I might collapse the building on you, combust you down to ashes, reinvent you as ... as maybe fiddler crabs ... the possibilities are endless."

Tho: "And we're helpless to stop you. You're saying there's simply nothing we could do to stop you?"

Bel: "Quite. Allow me to demonstrate. Captain, please pull your service revolver and shoot me."

[Belbin's cajoling at this point went on for some time. Eventually, not so much to humor him, but more to frighten him into silence, the captain did attempt to bring forth his weapon. He could not. His limbs were frozen in place, as were my own. I am certain Officer Daniels will report the same sensation]

"You see, Captain Thorner, friend of Anton Zarnak, I am completely safe. If you try to rise, looking to defend yourself with physical violence, you will find you can not. My power is infinite at this point, and you are well within the boundaries of my infinity. Your aide, poor Officer Daniels, so less experienced in these matters, I have reduced to a puppet.

"Dr. Zarnak's mind I have entered as well. No spells can he utter. No hand gestures can he make. I set these precautions into motion before you even entered the room."

"You're telling me you actually watched his handcuffs disappear— link by link—right there in front of you?"

"Yes, your honor."

"No sleight of hand, no stage trickery?"

"No, sir."

"And you really did try to pull your weapon?"

"If I could have gotten it out of its holster," said Thorner, "I would have shot him then and there."

The judge stared, unblinking. He could not have imagined such a response coming from the seasoned commander. Thorner was the most highly decorated officer in the city. Reis knew him to be extremely capable and cool under pressure. Without questioning him further, the judge turned back to the report, picking up where he had left off.

Tho: "So, when exactly will all this eliminating take place?"

Bel: "As soon as I have ascertained what exactly your friend, Dr. Zarnak, is up to."

Tho: "What do you mean, Tidril?"

Bel: "Captain, you play the game well, but there is little you can do against one who can read minds. Do not look surprised. Surely you must understand that one who can pierce the veils between dimensions can peer into the thoughts of mortals. Or should I say, most mortals.

"Dr. Zarnak is clever enough to shield his thoughts from me. Even immobilized as he is, it is certain he is trying to find some way past your shared predicament. Aren't you, Anton?"

Zar: "There is no need to."

Bel: "Really?"

Zar: "Yes. I've already taken precautions against you, Tidril. How could I not? I have observed you, obscenely licking at Azathoth's teat, suckling power. When I was called here to observe you, I knew things would come to a moment like this. You are too careful a being to expose yourself by accident. Any creature that can whisper in Azathoth's ear without bringing about its own end is certainly capable of tip-toeing around the police.

"No, I assumed you wished to be captured. And, considering that you are a creature without remorse, such meant you had something in mind."

Bel: "How amusing. The good doctor lives up to his reputation. And how will you accomplish this?"

Zar: "I will wait until you are distracted with some moment of foolishness, and then I will cause you to cease to exist."

Bel: "I believe you might. And wouldn't that be foolish on my part, to allow you to use my own flamboyance of the moment against me. Very well, Dr. Zarnak, friend of Captain Thorner, perhaps I should put things to an end here and now."

[So saying, Belbin smiled and raised his hands. At this point the building began to shake.]

Zar: "Officer Daniels—fetch Mr. Belbin some tea."

[At this point Officer Daniels pulled his service revolver and fired, shooting Tidril Belbin between the eyes. The priest died instantly. The earthquake his summoning began faded as quickly as it had begun]

Reis rubbed at his burning eyes. Looking absently toward the window of his chambers, not focusing on anything, not looking at the others in the room, he asked;

"What did you do, Zarnak?"

"Belbin was correct. I had observed him on Azathoth's plane. It is my duty to watch for such creatures. When I was summoned here, I suspected the possibility Belbin was ready to make some sort of move. Before going into the first observation room, I spoke to Officer Daniels, giving him what you might call a post-hypnotic suggestion. I told him that if I ordered him to get some tea for anyone, he was to pull his weapon and shoot to kill."

Reis closed his eyes. It was all far beyond him. He was a good judge, a good weigher of evidence with a sound talent for gauging the truth in a man's voice. Thorner, Zarnak, Daniels, none of them were lying. As much as he wanted to believe they were, he knew they were not.

"How long will it take for you two to produce an alternate report?"

"Already done, your honor," responded Thorner, his tone level. "Pretty much reads the same. Says at the end that Belbin broke his cuffs, strength of a madman, that kind of thing. Says he turned over the table, got his hands around my throat. Officer Daniels was only doing his duty."

Tears formed in the judge's tired eyes. Such a simple deception. And, it was not as if he had not protected the police in the past. The court appointed lawyer would buy it—surely. The papers, the radio stations, of course they would accept it. It made the perfect end to the story—mad killer forces police to kill him. All neatly tied up.

Reis rubbed at his eyes once more. The horrible heat had dropped considerably. It had been building for weeks, every day a few degrees hotter than the one before, less than the day to come. Ever climbing, until, that was, the earthquake.

Earthquake.

The judge's body sagged. Perhaps with the happy ending, with the madman and all his terrible secrets to chatter about, with the earthquake and the still mounting property damage and loss of life, perhaps no one would notice his signature on the case. Perhaps no one would question his ruling, perhaps—

"Zarnak," Reis asked, eyes still closed, ears carefully listening for the answer to come. "Was he really as powerful as he thought he was? I mean, he claimed to ... to be like a human atom bomb. Was he? Could he? I mean—"

As the judge's voice quavered, Zarnak answered quietly, soothingly;

"He was just a madman, your honor. One the good police of New York City dispatched with their usual aplomb. Really, nothing more should be made of it."

Softly, the report on Tyler Reis' desk was replaced with another. That done, the two men withdrew from the judge's chambers, exiting out into the hall. As they made their way down the hall, Thorner asked;

"Is that what he was going to do, when he started the earthquake runnin'? Was he goin' to Hiroshima the city?"

Zarnak thought for a moment. His friend had seen so much over the years, dealt with so many sinister nightmares. It was true that Thorner was a strong man, and a good one. But Zarnak knew all too well the kind of fear atomic devastation brought to the mind once it was actually understood. Deciding his friend needed distraction more than truth, he offered;

"Perhaps we should just go and get ourselves a little drink.

With a shudder, the captain nodded, adding;

"Perhaps we should go and get ourselves a lot of little drinks."

Dr. Zarnak did not argue. Reaching the front door of the courthouse, the two stepped out into the waning daylight, the smell of smoke and the howl of sirens still thick in the air.

*Authors tend to get pigeon-holed. There are many who only know CJ for his hardboiled fiction. Others believe him to restrict his prose to the writing of Lovecraftian mythos tales. Then there are those who believe he only writes thrilling horror/action stories. Not that he does not do all of the above, but he also likes to give people a good laugh. To that end, one of the humorous outlets he created was the television show **Challenge of the Unknown**, a news venue where the investigative reporters look into the supernatural. They were meant to fill a market-need, to cater to what the network considered the whack-o portion of the audience. And then, they started opening crypts, and things started walking out. It's been laughs ever since.*

Ladies, Gentlemen, and Children of All Ages ...

"There's no business, like show business; like no business I know."
— Joseph Goebbels

"**I**'m tellin' you," the man shouted again, "I *saw* it!"

To the casual passer-by, he was a mild curiosity, but no more than that. Staggering through Grand Central Station, the fellow moved from person to person, slowly becoming somewhat calmer with each rebuff.

"But, I did. I mean it. I really did. He was there, just like you or me, and then, and then ..."

No one answered him. No one looked in his direction. It was New York City, after all. There were certain instinctive protocols programmed into its natives' genetic code that kept the city's children safe from one another. The chief of those safety features was disinterest, and it was running at full throttle through the famous train station that day as the frazzled man made his way from person to person.

"He did; he did. I saw it. He changed ... I—I ..."

His voice was almost a whisper by that point. His outbursts, his wild-eyed commotion, nearly forgotten—by the crowd, by those closest to him when it started. By himself, even. His standing in the community remained undiminished, of course, for he lived in Manhattan, where it was understood you could, in the always-colorful parlance of the street, "just wig out" once in a while and not have to expect repercussions.

But still, he thought, I really did see it.

"Of course you did."

The wild-eyed man, so very nearly calm, so very nearly ignored and disbelieved back to a state where he could return to what society was terming "acceptable behavior" those days, responded instantly to the tiny offer to return to near-slobbering panic. His head whipping around, beads of sweat flying from loose strands of his hair, he sputtered wide-eyed;

"You believe me?"

"Shouldn't I?"

"No—Yes! I mean, it's just ... everyone else was ignoring me, they didn't believe me. I tried to tell them ..."

"It's not that they didn't *believe* you, my friend," said the smiling man, trying to both block the other's view of the cameraman behind him while not actually obscuring the shot. "It's that they didn't get the chance to, because they didn't want to *listen* to you." As the hysteric managed to calm himself and yet grow more excited at the same time, his audience-of-one told him;

"No one wants to listen to someone screaming in the streets. That's so, so eighteenth century. They like distance from their announcements now. And they like filtering. In a world where every other thing you come in contact with has a message on it—not just advertisements in magazines and movie theaters, on TV screens and the sides of buses, but on every cereal box, tube of toothpaste and pair of pantyhose."

The shouter was now calm, his attention completely captivated by the handsome man who had stopped to listen—the one doing all the talking.

"For their own sanity they don't want to get involved. They can't. People are losing it second by second; that's why they rush through their days as if their lives depended on it—because they do. Stop their routine, shatter their rote procession, and you'll push half these tourists on their noodle."

The silent shouter nodded—understanding.

"These people all around us, they live in deadly fear that just another ounce of crazy added to the nightmarish load they're already carrying around will be the shot that shatters their spine. But, once they get home, have severed the bonds of family and community and locked themselves away with their one-eyed best friend, the cyclopean guardian waiting for them in their safest of vantage points, removed from the maelstrom of life, they can plop in front of the monitor of their choice and view the world's nonsense refined down by a million hands to the best-of-what's-out-there."

The speaker stared into the wild man's ever-calming eyes, smiling as his entire body language assured the hysteric that despite how he felt about himself, that he was important. And, as the thought began to sink in, the speaker confided;

"You know it's the truth. Someone shouting in the streets, they're to be avoided. But, someone shouting on *television* ... now that someone they'll listen to."

"But," the wild-eyed man who believed he had spotted some fantastical occurrence, and yet had not noticed the cameraman filming him, asked, "I'm nobody. How, how could I get on television?" His smile growing to the point where it seemed to anyone looking on that it must be injuring its wearer, the audience-of-one replied;

"I'm so glad you asked."

"Well, that makes three."

Marv Richards, handsome, wealthy, and winner of the Most Self-Absorbed Capitalist award for the year it was discovered his production company cut him a check for that period of time he spent viewing home movies of himself, calling it "character research," attempted mightily to seem involved in the meeting.

"So then, we're ready?"

"Yes, Marv," answered Lora, his much-more-than an assistant. For two seasons she had been there in the background, making certain the anchorman/producer managed to stay on the air. She covered for him during his many absences, placated sponsors, intervened with standards & practices, and in so many ways made production of his show, *Challenge of the Unknown*, a smoothly efficient machine that Richards himself barely had to do any more than show up on the set on the right day.

Challenge was the only television news show to exclusively feature media coverage of the strange, the occult and the bizarre. Spring Heel Jack, UFOs, pygmy ant riders, books of magic, vampires, haunted houses, crop circles, white witches, black witches or *whathaveyou*, if there was a mutilated cow carcass to show to the world, or a spooky crypt to open on national TV, Marv Richards was the man who would be hosting the event.

"If your highness could manage to squeeze a little work in this week..."

"You cut me to the quick," responded the anchor, checking out his lesser profile in the wall-length mirror behind Lora. "You savage me, tart. Did I not personally get this werewolf story rolling? Personally. Footage in hand already. Personally."

"Yes, Marv," answered Lora in a tone implying she might be less than impressed, "we are aware of the monstrous level of your dedication. The fact that you could ignore a man screaming about seeing the wolfman in the middle of Grand Central Station until your cameraman pointed him out, suggesting to you that you might want to look into it, hardly dampens out enthusiasm for your talents."

Lora did not know which infuriated her more—Richards seeming total lack of commitment to his own show, or the fact that when called on such things he merely smiled, freely admitting that such was the nature of his character.

Still, a voice within her mind whispered, it's a good job. The hours might be long and Marv might be a pain, but the pay is good, and the job security is fantastic.

A sour giggle escaped her lips at the thought that anyone might try and take her job. So far the show had nearly killed her three times, gifted her with two nervous breakdowns and one full blown psychotic incident. That she still had her looks despite the fireball mountains of stress that swirled around her from 9:00 to whenever every Monday through Friday she simply chalked up to youth, luck and good genes.

And then there was the fact that after all she had been through, she might not even be able to keep the job she had worked so hard to carve out for herself. Thinking she would find no better time, there in front of the rest of the crew where the embarrassment of her words might help make them stick for once, she added;

"However, as I've told you several times now, Mr. Abrams isn't happy with what he's been seeing lately. There's been a lot of talk upstairs with things like 'non-renewal' and 'cancellation' in it. You might want to start taking things more seriously. At least for a week or two."

"Please Lora," answered Richards, "we've so much to do, and here you are wasting time with idle rumors. Enough of that. Aren't we finished yet?"

"Soon enough. Let's get the blocking done for this week and we're finished—here, that is."

The anchorman's left eyebrow arched itself. Suspicion curving his spine and cooling his voice, he whispered;

"Can we review that last phrase, let me get some playback on that ... 'here, that is' ... yes. That part. Could you review that part for us?"

"But, Marv," Lora cooed with the innocence of a government agent trying to assure citizens that they were only 'there to help,' "you still have to do your follow-up interviews with this werewolf of yours."

Richards froze, trapped by his own rules. He had indeed proposed the werewolf piece.

Damn, he thought, he knew he hadn't wanted to stop there in Grand Central; had known deep within himself there was a good reason to not find out what the hysteric was yammering about.

"You bring it in, you do the spin."

His lips twisted into an ugly shape as he heard his own words quoted to him. A glance at Lora showed him quite clearly he was not going to be able to get out of this one. He had created the trap which had just sprung shut on his leg and he knew all too well it contained no weaseling room. He had created the rule just quoted to keep himself from having to chase down every idiot lead anyone discovered; it had cut his legwork down to practically nothing. Until, of course, he went and forgot himself and actually acted like a newsman for once.

"So," asked Lora, straining not to laugh, "when do you think you'll have some footage for us?"

"Tell us, Mr. Sample, when did you first know you were a werewolf?"

"Oh, no. Not you—again...?"

It had been a long and grueling week for Marvin Richards. Of course, it had been a longer one for his cameraman, Santo Tiega. Santo not only had to carry all the equipment, extra bags, water bottles, et cetera, for the two of them, but he also had to keep his 57.8 pounds of video equipment focused on Richards while he did so, and continually listen to the anchor as he complained about Santo's diabolical nature, a reference to the cameraman's having gotten them into the pickle of having to work for a living for once.

"Come, come, Mr. Sample, we do our research here at *Challenge of the Unknown* with an eye toward accuracy. We're not accusing people of fraud or insider trading on this show. We're a public service, protecting the public from the terrors from beyond. So, I'll ask again ... how long have you known that you suffer from the curse of the lycanthrope? That you are in fact, a bono-fide werewolf?"

Darell Sample was an average man—not too old or young, neither well-muscled, neither soft nor flabby. His hair defied category—sometimes sandy, sometimes gray; sometimes thin, sometimes full. Whether it was a trick of the light, the way the wind played with it, some facet of his barber's special touch, or something else, there was no way to tell.

"Will you please leave me alone? I'm a very patient man, but even I have my limits."

This was the third time Marvin Richards and Santo had ambushed the man three eye-witnesses had claimed turned into a werewolf before their eyes. The man in Grand Central Station, Feldon Meyes, a management trainee at a local coffee shop, had given Richards a fairly good idea of where to search for folks who might back up his story.

"I'm warning you, Richards," said Samples, raising his voice higher than any of his neighbors had ever heard it before, "I have a lawyer. I'll send him after you. This is harassment."

"This, Mr. Samples, is freedom of the press in action. Look it up, it's in the Bill of Rights."

"The Constitution," whispered Santo, but he was ignored by both men who continued to bluster at each other while the suburban crowd about them grew larger and larger.

Meyes had actually given Richards five different ideas, one of which had panned out. Of course, that last one had taken so long to show results, maybe they all might have if the anchor had put as much time into any of them as he had the last one. But, as was his usual way, he had put as little effort into any of the first four as possible until, with but one place left to try, he had finally gotten serious and canvassed the last chance he had until it had borne fruit.

A mother, Mrs. Doris Feenie, with a gurgling child in her arms, no less, and Ms. Ti'bu Lee, a quite attractive Asian in her early twenties that Santo put more effort in making look good on camera than he had his own wife at their wedding. Both women corroborated Meyes' story, one of them, the photogenic Ms. Lee, having a name to put with the description. Ms. Lee's family ran a dry cleaning operation where Mr. Sample brought his clothes. Confirmation of repairs needed and great quantities of unidentifiable hair were mentioned. Richards and Santo captured every word with a warm and loving satisfaction.

"Do you rampage every full moon, Mr. Sample?"

"I'm not listening to you. I am not speaking to you."

"Of do you have some degree of self-control? Could you possibly be a shape-shifter rather than a true lycanthrope?"

Suddenly spinning around, Sample stalked back toward Richards. His fingers clenching and unclenching, the anchor was uncertain what the smaller, but extremely intense man was about to do. Making a fist of his right hand, Sample shouted;

"Get away from me. Get out. Get out of my neighborhood."

"It's still a free country, Mr. Sample," answered Richards, backing up some nonetheless. "Despite whatever plans you and the rest of your monster brethren have in store for us."

Sample stopped and stared as if Richards had hit him with a water balloon, then begun doing a falsetto rendition of "I'm a Little Teacup." The shock on his face seemed as genuine as was humanly possible to generate. Santo lovingly caught every nuance of it, mentally making space on the shelf in his den for a second Emmy. His fist uncurling, defeat crumpling his average body, Sample turned away from Richards, walking sadly to his apartment building.

His thick sandy hair suddenly seeming thin and grey, the average man disappeared inside without saying another word. Watching the door close behind him, Marv Richards smiled. He was glad he had gotten out of the office for once. The show always got so interesting when he did some field work. And, with that Saturday's broadcast coming ever-so-conveniently on just the day he wanted it to, lunarly speaking, he was busy within his mind making room for his next Emmy as well.

The candy blue light specific to televised special effects had introduced that week's episode of *Challenge of the Unknown* nearly forty-five minutes earlier. Lora sat in the booth, working to coordinate all the various teams needed that night, summing up her frustration in the threatening murmur;

"I hate you, Marv."

"Get in line," added one of the others in the booth, dragging chuckles from all the rest.

"These live remote shows are a pain in the ass."

Everyone agreed with the sound man's comment, although, technically the show had not yet shifted over to remote. Indeed, up until only a few minutes ago they had been merely running the previously taped portions of the show. Footage of UFOs buzzing Mexico City—

What is it about that town, wondered Lora for the thousandth time.

A speculation piece on the new lake monster rumored to have moved into Lake Erie—a revisiting of four once-haunted sites which the *Challenge* team had previously covered as each of them had been de-ghosted—and, when they returned from commercial, Richard's insane werewolf piece would begin. Frantic, Lora cut to the anchor on location.

"Marv," she shouted shrilly, the decibel she reached making his normally calm eyes bug out for a moment. "We still have time to drop this."

"Relax. Everything is under control. It's going to be fabulous."

"We've got that footage of those mummies from the Andes those professors swore moved from one side of their room to another. And, and that reporter who keeps chasing that big green monster from city to city..."

"Lora," the anchor broke out his #4 voice, the one he reserved for those moments when he absolutely had to make someone do something as quickly as possible, "enough. My show. My responsibility. You do a wonderful job when I don't feel like working, but I'm the fellow what built this bit of cable time waste into a big breasted mama of a show with a national following."

"Yes," his assistant agreed, "and Abrams says if this doesn't pan out, he's ripping up your contract."

"And my watch says you should be cuing my tape in four seconds."

"Please, Marv ..."

"Three ..."

"The mummies...?"

"Two ..."

"Please!"

Richards said the word "one" even as Lora pointed off the items to play on the go roster to the coordinator working the board next to her. Smoothly, the pre-recorded, sharply edited segments rolled across the screens of America, one after another. First Richards' introduction to the idea of were-creatures, followed by reports of such a beast being ignored by the authorities. Then the focus shifted to the ceaseless courage of the dedicated *Challenge* staff as they tracked down leads until they found, in order, Mr. Meyes, Mrs. Feenie and Ms. Lee who had pointed them in the correct direction.

As the show played on, Richards and Santo made their way up the street and into Sample's building. Three other camera units positioned around the area powered up, confirming their feed deliveries with Lora. The anchor had no fears of getting into the apartment complex—that had been arranged with the doorman more than a week in advance.

Of course, Sample might have chosen to be elsewhere that evening, but Richards had been prepared for that as well. When the inevitable investigation by the authorities was made (the anchor was, after all, forever setting this or that hobgoblin loose), it would be shown that a team had kept the suspected Lon Chaney Jr. stand-in under surveillance every moment for the last four days. As always, Richards the showman had covered his bets.

And now, the anchor thought, his hand about to come down on the door to Darell Sample's apartment, it's show time.

Across the country, those tuned in to *Challenge* saw a pre-recorded Marvin Richards who told them they were about to shift to a remote, live location where Mr. Sample, whom they had just watched denying repeatedly that there was anything the least bit canine in his genetic background would be exposed for what he was. Knowing that phonelines everywhere were about to explode as the show's millions of die-hard fans punched up the numbers of their less committed friends, letting them know they simply *had* to tune in to *Challenge*, the pre-recorded Richards recapped all they had seen up until that moment. As he continued, twenty seconds from end-tape, Lora's voice sounded in the anchor's ear one last time.

"Swear to me, you bastard," she whispered, "tell me right now you know what you're doing."

"Sweetheart," Richards answered happily. "You don't know how good you make me feel, worrying over poor little me like that."

"Marvin ..."

"Just cue Harry to be ready to drop in any voice-over we might need. Santo's feed is clear, and I'm going in."

His name ringing in his ear, Marvin Richards knocked on the entrance to apartment 9C. The door opened quickly enough, answered not by any kind of were-nasty, but the same average man who had been pleading to be left alone through the last three taped segments.

"You."

The single word was a thing of weariness, of shattered defeat. "Go away, you stupid, stupid man."

"Can't do that, Mr. Sample," answered Richards, holding his travel mike out before him. "We're here to make history."

"Forget it," snapped Sample. "You lose, Richards. Can't you see you've got nothing? You coming here just makes it easier for me to sue your ass. Look at me, you idiot.

"Look at me!"

It was easy enough, of course, for even the simplest of viewers to discern Sample's meaning. It was well past sundown all across the country. Richards' pre-recorded self had made certain everyone understood that their evening sky that night was being graced by the fullest of full moons.

"There's a full moon tonight," the average man shouted. "Well, do you see any changes? Are my ears pointed yet? Do I have a tail? Am I salivating for your blood, covered in hair, bursting out of my clothing? Anything—*anything at all*, you asshole?" In response, Richards turned toward Santo, telling his audience;

"Numerous cultures which embrace the legend of the werewolf claim that those stricken by this terrible curse are helpless in its grasp—that the setting of the sun, the revealing of a full and silvered moon is an inescapable, automatic trigger ..."

Doing his best to keep both men in camera, despite the awkward angle forced upon him by the narrow hallway, Santo whispered into his mouthpiece, cuing one of his fellow cameramen on the outside that it was time for him to point his lens skyward. Hearing the response in his own earpiece that the needed picture was captured, Richards continued, saying;

"But there are others that believe one can be shielded from the light of the lunar sky and thus deny their curse." Pulling out his ringing cell phone, knowing who was on the line simply by hearing the opening notes to "Bad Moon Rising," the anchor flipped open his picture phone, aimed it at the average man, and said;

"What do you think, Mr. Sample?"

And suddenly, before the eyes of the nation, Darell Sample seized his chest and began to writhe. As the reflected rays of a tiny but extremely full moon bathed him, Sample began a startling transformation. His ears stretching, sharpening, his canines extending, eyes glazing over. In but seconds his clothing was ripping, the beginnings of a tail forcing its way upward out of his pants. His hair-covered mouth dripping saliva, Sample threw back his head and howled—

"I'll give you this much, Marvin," whispered Lora, watching a delighted Abrams slapping various members of the crew on the back, "this is some great TV."

"This is incredible, ladies and gentlemen." Richards could not answer his assistant as he needed to stay focused on their audience. Stepping aside, he surrendered Santo's camera to give the transformation center stage. Across the country jaws dropped further as Sample's clothing simply exploded away from his swelling body. "And there you have it, as you can see, as promised, live before your eyes, an actual case of now authentically documented lycanthropy."

Richards continued his commentary while all around the nation people bellowed at their television sets, screaming at the anchor to stop talking and start running. Second after second, as Sample's transformation continued, muscles knotting, veins popping, every aspect of the were-beast growing more monstrously spectacular with every passing moment, Richards simply continued to comment on what they were seeing, as well as supplying background commentary on legends of were-creatures from around the world.

And then, suddenly it seemed to dawn on Santo, Richards, and Sample, all at the same instant, that perhaps the scene was about to change.

"Oh my God," came Lora's voice in Richards' ear as she stared into the eyes of the hulking, hairy shape grinding is claws into the ruins of Darell Sample's clothing. "Run, Marv—*run!*"

Richards threw himself backward, clearing the doorway a split second before Santo, the cameraman following a degree of time shorter as the werewolf smashed into the door frame. Too large to exit straight on, the crazed creature shattered the molding around the doorway, splattering plaster and splitting the door itself with the force of his leap. As the news team retreated to the elevator, the beast took out its frustration on the door, ripping its remains from its hinges, tearing the pieces apart and throwing them against the wall across the hall.

Heroically, Santo kept filming while Richards pressed the down button repeatedly. He captured the explosion of wood and metal as it flew from Sample's apartment, much of it not bouncing off the wall across the hall, but becoming imbedded within the wall instead.

"Com'on," said Richards, pressing the button again. Then again. And again and again and again. "Com'on, where are you? What's the delay—this building's not that tall ..."

On her end Lora had already called 911, giving them Sample's address and reporting an attempted murder in progress. She told them some kind of beast was loose in the building, making certain the feed from Santo's relay could be heard over her phone. To those viewing the situation in the hallway, it did not seem possible they could arrive in time to be much help.

Such speculation seemed prescient as, his rage with the door passing, the werewolf pulled itself through the now enlarged doorway and turned in the direction of Richards and Santo. Just at that instant, though, the elevator finally arrived. Not hesitating, the two men leaped into the tiny box, the anchor desperately searching for both the Lobby and the Close Door buttons.

Sample's building was an older one, the kind where the individual floor's door slid shut first, followed by the elevator door a moment later. The news team could hear the thing outside coming down the hall through the first door. Then, as the elevator's door finally began to slid shut, savage claws the size of potato peelers slashed through the outer door.

"You know," Richards said, sounding serious, "I'd really have loved to know what the final numbers for the evening came in at." Santo stared at the anchor for a second, then whispered to his wife through the ether;

"You were right, honey. I shoulda gone back to PBS."

Even as the outer door was ripped away, the elevator began its slow descent. Acting with sudden inspiration, Richards popped the top panel of the elevator so Santo could keep filming. The cameraman aimed his camera upward, focusing on a scene which literally made his heart skip a beat. As he watched, two large and powerful hands reached out and grabbed hold of the elevator cable.

"Hey c-chief," said Santo, his professional hands not so much as twitching even as his voice stammered badly. "W-Were you, you, expecting anything like *this?*"

The elevator came to a crashing halt, accompanied by a terrible sound of grinding metal and the smell of burning wire. Richards began pressing every door button, hoping for any kind of exit, but the electronics of the ancient device had been shorted out. The elevator was still moving; the problem was its direction.

"He's goddamned pulling us back up. *Up!*"

Inch by inch, the small box was hauled against its will back up through its shaft. Minute by minute, the horribly powerful arms of the were-thing grew larger and larger. The sound of its labored breathing echoing downward to them, Santo supposed;

"Perhaps he'll grow too tired to get us the whole way there."

"You're so optimistic," answered Richards, somehow managing a smile. "How'd you ever last this long in television?"

And then, the werewolf had finished its work; it had pulled the car all the way back. Still holding the cable tightly with one hand, it reached for the tiny opening on the top and gripped the edge. Giving out with a terrible roar, it peeled the top of the elevator back like so much cardboard. Then, its eyes staring directly into one hundred and fifteen million American homes, he roared at the two men below him and began to clamber down into their tiny box.

"Richards, you are the trickiest, the luckiest goy bastard I ever had the good fortune to hire."

"Well, thank you, Mr. Abrams," said the anchor with mock humility. "It's always nice to be appreciated."

The buzz in the production meeting room was finally dying down. The evening's telecast had been an overwhelming success. Audience share had grown by the split second—internet chatter was exploding off the charts; the *Challenge of the Unknown* website could barely stay launched under the devastating number of hits still pouring into it.

"This is the kind of stunt that gets you a third season, you know."

"Really, Mr. Abrams," responded the anchor with a sincerity so believable the studio head almost caught himself believing it, "well, I guess that's just what comes from trying to do a good show."

Abrams thought for a moment over protesting Richards' attitude, then decided anyone willing to face a half-ton of muscle, fangs and claws deserved a bit of their own. Laughing at the anchor's studied lack-of-understanding, the studio head slapped him on the back, then headed off to see which young, pleasant-looking production assistants wanted to get ahead in their careers that night. As he did, Lora took the moment to spend a quiet moment with Richards.

"Feeling smug?"

"Who, me?"

"Oh, come off it, Mr. Innocent, take your bow. That was pretty impressive stuff out there tonight." The anchor sat back in his swivel chair, tilting his head so he could pour another few fingers of Scotch down his throat. Then, suddenly, his eyes narrowed. Holding his glass at the ready for a moment, he said;

"Why, you were worried about me, weren't you?"

"Doesn't do much for a gal's career if the star of the show gets torn to bits."

"That's true," agreed Richards. "But I think there's more here. I think you were really worried about me."

"Who wouldn't be, you moron," she snapped. Taking a sip from her own drink, she added, "you scared the hell out of me tonight, you whack-job."

"I scared the hell out of America tonight, sweetheart," the anchor said smugly. His trademark smirk spreading across his face, he added, "And now that I've done my part for the show for this season, getting us renewed, don't be asking me to do any more heavy lifting until next season."

"You bastard," Lora snapped, "if I hadn't called 911, if those cops hadn't taken the stairs and started pumping lead into that thing ... if, if..."

"'Pumping lead,'" Richards quoted the young woman, his voice going soft, "someone's been reading too many hardboiled novels. Look, everything worked out for the best—right? The cops drove Sample off, the city is already trying to sue us for staging a hoax and the government has already closed his apartment building down for investigation. This thing will be over-the-top for weeks. We got everything we wanted, and everything turned out all right. Didn't it?"

Lora stared at the anchorman for a moment, a rush of past nightmares experienced since she had begun working for him racing through her mind. Finishing her drink in a gulp, she thought;

Well, at least this time I'm not strapped fast to a gurney screaming.

Setting her glass down, she gathered her things and stood up to leave. Turning on her heel, she walked away from the table, throwing over her shoulder;

"I've quit better jobs than this."

"So have we all, sweetheart. So have ..."

Richards was interrupted by the ringing of his cell phone. Recognizing the programmed ring, he clicked it on immediately, saying in a hushed voice;

"There's my star. How you doing? You all right?"

"Oh sure, Mr. Richards. Bullets can't hurt me in this form."

"Where are you?"

"In the park. I—zzzz-buzittup—" The anchor waited while Sample did his best to manipulate his cell phone with his massive paw. After a moment, the heavy, growling voice returned;

"I have a spot I like; I've used it for years. Everything's fine on my end. How about yours? Everything okay?"

"Golden," answered Richards. "My end is perfect. And calls in have told me your's is, too. Those producers I told to watch were very impressed."

"Really?"

"Elwardo Baptiste in Spain, he wants you as soon as you can start. And Fellipi, the Italian, he has a contract ready to build a trilogy of horror movies around you. And that looks like just the beginning."

As the still-transformed Darell Sample growled enthusiastically into the phone, thanking Richards repeatedly for helping set up his big break, the anchor simply sipped at his Scotch. Indeed, ever since he had first tracked the werewolf down over eight months ago, he had been planning that night's show and how it could work to his best advantage. Yes, he had received numerous calls for Sample as he had promised. But, he had also received quite a number of calls Sample had promised to him.

As Richards had been able to arrange for quite an audience for Sample's performance that night, so had the not-so-average-man for the anchor. Special effects were expensive, and Sample had plenty of friends who could use the exposure offered by *Challenge of the Unknown*.

Leaning back in his chair, Marvin Richards took another long drink from his glass. As satisfied as he could be with himself, the anchor glanced at his reflection in the wall mirror. Even his bad profile looked good right then.

"Oh, it's true," he said to himself. "There is no business, like show business ..."

His cell phone stopping him from taking his song cue, he flipped it open and clicked it to life, asking;

"Yes—who've I got?"

"Hello," a vaguely European voice responded, "is this Marvin Richards? A mutual friend told me ... that, ummmm ... you might possibly be interested in meeting a vampire? Yes?"

Oh, thought Richards, switching to his most earnest and sympathetic personality, it's going to be a great third season.

If there is one thing CJ loves to do, it's work with other authors. In his time he has written stories in Brian Lumley and Ramsey Campbell's universes, collaborated posthumously with Robert E. Howard and H.P. Lovecraft, and teamed-up with modern luminaries such as John L. French, Patrick Thomas, and John Sunseri. Beyond all of these, however, he is best known for working with one individual in particular. The pair have created three series together so far, and there will probably be more to come. The following, however, is one of their best efforts, and the one they have yet to top.

Eye to Eye

by
C.J. Henderson
& Bruce Gehweiler

"He who fights with monsters might take care lest he thereby become a monster. And if you gaze for long into an abyss, the abyss gazes also into you." — *Nietzsche*

TAYEGUE, HONDURAS

"Jesú Cristo, I tol' you shut up, bitch!"

The man's hand snapped, open fingers slamming against the side of the woman's head—face struck, cheek stinging, skin inside her mouth shoved between her teeth, taste of blood. The woman's eyes closed, then snapped open, brimming with tears.

"All I said was our little girl, your daughter," the woman said fearfully, "thinks she saw something outside, maybe even inside. Maybe ..."

"Don't say it," the man threatened. His fear almost caused him to strike his wife again, but dread stayed his hand. A head and a half taller than the woman, four pounds shy of twice her weight, still the thought that what she was saying might be correct shattered his courage.

"Inside?" He repeated the word with a tone so frightened it implied he did not understand its meaning. Terror had seized the weak man's spine and rattled it, stealing his breath, making his hands hurt.

"Inside ... *here?*"

The woman nodded, taking an unconscious backward step, still wary of her husband's terror. The man stared at his wife, then looked about as if he expected to see the unnamed terror there in the room with them. His eyes moved from shelf to shelf, from the stove to the sink, under the table, up to the lightbulb swinging overhead—everywhere. Sweat rolled down from his unwashed hair across his forehead and into his eyes. As he rubbed the stinging dribble away, he whispered;

"Where? Where is she?"

"In her bed."

Swallowing air, the man picked up the butcher's cleaver from the counter. Heavy it was, and sharp enough to prop up the man's fragile will as he left the kitchen, heading for the back of the house. He walked slowly, his head constantly turning, staring about him, analyzing every shadow. His ears strained at every noise; his eyes hurt from the strain of not blinking. The man's steps were jagged, uneven. He fought the leaden quality he could feel creeping through his body, slowing his pace, making him ache.

Then finally, he reached the children's room. His hand trembling, he reached out for the door knob. It was an old-fashioned, enamel piece of hardware, one with a large chunk broken out of it. It did not matter than it did not turn properly; the seventy year old mechanism no longer lined up with the worn catch plate in the door jam. For the last two decades the lock had merely been an affectation. His teeth jammed hard together, the man slipped his free fingers around the knob and pushed the slightly warped door open, illuminating the room beyond with the light from the hall.

Inside he saw nothing out of the ordinary. The girl lie on her pallet, making no noise. His two sons lay in theirs. Quietly, the man entered the room, walking softly over to his daughter. The last few paces he walked backward, looking about the room for signs of ... anything.

Going down on one knee, he stared at his wife waiting in the doorway, reaching behind him toward his daughter. As he pulled her thin sheet back, his eyes stayed busy stabbing the shadows throughout the room, looking for anything that might be amiss. Then suddenly, as his fingers brushed his daughter's body, he felt the wetness at the same moment his wife's eyes went wide.

"Madre de Dios!"

Turning, the man brought up his weapon even as the small figure leaped forward. His wife erupted, her hands waving before her face. Her first screams were prompted by what she had seen. They were followed by those prompted by the feel of tiny hands grabbing at her legs and buttocks from behind. Her husband screamed as well, screamed as fangs bit into his arm, his side, his thigh; screamed as he felt the blood draining from his body—screamed as he finally saw what was biting him, how many of them there were, how hungry they looked.

Swinging his butcher's tool, he splashed what might have been a head against the floor and then ran for the door. He grabbed his wife's arm as he went past, pulling her from the doorway, down the hall, out of their home. Scarlet oozed from their wounds as they ran, and ran they did. They were not retreating, but fleeing for their lives in terrified, primal human panic, their home and children abandoned.

And, behind them in the dirt roadway, red eyes glowed, and the hunting horde gibbered as it moved forward methodically, dreaming of blood.

RALEIGH/DURHAM AIRPORT, NC

"So, just what is this all about, anyway?"

Dr. William Boles, a leader in the field of Para-Psychology, and Dr. Hugh Blakley, one of the world's most respected Crypto-Zoologists, sat next to each other in the jet aircraft they had managed to reach only minutes before take-off. Of course, they had rushed like madmen only to then discover that they would have to wait an additional hour on the runway while a stormfront subsided. Not the kind of men given to wasting time, however, they used the opportunity to their best advantage.

"You've read the telegram," Blakely replied. "You know as much as I do now." Blakely, a tall, lean man with dark eyes and a heavy jaw spread his hands out before him in a manner that emphasized what he had just said. Boles frowned and folded his arms across his fragile chest, one hand clutching his chin, his eyes closed. A smaller man with a slender frame and light blue eyes, he looked almost boyish next to Blakely's well-muscled frame. When he finally opened his eyes once more, he asked;

"And you have faith in this communication?"

"Professor Pierce knows her stuff," Blakely said with assurance. "She's not one to get caught up in hysterics."

Boles nodded. He knew the plump geologist slightly, but enough to agree that she was no one's fool. Still, the Para-Psychologist asked;

"What's she doing down in that region, anyway?"

"I had just enough time to call the head of her department before I had to bolt. He said she's on a two year research study of the volcanos of Honduras."

Boles continued to frown. A fastidious man who liked detailed plans and precise schedules, he was not pleased by how his day was progressing. On the strength of the telegram he had just perused, Mr. Gordon S. Pimms, school chancellor for Duke University, the institution where both he and Blakely worked as tenured professors, had ordered them to Honduras immediately. A rapid search had shown the next plane they could catch to be the only even semi-direct flight for two days.

"I don't see why we couldn't have waited until the next plane," fumed Boles, still angry over having to leave with only the clothes on his back. "How am I supposed to work without my equipment?"

"I know how you feel," answered Blakley with an actual touch of sympathy in his voice. "But we've got Pimm's go ahead to spend like sailors on leave once we get there. And anything we request will be sent down on the next plane, so ... I guess it's not too bad."

Boles snorted, unfolding his arms only so he could refold them more harshly in the opposite direction. Blakely thought to say something further, then decided against the idea. He and his colleague might have a common enemy for once in Pimm, but he was certain it would not be long before they were sniping at each other once more. Seeing that Boles had re-closed his eyes, he applauded the idea by closing his own. Pierce's telegram had been short and to the point.

Incredible trouble STOP News contained
so far STOP Send Blakely and Boles STOP
Chance of a lifetime   Gail Pierce

The Crypto-Zoologist allowed his imagination a bit of freedom as he stared at the backs of his eyelids. Something had happened where Pierce was working that apparently no one else knew about, which had caused some kind of major problem, a problem involving either some unknown creature or the supernatural.

Or both, his mind whispered.

Wondering what they were going to find when they arrived in Honduras, Blakely felt the tension in his shoulders suddenly release as the plane finally began its last taxi before take off. As the tons of metal threw itself into the air, the professor relaxed. Whatever Pierce's "incredible trouble" was, he was certain they could handle it. Of course, he had also been certain when he had gotten out of bed that morning that he was in for an uneventful day.

ON THE ROAD FROM TEGUCIGALPA TO JUTICALPA, HONDURAS

"All right, Ms. Pierce," snapped Boles, his body lifting from its seat in the geologist's jeep every time she hit a bump in the rutted roadway. "We are away from the airport. No one can hear us. I can barely hear my own thoughts over your machine. Now, will you kindly, finally, tell us what this is all about?"

Pierce chuckled, looking over her shoulder at the bouncing Boles in her backseat. Blakley, sitting next to her in the front passenger seat of her antique vehicle, did all he could to contain his amusement.

"Dr. Boles," she said, "I sent for you two because three days ago several adults and five children were killed in an extremely rural area outside of my dig. The survivors say it was the work of El Chupacabra."

Boles stared blankly. Blakley whistled with delighted surprise. After a moment, the Crypto-Zoologist explained;

"My field. El Chupacabra is the Loch Ness monster of Latin America. Small things, and by small I mean three to four feet tall. The name literally means 'goat sucker.' They got it because that's what the first ones spotted did—literally sucked all the blood out of some goats."

Boles nodded his head at that point, explaining that he had heard of the creatures. Pierce, a jovial woman in her mid-forties, called over her shoulder;

"Yeah, we all 'heard' of them, but trust me, seeing is believing."

"You saw one?" Blakely's question was tinged with shocked excitement.

"Yeah," replied Pierce. "And when we get where we're going, so will you."

Between the noise of the doctor's vehicle, and the danger in distracting her on the shambles of a road, the party decided that all further questions and speculation would be put off until they reached the village where the disturbance had taken place. Once there, Blakely insisted on being taken immediately to the remains. As he was lead to a shanty constructed mainly of scrap plywood and cinderblocks, he pulled a heavy .45 revolver from his pack.

"Wherever did you get that?" asked Boles, staring at the long barreled weapon.

"Picked it up at the airport," answered the professor. Pulling loose a faded ammunition box as well, he began wiping down the brass on the shells before loading them as he said, "Got it while you were looking for toiletries."

Boles merely nodded. He had not yet seen Blakely go into the field unarmed. He also knew at least seven people had recently been murdered in the vicinity. Boles might not greatly enjoy the company of the Crypto-Zoologist, but Blakely's insistence on having a firearm nearby had proved valuable in the past, thus he allowed the incident to go by unchallenged.

Inside the shanty, Pierce lead them to a table off to one side upon which something had been covered by an old burlap bag. Pulling aside the covering, the geologist said;

"Now, boys, tell me I shouldn't have called you."

Blakely whistled. Boles stood with his mouth slightly opened. There on the table before them lay the remains of what could only be described as El Chupacabra. Blakely immediately moved forward and began to study the carcass. The thing was nearly four feet in length, covered in dark gray, scaly skin. It possessed a crest of spines running from the base of its neck to a point halfway down its back. These were flanked on both sides by a set of leathery wings. The creature's head had been caved in, but the Crypto-Zoologist could still discern that it had sizeable fangs, and oversized black eyes.

"So," asked Boles, "is it a Chupacabra?"

"It'll do until one comes along."

"Then the way I handled this," started Pierce, "keeping things quiet, getting you two down here ... I handled this okay?"

"If you interpreted all of this as a way for Duke to put itself on the international map like a big dog," answered Blakely, still engrossed in examining the small body before him, "you did more than 'okay.' Prestige, publicity, money ... Lord, if we could capture one of ..."

Turning to Pierce, Blakely started quizzing her rapid fire, asking how they could get the supplies they needed, when he could question witnesses, inspect the scene where the creature had been killed, see the human bodies, et cetera. The geologist slowed him down, handing him a pad and pencil, telling him to make a list of the things he needed. She assured him that when he was finished she would send an aide back into Tegucigalpa for anything he wanted and that after that they would take care of the rest.

Blakely wrote as fast as he could.

TAYEGUE, HONDURAS

While one of Pierce's research assistant's drove back to the capital city, the geologist took the newly arrived professors to the small village where the attack had taken place. It was a tiny place, four rows of simple homes clawed out of the jungle along the main road from Tegucigalpa to Juticalpa. It was less than a shanty town, merely a place where a few families had gathered together and decided to form a semblance of a community.

After inspecting all the sites where the locals had seen or confronted the attacking creatures three days earlier, Blakely and Boles were introduced to Ulises Guayaga, the man who had killed the thing they had inspected on Pierce's table. Blakely's Spanish was more than adequate for the interview. He spent a great deal of time with the man, leaving Pierce and Boles to question those others who had actually returned to their homes. As the sun began to set the three compared notes.

Their reports all seemed more or less to coincide. Descriptions of the Chupacabra and their actions matched more or less. Everyone agreed that the creatures seemed to come from the Guayaga house, and that Ulises had slain the corpse Blakley had already examined.

"You seem to make a favorable impression on Ulises," said Pierce as the three settled down to a quick dinner. "Not that easy for most Yanquees."

"Probably because they can't mask their revulsion over his quaint ideas on paternal guidance." When Boles simply stared, his partner explained, "Ulises is from *Dulce Nonbre De Culmi*. He's got strong Indian blood, *los Payas*. Thinks of himself as going all the way back to the Mayans. Thus despite his status in life he feels he should be accorded great respect since he's got such an illustrious set of ancestors."

"And the parenting part ..." asked Boles.

"He beats his wife and kids to relieve his frustration," answered Pierce, matter-of-factly. When the professor allowed his shock to show, the rotund woman laughed, shrugging off his objections with an amused wave of her hand.

"Please, professor," she said, "this is *Olancho*. Haven't you heard; everyone here is crazy. You stay long enough, you'll be crazy."

"Too late for poor Boles on that one," joked Blakely. As the Para-Psychologist fumed, Pierce interrupted, saying, "Ulises, he's *el es tau picaro*, one of the dirt poor. This isn't the States, boys. Here they sell their children when they can't feed them." Turning back to Blakely, she said;

"Still, Ulises was very forthcoming to you. Sure you didn't use anything on him besides your considerable charm?"

Blakely held his hand to his mouth to feign surprise, then fanned himself comically while he said, "Why ma'am, you'll turn my head with such talk."

Boles grimaced while Pierce simply stared, unable to hide a widening grin. With a double shrug of his eyebrows, the professor reached into his bag and pulled forth a bottle of Old Grand-Dad, twin to the one he had given Ulises.

"I may have introduced him to the charms of Kentucky Bourbon."

When Boles simply stared, Blakely said, "Hey, maybe you can't get a gun onto a commercial airliner anymore, but there was no way I was going into the bush without a few trade items."

"Huummmmm," murmured Pierce, approvingly. "You don't spend a lot of time in the classroom, do you professor?"

"Yeah," he admitted. "Chalk dust allergy. I was going ..."

Blakely went quiet as a terrible croaking sound shattered the darkness. Boles jumped so badly he spilled his beans and bread. As Blakely started to finish his joke, his colleague shouted;

"What was that? Is it those things? Are they coming? Get your gun out!"

Greatly amused, Blakely strolled away from the open tent where the three had been dining and moved off into the brush. More of the terrible screams were heard as he disappeared into the shadows. After a moment the Crypto-Zoologist returned, his hands cupped together. As Pierce continued to calmly eat, Blakely opened his hands before Boles' face.

"Here's your monster, William." Boles stared at a small, gecko-like creature. "The pichete. Noisy, but harmless."

Blakely released the reptile which scurried off into the night, throwing another great howl over its shoulder as it disappeared. Boles said nothing, his stiff embarrassment amusing Pierce and Blakely to no end. The situation was not helped when the professor, realizing that his rushed departure had brought him to the Honduran jungle with nothing to sleep in, had to borrow a shirt from the much larger Pierce. She lent him a T-shirt that was tight on her, one emblazoned with the legend "I WISH THESE WERE BRAINS." Boles accepted what on him would be a nightshirt that would reach to his knees as graciously as possible. He then retired for the night, leaving Blakley and Pierce to chat peacefully.

Their peace did not last all that long.

Less than forty-five minutes later Boles came out of the tent where he had gone to sleep at a full run, waving his arms, screaming into the night. Tripping over one of the tent's guide wires, he went down in a tangle. Before he could regain his feet, Blakley had reached his side. Grabbing his colleague, he held him firmly, shouting;

"Boles, snap out of it! Wake up."

By the time Pierce and several of her students had reached the spot where the two men were, Boles had recovered himself. While he made his way to his feet, Blakely explained;

"William gets visions, and I must admit I've learned to trust them.

In fact, I was surprised when he didn't get one as soon as we saw the body earlier, to tell the truth." Turning to the shaken man, Blakely asked, "What is it? Did you see something?"

"Them."

The small crowd turned, following the direction of Boles' pointing hand. Coming at them through the darkness they saw a dozen sets of glowing red eyes. All remained transfixed for a moment as the hopping, hissing forms drew ever nearer. Then, suddenly a female voice screamed and everyone began moving.

Two of the students actually ran into each other, one falling down, the other running off into the jungle. Pierce swung her flashlight about, cracking one of the beasts in the side of the head. As a research assistant cried out, one of the chupacabra biting into the young man's thigh, Blakely pulled his weapon and aimed for the midpoint between the closest set of glowing eyes. He squeezed his trigger three times, killing two of the things instantly. As their fellows died, the remaining creatures suddenly veered off and disappeared into the night.

Shaken, the entire camp gathered around Boles who still lie in the dirt where he had fallen.

"Good thing you woke up in time," said Blakely. As wounds were tended and people were hushed, he added, "This could've been a lot worse that it turned out thanks to you." Boles grabbed his colleague's arm with urgency.

"Ulises," he said in a whisper, terror in his voice. As the others began to pepper the air with questions, Blakely waved his arm violently, quieting them. Turning to his partner, he asked;

"What about Ulises?"

"It was supposed to be worse. Ulises ... he's the one. Called them. Called them here to kill us."

After a few more questions, and a quickly downed four ounces of Old Grand-Dad, Boles explained that he had dreamed of Ulises, seen him stewing in anger, seething. Then, in the vision, the Chupacabra had entered the scene, leaping into sight through a crack in the air. As they danced around slaughtering everything in sight, Ulises had merely smiled.

"That was when I woke up," Boles explained. His hands twitching, he said, "he's a focal point. It's, it's ... not split-brain, not that ... more like, like a poltergeist manifestation."

The small group around Boles said nothing. Several raised an eyebrow. Undaunted, the professor explained, "In the late nineteenth century researchers proved poltergeists aren't ghosts. The activity surrounding what is known as a poltergeist is really the work of a mentally disturbed mind. Not insanity, no. No—just a disturbance, like puberty. So many poltergeist come where there are children entering puberty. Frightened. Uncertain. It's the stress, you see ..."

"Yes, fine," snapped Blakely. "But what's that have to do with Ulises?" Boles blinked hard, trying to focus his attention.

"He's calling them," the professor said softly. "Through his unconscious. We all can, you know." As Blakely and one of the students helped Boles into a chair, the professor continued to lecture, his voice hushed.

"Roger Sperry, experimenting at Caltech, working with split brain patients, he found out. Two halves of our brain, the left half is where our day-to-day self exists. The right half, the dreamer, it's another person—what it does, we don't know about, can't control. What Hesse was talking about when he called our two aspects 'man' and 'wolf.'"

As Pierce illuminated the area by lighting two lanterns, Blakely knelt next to the now sitting Boles, working to keep him calm. The Crypto-Zoologist had been with his colleague during a number of his psychic episodes, but he had never seen the man so shaken by one of the experiences.

"Seems silly to think children can get so upset their minds can make things fly through the air, start fires, break mirrors, but is the thought of ghosts tormenting people for no reason any less silly?"

"But how do they do it," asked Blakely. "Where does the energy come from?"

"No one knows," answered Boles. "Maybe the energy of the human body, or the Earth itself."

"And you think Ulises ..." Pierce paused for a moment, then continued, "'made' these things with his mind somehow?"

"No. He didn't make the creatures. He made a doorway."

It all made a certain sense to Blakely as he moved quietly through the dark. Boles said that it was usually children who were found at the center of these occurrences, but not always. Adults could cause them as well. Especially adults under great amounts of stress. Resentful people, angry ones, proud ones—with their backs to the wall, any might possibly be a candidate for such activity.

So take one highly resentful Ulises Guayaga, thought Blakely, unable to feed his children, smarting from the notion he's descended from kings, seeing us Americans coming in to do what we want with his country—his Mayan country ...

Blakley saw the pieces falling into place. If the man were unconsciously looking for a cure to his problems, El Chupacabra could be it. Vampires that quietly drain their victims of blood, a painless, merciful way for him to rid himself of his children. He gets rid of his kids, Blakely reasoned, and everything's good. Then, a few days later more Yanquees show up. Once he sobers up, he starts feeling used, works up a little hate, and before you know it his subconscious has sent a hit squad to wipe us out in our sleep.

The professor did not want to believe Bole's theory. If it were true, then the Chupacabra were not a new species, they were alien invaders, let into the world on occasion by frenzied, hate-filled minds.

Still, he thought, it makes sense. No Chupacabra spottings before 1975, then everyone is seeing them. Maybe this is where big foots come from, Nessie, everything. One disgruntled whack job dreams up some creature, then all the lesser minds feed into the nightmare and the things are with us forever.

Blakely listened intently to the jungle to both sides of the narrow, dirt road. Making his way with only starlight as his guide, he kept to the center of the road as he thought;

It makes sense, though. Look at el Chupacabra—wings but no balancing tail, not even vestigial. Reptilian, but active at night. Lower and second thighs, elevated heels, and yet they walk upright—when they've not flying, according to some reports. Black eyes that glow, it's the bride of the platypus, by way of Roswell. But then ...

Blakely let his thought drift as he spotted a glowing disturbance some fifty yards ahead. Pierce had driven him from her camp to the main road. Not wanting to announce the fact he was coming, he had told the woman to wait for him there and then proceeded on foot. The odd light was coming from where he expected to find the town of Tayegue.

"Okay," he whispered, "Show time."

The professor stopped long enough to free his weapon's cylinder. Running a comforting finger over its six chambers, he made certain each held a cartridge, then slid the cylinder back into place, holding his hand over the loading gate to muffle its slight noise. Swallowing, he moved forward once more. And then he stopped. Terrified.

As Blakely looked all about him, he saw Chupacabra everywhere faintly illuminated by the starlight. His eyes went wide as he saw them sitting on the ground, or in the trees, hundreds of them. Possibly thousands.

The professor stood frozen, blood slowing in his veins, wondering if any of the things had seen him. Though the evening temperature was barely seventy degrees, Blakely found himself covered with sweat. Instantly he saw the sad comedy of his situation. One man, with one gun. Six chambers holding six shells. Even if he scored direct hits with them all ... even if he could expel his spent brass and reload ...

There are thousands of them—*thousands* ...

And then he realized what was wrong.

Their eyes, he told himself. They're black. They're not glowing.

Cautiously, his body shaking, mind white with terror, he took a step forward. Then another. Nothing noticed him.

They don't see me, thought Blakely. Or they don't care.

The professor had no idea why the Chupacabra were ignoring him. He decided he did not care the reason.

So, that gives me two choices, he realized. Turn around and get out of here before something happens, or keep going.

Professor Hugo Blakley was not by nature a warrior. He was a scientist. He was an extrovert, true, but not enough of a one to run into a burning building to save a baby. That, he knew, was what the fire department was for.

So, he asked himself, what exactly do you do when there is no fire department?

Slowly, the Crypto-Zoologist took a step forward. Then another. Another. After a few more steps he found himself hurrying. Then running. In only a handful of moments he reached the tiny niche in the jungle known as the town of Tayegue. The entire way there he saw Chupacabra everywhere.

Six chambers, six shells, he told himself once more, and then stepped around the home of Ulises Guayaga to see for himself what was creating the distorted glow shining through the trees. As he came around the crude shanty, the professor saw a sight so bizarre that at first his mind could not comprehend it. Yes, he had seen such things in movies, on television, but you could see anything there. This was something he was seeing outside the cinema. This was real.

Is it? The question echoed in Blakely's head, making him almost giddy. Is it real?

There before the professor hung a crack in time, a crackling fissure in reality. Or, as Boles had called it—

"A doorway."

But, his brain hissed, a doorway to *where?*

As Blakely stared relentlessly, unblinking, his mind finally began to take in details. The portal was insubstantially solid, a vague, purplish oval of pulsating energy, from which came one Chupacabra after another. Staggered by what he was seeing, Blakely put his hand over his mouth as he began to titter. Out of the doorway, besides the ever growing army of monsters, there also flowed a mist, a thick veil of green and scarlet swirls that smelled of almonds and spoiled milk. As Blakely peered into it, he began to discern a background landscape far in the distance, one filled with cyclopedian towers and inverted pyramids.

Ulises ...

The thought sent Blakely stumbling for the Guayaga home. He entered the hovel silently, searching for the man responsible for everything that was happening. He found him sleeping on a dusty pallet, snoring loudly, a mostly empty bottle of Old Grand-Dad clutched in his hand.

Okay, fine, he thought, shaking, all of him shaking, I found him. So what? So *what?* What am I supposed to do now? What am I supposed to do?

Six chambers, six shells.

As his brain whispered the words to him once more, the professor pulled his weapon. He could do it. Before any more Chupacabra came into the world, before any more alien vampires entered his plane of existence.

Just pull the trigger, he told himself. Once this guy wakes those things up, once his hate sets off their alarms, gets their headlights glowing red, then who knows how many more people are going to die. Who knows?

The professor aimed his gun at Ulises' head. Swallowing hard, he began to put pressure on the .45's trigger. He knew Ulises Guayaga was not responsible for his actions. He had not consciously called out to the Hell-things all around them to come and slaughter his children and neighbors. Nor had he called them and sent them to Pierce's camp.

Not on purpose, thought Blakely. No ...

But he had sent them. And once he had called forth enough of them this time, he would send them out again.

Only, wondered the Crypto-Zoologist, where will he send them this time? Who's the target this time? How many more have to die to satisfy this guy's hate?

The .45 doubled in weight. Blakely grabbed his wrist with his free hand, trying to hold the weapon still in his shaking fist, trying to steady his aim.

He has to die, the professor's mind whispered to him. There's no other way.

Blakely's teeth chattered. His stomach churned. In his hand the .45's hammer had moved halfway to the point where it would snap forward and expel the first shell from his weapon. Second by second it crawled backward, the Crypto-Zoologist struggling to finish the deed his brain kept screaming at him to accomplish as quickly as possible.

The needs of the few versus the needs of the many, he reminded himself. Or the one.

And then, another voice from his mind posed a question.

If you kill him, what happens to the Chupacabra?

Blakely froze. What *would* happen? Would they disappear? Would they go on the attack? Either scenario was just as likely.

Make up your mind, you son'va bitch, he snarled within his head. *Think—think!*

Blakely looked down at the snoring man once more, then at the fanged horrors all about him. The things were being called by Ulises. They were coming to him.

Then, a voice from the back of the professor's mind said, won't they keep on going to him, no matter where he is?

His clothing glued to his body by sweat, Blakely suddenly shoved his weapon back into his belt and went down on one knee. Gently, but quickly, he lifted Ulises from his pallet. The Honduran was not a small man, but neither was Blakely. Adrenaline pumping, nerves shattering, the Crypto-Zoologist retreated from the shanty with Ulises in his arms running straight for the portal.

Halfway there, the drunken man began to stir.

"Puchica," he mumbled groggily, slurring the word. "Porque me estan levantando ..."

Reaching the edge of the pulsating disturbance, Blakely hurled his burden into the mist. Ulises Guayaga did not fall to the ground. Instead, his voice came from beyond the portal's edge, from within the green and scarlet mists—his words broken, tone frightened. A growling came to Blakely's ears next, followed by terrified screams.

All through the jungle then, for miles in every direction, black eyes opened, instantly pulsing to the color of hot coals. As the screams turned into a undying series of shrieks, the tens of thousands of Chupacabra suddenly became animate, all of them making straight for the floating doorway. As Blakley staggered back toward the shanty, the hissing creatures hopped and flew, slamming into each other, crawling over one another, all of them furious to clamber back into their own dimension.

In seconds it was over. The Chupacabra were gone.

Blakely stood in the doorway of the hovel, watching as the purpled oval pulled in on itself and disappeared. Weakly he slid to the floor, laughing at his tears. As the smell of urine came to him, at least a part of his mind knew whose it was. His head bobbing on his neck, the Crypto-Zoologist screamed into the night, then pulled the .45 from his belt. He stared at it for a long time, laughing over the uselessness of it.

Then, as he raised it to his head, his mind a whirl of nonsensical thoughts, he felt a hand on his wrist.

"No, not today—okay?"

Smiling up at Pierce, the professor allowed her to remove the weapon from his hand. And then his eyes welled with tears, sending them streaming down his face, all of them working to drown his growing laughter as his mind wondered exactly how many more people were feeling as stressed out as Ulises Guayaga that morning.

Now we return to the Nardi Agency. As we said earlier, CJ's original intent with these characters was to return to a simpler kind of story, where normal individuals attempt to turn the tide against adversaries which, while they might be fearsome, were not actually invincible. Of course, as any long-time CJ readers know, his characters don't get to just stick their toe in the water for very long. Here's what happened to the Nardi Agency when it finally leapt full-force into the pool.

Cruelty

"Weak men are apt to be cruel."
— George Savile, Lord Halifax

"Oh, Mr. Nardi, sir, oh my goodness. Thank God you've come."

The speaker was a painfully thin gentleman, the kind one could determine at a glance could consume several hundred thousand calories a day and gain no weight. It was an attribute that would have made him a thing despised most everywhere in modern America, if it were not for his eyes.

"It's all right, Mr. Clemmens. "It's my job."

His eyes were deeply worn pits, tired, frightened orbs that let one know their owner never slept well, never had time to relax, never found a moment designed to allow him the luxury of a smile.

"Now tell me," continued the newcomer, forcing his way through the ever-growing throng to join Clemmens in the building's interior, "what's gone wrong?"

"Oh, Mr. Nardi, it's something terrible. Ghastly. It's been so long since anything like this ... oh, good heavens—"

As the thin man reached for a badly dampened handkerchief in his suit coat's breast pocket, Nardi stopped their forward movement. Giving

Clemmens a moment to dry his brow, the newcomer said;

"Listen, take it easy. Calm down. I'm no doctor, but I walked the beat long enough to know the look of someone beggin' for a stroke. Now, stop talkin' for a second and take a deep breath. Then take another. Relax for me, okay?"

Frank Nardi was the head of Nardi Security. A twenty-year-man with the NYPD, he had taken his pension and fled the chaos and horror of the Big Apple for the calm and serenity of the New England countryside. Deciding on Arkham, Massachusetts, as his new hometown, a placid, historic burg just big enough to support his plans, he had opened a private security firm with three other retiring officers.

"Thank you, Mr. Nardi, I feel better. But I am afraid you will not share such feelings when I explain what has happened."

Harold Clemmens was the president of Miskatonic University, final signer-off on all decisions, final arbiter of all disputes, final check on all balances. It had been his decision to bring in a private security firm to add another measure of safety in reference to the school's library, a repository known for containing the largest collection of rare occult material in the western hemisphere.

"Try me."

Nardi and his people did not guard the library like foot soldiers. No, Clemmens was much a visionary, and he had hired the firm based on information about its background. What Nardi and his people did was merely keep their collective ears to the ground, listening for any hint of possible break-ins looming in the library's future. Over Miskatonic's two hundred plus years, its wealth of rare and exotic texts had attracted all manner of thieves, some rumored to be more than merely mortal.

Determined that there would be no more such incidents during his watch, Harold Clemmens had offered Nardi a healthy retainer to monitor the underworld and to protect the library from further incursions. Although the ex-police detective was loath to take all the credit for the relative quiet the university had enjoyed over the past year, there had not been any unwanted intrusions or thefts since his company had been on the job.

"We've been preparing the Exhibit Museum for a rather impressive show. As well as the finest selection from our own stores, it is to have pieces on loan from major museums and private collections around the world. Magnificent."

"The Egypt show, right? The one Tony was overseein' for you?"

"Yes, yes," answered Clemmens, almost too quickly. As the pair started walking again, he continued, saying, "Your Mr. Balnco was most thorough in his execution of his duties—perhaps too much so."

As the university president continued to chatter, Nardi listened with a part of his mind, another section working to piece together a sense of what was happening. Miskatonic was no sleepy little backwater school. It might reside in a small town, but then so did Harvard and Princeton. As Ivy League as any campus, its yards were usually bristling with activity. But, Nardi knew, not the kind of activity through which he had made his way moments earlier.

Something had happened inside the Exhibit Museum—of that he was certain. Something big.

Something bad.

There were too many people on campus, too many non-students. They stank of curiosity, an odor Nardi remembered well from his days on the streets of Manhattan. They were townies, so far, but there was a terrible certainty working through his nerves that told him that would change—soon. Next-town-overs were probably on their way. And the media. Of course, the media. He could tell from the sickening nerve vibration slithering through the halls that whatever this bad thing was, it was one more than large enough to slap cameras in hand and focus attention.

"There's no way to describe ..."

Clemmens stopped speaking, going for his handkerchief once more. Nardi knew things were beyond horrible. When skinny men sweat, his captain used to say, things are in the shitter.

"At least," thought the security man, "he didn't walk us to the library. Whatever the problem is, it ain't our fault."

"Please, brace yourself, sir," said the university president. Stuffing his soppingly useless handkerchief back into his breast pocket, he pushed on one of the main doors to the Exhibit Museum, adding, "the Egyptian exhibit I was telling you about is this way."

The pair moved forward in silence from that point on. Although his agency's responsibilities to the university centered only on the library, Nardi had made it his business to know the layout of the entire campus. Indeed, after only a few years in Arkham, he had practically the entire town memorized.

"Come in handy if I ever want to get a good job," he mused, "like a cab driver."

As the two men entered the Exhibit Museum, Nardi had no problem spotting the epicenter of the university's current problem. A pair of large metal doors stood closed before them, a large throng of people clustered around it. Three campus security guards stood before it, barring them entry. The crowd parted for the on-coming Clemmens, as did the guards. Stopping just before the door, the president ordered the security men to disperse the crowd, to use force if necessary. As they proceeded to move the intruders outside, Clemmens turned to Nardi and said;

"Franklin, you have done Miskatonic a number of fine services since we brought you in on retainer. I will not bandy words coyly with you now. Mr. Balnco is inside, behind these doors. He discovered ... an intruder, of sorts."

"Of sorts?"

"Please, you know what kind of town this is, the kinds of things that go on here. He came across something, something inside. Something evil. On the surveillance cameras, it appears to be just a man, just an ordinary man. But ..."

"But it ain't—right?"

Clemmens hung his head sadly, his bony shoulders drooping even further than normally. Unable to meet Nardi's gaze, he simply muttered;

"The cameras can't reveal exactly what has transpired within, but ... something terrible has happened to Mr. Balnco. I've spoken to you often enough to, to appreciate the type of man you are. Before we alerted the authorities ... I knew you would want to go in first."

Nardi nodded. Glancing downward, staring at the floor, not seeing it, he took a deep breath, then reached for one of the massive doors. As he began to push it open, Clemmens hand touched his wrist.

"You don't have to go in there, sir," the president told him. "Indeed, I would strongly advise against it."

"You did right to call me," answered the former police detective. "I talked Tony into comin' here. It's my responsibility."

Clemmens stepped back, allowing Nardi access to the exhibit hall. Letting him know he would be returning to his office to call in the proper authorities, the president watched the security man pull the large metal door open, watched him pass through it, then watched for several long seconds as it glided quietly back into place. Clemmens stared at the solid, silent bronze for another handful of moments, then turned and walked nervously away, returning to his office to, for all he knew, call more men to their doom.

"Tony, where in Hell are ya?"

Nardi moved forward slowly, not so much cautiously, but with a certain wary prudence. He had no idea what had really occurred within the hall, but somewhere within lurked one of his partners with someone, or something, looking to do him harm. Best he lead as he would have back in Manhattan, as if there were nothing to fear.

"God how I hate this town," he thought. "Ghosts, vampires, the goddamned walkin' dead. Of all the towns in New England, I hadda pick the capital city of the Twilight Zone."

Nardi knew, of course, that Arkham was not the only dark place in Northeastern America. He had heard the tales of the enclaves of fishfolk all up and down the Massachusetts' coast. Numerous other stories as well. Still, what was supposed to be a quiet, Mayberryesque escape from the dread concrete reality of NYC had slowly unfolded into a black and nightmarish truth all its own.

"Looking for someone, Franklin?"

The voice came from Nardi's right, but also from below and above, from all directions.

"Whatever that was," his mind hissed, "it's too our right."

"I'm looking for my partner," answered the security man, turning to his right. "You seen him?"

Nardi was rewarded with the sight of what appeared to simply be an ordinary man. Middle Eastern in appearance, lanky, well-dressed, seated casually on the corner of a display case. Walking toward the stranger, the security man remained wary as the figure spoke, telling him;

"I believe I have."

"Wanta tell me where?"

"Actually," replied the stranger, a thin smile cracking his immobile face, "I do." His dark, unblinking eyes flashing with a sinister spark, the intruder raised an arm, finger pointing to Nardi's left.

"I believe you were looking for Mr. Balnco, yes?"

Franklin Nardi turned, and the world rushed past him. Staring at the far wall, he saw a wriggling mass of flesh and bone, a blasted smear of nerves and bones, organs and skin, all jumbled, all tangled, writhing on the marble surface, suspended in some manner at which the security man could only guess. On the one hand, there was nothing about the horrid mass from which anyone might have identified a specific human being. There were no identifying marks, no familiar gestures or a long-familiar smile or twinkle from which might spring recognition.

And yet, there was no doubt within Nardi's soul that he was staring at his old friend—turned inside out, somehow still alive—suffering an agony as no man had ever known since the beginning of time. He stood before the pulsating wad, transfixed—helpless. Was Tony alive? Could he feel? Could he think? Could he be saved? What had happened, how could, why—

Questions mounted within Nardi's mind, spilling over one another, contradicting, pulling him apart, accusing the thing on the display case one instant, himself the next. His spine vibrating, limbs shaking, mind going liquid, the security man grappled for some unknown amount of time, desperate to simply control himself, to find a direction in which to funnel his energies before they twisted free from his control.

Finally, his brain clearing to the point where he could grasp some small amount of control over his faculties once more, he spun around, beginning to shout, syllables of fiery hatred tumbling up his throat. Then, a millisecond before they could become words, he slammed his mouth closed, drowning their emotion.

"You are a clever ape, are you not." The intruder was not asking a question. "Moreso than poor Mr. Blanco."

"What-what ... what happened here?"

"Relying on your training ... yes, very good." Uncrossing its legs, the humanoid figure of a man of Middle Eastern extraction slid forward off its seat. Moving toward Nardi in a non-threatening manner, it said;

"He said I did not belong here. He was wrong in this assessment. I dismissed him."

"You—"

Once more, Nardi threw an iron grip over his emotions, strangling them, beating them back. Denying them, casting them aside, forcing them into submission before they earned him the same fate Tony's most likely had earned for him.

"Mr. Blanco did not understand my importance in the shaping of Egyptian history," said the intruder. "I am not certain you do, either, but you are willing to show respect—enough to keep yourself breathing, anyway." Smiling once more, the intruder gestured toward the shivering mass hanging against the wall, then said in a whisper;

"Of course, I suppose Mr. Blanco is still breathing as well." The stranger then sat down upon the air beneath it, stretching out its limbs as if in some manner of invisible recliner. "Do you think that is a kindness on my part, Franklin? Allowing him life? He breathes and thinks. If he thinks, he is—correct? That is what your species believes—yes?"

Nardi staggered, reeling from what he had seen, what he was hearing. Crippled, impotent, the security man did not know what answer to make, even how to make one. As he stammered without sound, his mouth moving, tongue unable to find sounds to expel from his mouth, the stranger added;

"Tell me, Franklin, honestly ... do you think me cruel?"

Nardi's mind was swimming, struggling to find the means to response. Yes, he told himself, he had encountered strange things since coming to Arkham, but nothing like what hung before him on the far wall. Neither that, nor the casual being responsible for it. Swallowing hard, balling his fingers, the security man was about to force some jumble of words from his throat, when suddenly a voice rang out from the doorway.

"Mr. Nardi, could you come here, please?"

"Clemmens," he thought, his desperate mind struggling to center on that one piece of tangible reality. "It's Clemmens." Closing his eyes, blotting out everything but himself and the university president, he called out;

"Yes, sir, can I help you?" When Clemmens repeated his request for Nardi to join him, the security man turned to the intruder once more. Opening his eyes, he managed;

"Could you excuse me a moment?" With a gracious nod, the stranger dismissed Nardi, turning its attention back to the display. Walking briskly, but forcing himself not to run, the security man found his employer waiting for him on the other side of the main door to the hall. As Nardi joined him in the hall, Clemmens said;

"You were in there over an hour—" The security man began to protest, then realized he had no actual idea how long he had stayed frozen before the sight of his partner. Conceding the point, he asked what Clemmens wanted.

"It's become a madhouse outside. There are all manner of people outside, demanding entrance."

"Worse," said another voice. "We've got this to contend with."

Nardi turned, finding a young man—medium height, slightly over-weight, watery brown eyes, limp hair—holding a laptop up for his inspection. Noting that the device was connected to the Internet, the security man asked;

"And what is this 'this' we have to contend with?"

"Someone managed to hack into our security camera network here on campus. They downloaded this footage to YouTube." As Nardi stared in horror, he saw a blurred image of his partner, his splattered, inside-out partner, wriggling across the marble wall of the exhibit hall. Blood dripping, mouth screaming, exposed nerves shivering in the air-conditioning.

"It's already registered over 150 million hits worldwide since it was posted."

"People are flocking here by the thousands," added Clemmens. "The campus is overrun. Tens of thousands of dollars worth of damage to the gardens alone."

"My partner," answered Nardi in a growling whisper, his hand pointing toward the chamber behind them, "in there, dyin', sufferin', and you're worried about people steppin' on your goddamned flowers?" Making fists of his hands, the security man slammed them against his eyes, gouging them into his face as he screamed;

"What? What is it you want of me?!"

"Please, please, sir," said Clemmens in a soft, placating voice, "we need your help. We ... we don't know what to do." When Nardi demanded an explanation, the president told him;

"These crowds, this terrible thing that has happened, if they enter the hall, if they see, see for themselves ... the panic. So many in danger—"

"This couldn't have anything to do with your school's precious reputation, could it?" The younger man with Clemmens tried to interrupt, but the president silenced him with a stern wave of his hand. Turning back to Nardi, the older man said;

"Miskatonic has a reputation so blackened by the misunderstanding of the forces which roam this world that precious little could be done to it by what has happened to Mr. Blanco. But, sir, I beg you to consider, that thing in there, it wants something, of that I'm certain."

"Tell me, Franklin, honestly," Nardi heard the words of the intruder within his mind once more, "do you think me cruel?"

"It did ask me a question."

"Did you answer it?"

"Not yet."

Clemmens pulled at his narrow chin, relief flooding his eyes, pushing out his old fears, just as quickly washed away by new ones. Closing his eyes, taking several short breaths, the president bowed his head, pressing his lips together for a long instant, then finally addressed Nardi once more.

"Whatever answer it receives, that will decide everything."

"And the crowd," asked the security man, working to calm his own demons, "what about them?"

"We were hoping, I know you had experience back in New York with, with crowd control. If you could ... but, it's so much to ask, the crowd, the exhibit hall ..."

"Keep that goddamned room sealed," snarled Nardi. Running his hands over his hair, he started marching for the front door, shouting, "don't let anyone in there. I'll be right back."

Yard by yard, the security man stormed his way to the main entrance. With every step he felt his fear and confusions being consumed by a growing rage. As he neared the doors, he reminded himself;

"Don't get angry, don't let it use you. Think, you miserable wop bastard—*think*—'cause that's our only ticket outta this mess."

Reaching the doors, Nardi stopped for a moment, pulling all of his energy inward. Resisting the overwhelming urge to purge his mind of the horrors straining to assault him once more, he drove all thoughts from his mind, stepping away from the past, refusing the future. Living only in the moment, the security man took hold of one of the great bronze door handles and pulled.

Two Arkham police officers waited for him on the other side, their backs to him. Both male, both large, the pair were throwing all their energy into intimidating the swelling throng before them, to keep them from entering the Exhibit Museum. Ignoring them, brushing aside the tearing waves of curiosity stabbing at him from all directions, Nardi stepped to the left, jumping up onto the back of one of the two great granite lions which guarded the front entrance.

"Where are ya, ya prick bastard," he thought, his eyes scanning the crowd, "I know you're out there somewhere."

One by one, Nardi searched each face, looking for something he knew he would find. Somewhere in the crowd, he was certain, was the one person who could help him keep the situation from escalating into chaos. The security man had no idea who he was looking for—male or female, black or white, tall or fat or gay or whatever—he was not looking for an individual. Franklin Nardi was searching for an attitude. After six minutes, he found that for which he was looking.

It took him several more minutes of pointing and shouting to have the fellow in question moved to the front of the crowd. Once the youngster was at the front doors before Nardi, the security man stepped down from his perch, asking;

"Why do you think I wanted you up here?"

"I don't know," answered the younger man. Smiling as if he did not mind being lied to, Nardi responded;

"I need to take one person in there," he said loud enough for enough people to hear that his words were certain to be spread throughout the crowd, "who can verify what has happened and tell everyone else. Now, why do you think I chose you?" The younger man hesitated for another second, then pride forced him to ask;

"How did you know it was me that hacked the system?"

"Arsonists, bombers, hit-and-run drivers ... you all return to the scene of the crime." Almost bowing, Nardi pointed toward the doors, usher-like, bidding the hacker enter. "Let's go see yours."

"You mean I get to go in and check this thing out personal," he exclaimed with excitement. "This is wicked cool."

"Yeah," growled Nardi as the main doors closed behind them, cutting off the roaring protests of those left behind, "ain't it, though." The young man smiled, practically beaming as he said;

"And Haggerty said I was going to get in trouble. This is so totally awesome. So, what is that booger, anyway?"

"My best friend."

And then, Nardi back-handed the hacker and sent him reeling. Catching up to him as he stumbled blindly, the security man grabbed the younger man by the shoulder, almost lifting him off the ground, as he half carried, half-dragged him to the Egyptian exhibit hall. Finding Clemmens and his assistant still guarding the doors, he ignored their protests as he had those of his captive. Throwing open the doors, he tossed the young man inside, then turned to the president, saying;

"This fine fellow has business inside. Come in if you like, but I advise you don't."

Picking himself up off the floor, the hacker tried to run from the room, but Nardi caught him easily. Spinning him around, he dragged him across the room, screaming at him;

"Com'on, you little prick bastard. Come get that up-close look you were dyin' for." Shoving the young man up toward the two-hundred-and-eighteen pounds of meat and liquid oozing its way along the wall, Nardi bellowed;

"There it is, you miserable fuck! That was a man a few hours ago. A man with a wife. With kids. And you made this—look at him, *look at him*," Nardi grabbed the hacker's head, holding it steady so he could do nothing but stare forward—

"That's the image you gave to the world. That's the way you decided his kids should remember him. You're gonna decide that much about his life, then I think you ought to meet him." Grabbing the youngster by his shirt front, ignoring his cries and tears, Nardi shook the hacker violently, then threw him into the mass that was once Tony Blanco, screaming;

"Shake hands, fellas!"

The hacker fell to the ground, his voice coming out in one long keening screech. Hitting the floor, he skittered madly on his hands and feet like a wounded dog, curling up under a glass-topped exhibition table. As his shrieks muffled down into a mad series of groans, the intruder approached Nardi once more.

"So, sir," it said, its enigmatic smile still etched into the flesh of its assumed face, "what do you think? Am I cruel?"

"You're dangerous," snapped the security man, gasping for breath. Past his prime, with too many beers under his belt for such exertion, he panted as the adrenaline evaporated from his system. Staring at the stranger, he added;

"And curious, I think. But the strong aren't cruel. They don't need to be." The intruder nodded thoughtfully, as if placated. As it considered its next move, Nardi asked;

"Tony ... can you, like, bring him back?"

"I could," answered the stranger. "But with all he has ... ah, experienced, shall we say ... he will not be he that you knew."

The security man nodded sadly. Putting his back against the marble wall close to his friend, he slid down the stone until he was seated on the floor. Wiping at the sweat running down the sides of his head, panting heavily, he growled;

"Well, you're one goat-sucking son'va bitch, aren't ya?"

"Hummmmmmmm," the intruder mused, his smile growing wider. "Goat-sucking son of a bitch. Now I suppose I have a thousand and one names."

Stepping close to Nardi, the stranger bent down until their eyes could meet. His head slightly tilted, he said softly;

"You were correct, Franklin. I am not cruel. I am too indifferent to be cruel. But I keep visiting this world of yours, hoping to learn. I would have liked to have seen what that herd outside would have done with the proper encouragement."

Standing once more, the thing in human form shrugged its pretend shoulders, then made a gesture which caused the remains of Tony Blanco to reform into a lifeless, but recognizably human mass. After that it simply evaporated into a swirl of darkness, and then ceased to be. Franklin Nardi stayed where he was, tired and alone and filled with a horror he could not explain.

Under the glass-topped table, the hacker continued to whimper, a sound which in no way indicated he would be returning to rationality any time soon. In the hallway beyond, Clemmens and his assistant both sensed that their immediate crisis had passed. They had no idea why such a notion had come to them, they simply enjoyed the temporary moment of relief it brought them.

And outside, unknowing and uncaring, the ever-growing crowd trampling the flowers of Miskatonic University festered and growled in cruel indignation, complaining bitterly amongst themselves over the injustice of being forced to remain human.

*We told you earlier in this volume that Paul Morcey is the fan favorite character in CJ's Teddy London series. Actually, when polled, that is the overwhelming answer, but as much as the audience loves the exploits of the maintenance-man-turned-detective in the London novels, he hasn't generated nearly as many solo stories as the following character. Soft-spoken, intensely private, socially-crippled by a monstrous fate, CJ never thought he would ever use this sorrowful woman again after her first appearance. Despite the author's thoughts on the matter, however, she became an integral part of all the London novels, and even spawned her own short story collection (**Lai Wan: Tales of the Dreamwalker** available from Marietta Publishing). Here is the latest story written about her—*

The Moment After Death

> *"We sometimes congratulate ourselves at the moment of waking from a troubled dream; it may be so the moment after death."*
> — Nathanial Hawthorne

"I can't understand it."

Nine ...

The doctor repeated the words for the twenty-second time. Those around him had no better comments straddling the tips of their tongues, so they said nothing. After all, he was by far the best of them, and as they had all been made painfully aware by that point, the only comment he could come up with in reaction to what they all were witnessing was;

"I can't understand it."

Ten ...

The Asian woman in black and gray pressed the bell a second time. She knew she had waited the correct amount of seconds before pressing the device once more—knew so with certainty because she knew everything happening within the structure upon which it was mounted. With a touch of her hand to the building, she had sent out her awareness, felt everyone within. She could have, if she wanted to, seen through all of their eyes, invaded their brains and discovered what they made themselves for breakfast, learned their social security numbers, catalogued their drinks and drugs and other sins of choice ... if she had wanted to. It she had it within her to be that concerned.

She did not. Most of the people within the building she had no need for, did not care about, could not be bothered. No, she had come to see only one person—the person she knew had heard the second pressing of the buzzer, but who was not certain it was her buzzer which she had heard. With a gentle smile, the Asian woman pressed the small glowing plastic button once more.

"Hello," came an old and cautious voice. "Who is it?"

"You do not know me. My name is Lai Wan."

"Oh, what do you want?"

"It is a beautiful day out today. I have come to take you out for a walk, before the weather turns upon us."

There was a small hesitation, a quite normal, understandable pause for those who lived in New York City. True, the family neighborhoods of Brooklyn were far friendlier than those of Manhattan, but still, one had to be careful. After a moment, however, the old voice, minus some of its caution, sounded again, asking;

"Why ..." and then, in one of those whimsical moments none can explain, the question being asked faded and was reborn. "Can you wait a few minutes? I don't move very fast these days."

"Take as much time as you need," answered Lai Wan. Her fingers slipping from the speaker button, she added softly, "It is your time, after all."

It took Mrs. Muriel Benson some eighteen minutes to finally make it to the ground floor of her building. She had not been hampered by a need to add a great amount of outer layers. It was a wonderfully beautiful day, the kind New Yorkers long for, and then all too often don't notice when they arrive because of their hectic schedules. Mrs. Benson and Lai Wan introduced themselves to each other, after which, the older woman asked;

"Where did you want to go?"

"What I want," answered her caller, "the universe does not often grant. This is your day. You know how strong you feel this morning, and what you would use your strength to see. I thought it would be best if you picked our destination."

The old woman mulled the novel idea of doing what she wanted to do over in her mind for a few seconds, a certain giddiness seizing her. She had lived almost her entire life in the service of others. Indeed, after her husband had died, she had become almost lost without his needs to guide her daily routine. As her mind wandered over the local terrain, thinking on how far she could actually walk those days, she asked with a sudden excitement;

"Oh, could we go to the park? I used to love to walk there. It's so peaceful. Would you mind?"

Lai Wan assured her elderly companion that the park was an excellent choice. Of course, there were few who would have disagreed with Mrs. Benson, for the destination in question was no routine neighborhood corner of greenery. No, she lived close by to the Brooklyn Botanical Gardens, one of the finest civically-sponsored stretches of vegetation in all the world. Mrs. Benson had not been there in several years, despite her enthusiasm for the place. She walked slowly, hampered by her need for a cane. As they started out, she said;

"I've wanted to go back to the park for just the longest time now, but ... I don't know, by myself it ... it just seemed so far away."

"Many things seem distant from our grasp," Lai Wan answered. Then, as if struck by a sudden curiosity, she asked Mrs. Benson of her life—what she used to do, jobs she might have held over the years. The older woman responded, telling her;

"I was a teacher, for thirty-seven years. I taught history. They don't need history teachers anymore, you know."

"Why is that?"

"Oh, no need for it, don't you know. Not for real history. Not for what was important. Not for what pulled society together, made the world what it is today."

"What do they teach today?"

"Oh, all that political nonsense of theirs ... you know, now instead of knowing who conquered who, or when things were invented, or when places were discovered, it's all feelings. How does it feel to know you live in a society dominated by white males? Why are the words of this 1,000 year old African poet more important that those of Thomas Jefferson or Winston Churchill? If your choice was to steal from the poor and the innocent, or be a normal person, which would you choose?"

Mrs. Benson had to stop at that point. Her legs were trembling under her, her breath was short, her face red. Lai Wan took her arm with a certain amount of concern, then smiled, saying;

"I take it you did not agree with the changing times at the school board?"

"No, I did not." The answer came in a whisper. The older woman was tired out from her tirade, smiling at the fact the pepper and vinegar she thought long gone from her soul was still right there at the surface, waiting to be put to use. Nodding her head only to herself, she added;

"Bunch of communists. You ever have to deal with such creatures?"

Lai Wan had. As the two started forward once more, she told her companion of her escape from mainland China years earlier with her friend Xui Lu. Somehow, the story endeared the two to one another, and they both spoke quite animatedly about many things as their slow march through the streets of Brooklyn continued.

Indeed, the unexpected outing seemed to revive Mrs. Benson, and she let flow the torrent of her life. She spoke of her marriage, some sixty-five years earlier, and of the death of her husband, some fourteen previous. As they entered the Botanical Gardens, she reminisced on her college days, and her early days in teaching, and how happy she had been. As the pair slowly made their way past the Children's Garden, winding their way toward the park's magnificent central building, she said;

"Teaching used to be so wonderful. But these days, oouugghh, you know, I hate to say it, but the way things have changed, by the end, I was glad to go."

"Why is that?"

"Oh, just the way everything has changed so. Children in charge of the schools now. No respect for their elders; imagine, parents encouraging a system where the young don't have to obey authority. What kind of idiot couldn't see where that was going to lead?"

"The usual kind?"

Mrs. Benson smiled wickedly in response to Lai Wan's joke, then simply had to stop moving as she began to laugh. It was a thin kind of chuckle at first, the type of release an older person develops to keep from hurting themselves. The bit of humor hit Mrs. Benson too squarely in the heart of her beliefs, however, and after a few seconds she was swaying with laughter, teetering on her cane so violently that Lai Wan was forced to reach out and steady the older woman.

"I'm sorry," she said finally, when the cleansing attack finally passed. "I guess I needed a good laugh."

"There are none among us that does not need a good laugh now and again. Are you feeling strong enough to go on?"

Her elderly companion answered in the positive, then asked if they could sit down for a while. Spotting the park's compact restaurant area at the top of a nearby small hill, Lai Wan inquired as to whether or not Mrs. Benson thought she could make it that far. When she replied that she could go twice that far for a cup of tea, the two agreed that such a reward was worth the effort and headed for the outdoor cafe.

Conquering the summit easily enough, the pair found a table in the shade where the breeze seemed perfect. Lai Wan stood in the short line to get their drinks while Mrs. Benson rested. When she returned with the teas—one plain, one with milk and sugar—the two sat quietly, taking careful, lip-singeing sips, then fell back into conversation once more. Setting her tea before her, Mrs. Benson asked;

"So, I know you escaped from China, and that you used to sell real estate. You never married, but you once had a fiancé. You dress very conservatively, draped from head to toe almost like a Muslim, but you're not a modest woman. Your clothes are simple, but expensive, and your eyes flash with a desire that never gets met. Now, why is that?"

Eleven ...

"Not much gets by you, does it?"

"I was a teacher. Need eyes in the back of your head for that job. And you need a heart, too. One that listens to more than just words. Yes, we've only known each other a couple of hours now, but you did me a great kindness today, getting me out of the house ..."

"Surely your daughter—" Mrs. Benson cut Lai Wan off with a gesture. Taking a sip of her tea before speaking, she finally said;

"Marcey's a good girl. She takes care of me. All my bills are paid. She manages my money nicely. My rent is paid on time, all the utilities. When my legs got bad, she had my mail sent to her. She forwards personal letters, but everything else, she has computers taking care of it."

"People do not send much personal mail these days ..."

"No. And anyone who would write me is either dead or has the arthritis too bad. Marcey just didn't want me having to go down to the mailbox every day ..."

"Nor did she wish to come and do it for you." There was silence for a moment, after which Lai Wan apologized for her abrupt comment. Not content with her companion's forgiveness, she added;

"Not that it excuses anything, but I have sadly grown accustomed to being far too right about things, and not caring how I make use of the information."

"I've noticed," the older woman answered with a kind tone. "But it's part of what makes you so intriguing. So please, I'll ask again—"

Twelve ...

"What is it that makes you so different from everyone I've ever met?"

Lai Wan let a short breath escape her lips. A strong woman, still she needed to reach deep within herself for the ability to speak of her past without betraying the part of her that kept her emotions to herself. Tilting her head slightly, she made the briefest of nods, then said;

"Some years ago I was involved in an accident. A car and a bus, one or the other jumped the sidewalk, they tangled together, and their end result was that they pinned me to the wall of the building I had been passing. I was rushed to the nearest hospital, of course. I am told they broke some sort of rapid response time that day, but it did not matter. No one expected me to live."

"They were wrong, though."

Thirteen ...

"No—" answered Lai Wan sadly. "Actually, they were not."

Mrs. Benson simply stared. She knew the other woman had more to say, and that she needed a moment to prepare to say it. Taking another deep sip of her styrofoamed cup of tea, Lai Wan took in a deep breath, then finally told her story.

"I died on the operating table. The reports on how long I was actually gone vary from witness to witness. Most agree I was dead for a longer time than that from which it is possible to recover. And yet ..." She made a set of small circles in the air with her hands, as if to say, here I am.

"You poor dear ..."

"Oh, save your sympathy for a moment. The tale gets better." As Mrs. Benson warmed her hands around her tea cup, Lai Wan continued, telling her;

"When I was returned to life by whatever capricious fate decided it was necessary to do so, I was, well ... shall we say, 'gifted,' with certain abilities. They call this new talent I was given psychometry."

"My ... what's that?"

"The dictionaries politely called it the 'alleged art or faculty of divining the properties of an object, or matters associated with it, through contact with, or proximity to it.' It means I can tell you the history of a thing by touching it."

"Is that how you knew I wanted to get out of the house today?"

"Partly," responded Lai Wan, granting her companion a tiny smile. "You catch on faster than my doctors did." When Mrs. Benson asked what the psychometrist meant, she answered;

"When I came back to life on the table, I was still too weak to do much more than breathe. But, by the next day, I had begun to regain my strength—"

Fourteen ...

"And that was when I discovered my new abilities." Lai Wan shuddered slightly as memory reminded her how terrible life can actually be. It was a tiny gesture, but Mrs. Benson's teacher's eye caught it, and she felt a moment of fright because of it. Getting past her initial distaste, the psychometrist told her companion that she did not wish to upset her. The older woman, noting Lai Wan's discomfort, told her;

"Something tells me you haven't talked about this in a long time—maybe never. You just tell me as much as you want and don't you worry none about me."

"Long before I regained consciousness, they tell me ... I began to feel my surroundings. In particular, the bed I was in. The sheets covering it, the pillow beneath my head, the pillow cases ... all of it. Washing a thing may remove stains and odors, but ... it can not remove a thing's history."

Fifteen ...

Mrs. Benson nodded absently for a moment, then suddenly, she understood. As her eyes widened, Lai Wan confirmed;

"I was given an ability, but no control over it. As I lay upon the bed, so many bones broken, so many organs damaged, helpless, unconscious, this new power explored the mattress and all the rest provided for my comfort. It found the pain of so many men and women and children ... so many innocent victims ..."

"You didn't just learn about their suffering, did you? You felt it—experienced it. Yes?" Close to tears, Lai Wan nodded, admitting;

"Yes. I felt it all as they did. Every cut and burn. Every shattered rib and broken eye and missing limb. I suffered their cancers and other maladies as they did, endured the results of their falls and accidents—those that came from train wrecks, from burning buildings, from fights and anything else you can imagine. I felt their stab wounds, the pain of their gun shots, those attacked by dogs, those who were beaten, those who were raped ..."

The psychometrist's voice trailed off for a moment, her glistening eyes filling with a fleeting look of hopeless confusion. Her head down, voice soft, she added;

"And somehow, even worse, I bore the weight of those who came to see them. I was swallowed by the indifference of those who came to pretend to weep over them, saw their thousands of eyes sneaking glances at watches, felt their incredible boredom with being saddled with the terrible task of visiting a sick or dying loved one. Beyond reliving for the countless thousands their pain and monstrous suffering, past feeling their aching souls at the moment of death, as I died once more along with them, seeing again and again the glorious light I was denied, from which I was pulled back, the pain of the horrible multitudes that descended upon them, surrounding that hideous bed, that was the worst of all."

Sixteen ...

She did not tell Mrs. Benson of the doctor, the usually smug surgeon who stood next to her bed as she screamed weakly in her post-operation coma, saying over and over—

"I can't understand it."

She listened to him repeat the words seventeen times. He was by far the best of those in attendance, and yet all he could do was stare and stammer the same pointless phrase over and over as if he were a parrot. Putting her thin, tired hand over Lai Wan's, the older woman said;

"You poor dear ... it must have been awful."

"All in all," answered the psychometrist, "that is not a bad word for it."

Lai Wan moved her free hand to join the one held by Mrs. Benson. The older woman did the same, and the two sat for some time simply holding each others hands, reassuring each other silently that the worst the universe had to offer had passed. Eventually they broke off, returning to their teas before they cooled to the point of uselessness. Finally, her cup nearly drained, the psychometrist said;

"Lately, my powers have begun to change. Well, not change so much as expand—grow."

"What do you mean?"

"Recently, I have begun to experience a kind of future dream—I don't know what else to call it—where in I see things to come while I sleep."

"What kinds of things," asked Mrs. Benson.

"All manner," answered Lai Wan. "Most of what I see, I can not imagine why it is revealed to me. Earthquakes, floods, things which could not be stopped or prepared for if there were months. I know. I tried."

Quietly, the psychometrist related her attempts to warn governments about impending disasters. No matter what she did, she could get none to listen to her. Worse, when her predictions came to pass, she was investigated as if she were responsible for them. Not able to help herself, Mrs. Benson took her companion's hands in hers again, extending the only gift she had to offer, human contact. Lai Wan took it gratefully, continuing her story.

"I see smaller events as well, but still I am thwarted. What good is knowing this or that person on the other side of the world is going to die? I awaken in the morning sometimes, knowing that in five minutes a young boy will be struck by an automobile, or that in a half an hour a man on a camping trip will choke to death. It is as if cruel Destiny has determined to never stop testing me."

"Life can seem that way sometime," agreed the elderly woman.

"When I was cheated of Heaven, denied the Light and returned to this wretched world, that was not bad enough. No, I had to be sent back with abilities which frightened away my fiancé, which shoved a normal life completely from my grasp. Somehow I survived being gifted with the pain of ten thousand others, and managed to create a new life for myself. Shortly after that, I met a man named Theodore London who pulled back the curtains of the universe and showed me that there were horrors and monsters far beyond those of which I knew."

Mrs. Benson's eyes went wide of a sudden, her mouth forming the smallest of "os" for only an instant. Lai Wan held her hands, giving her back what comfort she could in the brief moment. Still holding the old woman's hands, she said softly;

"And so, now that I have become used to that knowledge, vicious Fate has given me these dreams. Such as the one it gifted me with last night ... of you."

Again the psychometrist saw what she had seen during her sleep. She saw the moment of Mrs. Benson's massive stroke, a swift and violent attack which would take her instantly—painlessly, without warning. At her age, it was the death for which most fondly wish. But, living as she did, no visitors, no friends, Lai Wan also saw what came next. The old woman's body quickly becoming the breeding ground of a plague of vermin. Thousands of insects born of her flesh, multiple generations in weeks, living within the safety of her walls. Although the dream did not reveal any specific details, Lai Wan could still tell that left to uninterrupted fate, the swarm would mutate to where they would be carriers of a mild plague. In the closely-packed quarters of New York City, hundreds of thousands would die in the first weeks. Millions more around the world would be sickened. She could not see beyond that point, but that had been enough.

Carefully releasing Mrs. Benson's hands, she made certain the teacher's now vacant husk would not topple from its chair. To all those around, the seated figure simply appeared to be an elderly woman enjoying the morning sun. Content that she had done all she could, Lai Wan finished her tea, the memories of her dream, of the plague averted, fading within her mind. Standing, she looked down at Mrs. Benson, and gathered her lace shawl about her as she said softly;

"Why Fate sought to condemn you to being the mother of agony, I do not know. But, being cruelly used after one's death ... that is something I know about."

Turning, Lai Wan made her way back to the stairs which led down out of the restaurant. Returning to the beauty of the park, every step she took falling within the steps of countless thousands who had gone before, all of them eager to inflict upon her their hidden fears and terrors and secrets which they had tried so desperately to leave behind, the psychometrist pulled in on herself and shoved it all away from her with practiced ease. Looking back at the restaurant gleaming in the late morning sun, she said;

"One of us is enough, Muriel."

And then she proceeded for the front gate, smiling at the lovely colors, delighting to the gentle scents of lily and pine, even as behind her the scream of a faraway table cleaner shattered the park's gentle quiet.

There is no doubting that CJ Henderson is known for creating groups of characters that lend themselves to multiple return visits. There are those rare instances, however, when he chooses to build an entire new universe for a single story. Although he almost always has a moral built into his tales, sometimes the social condition he has chosen to explore demands the utter attention of the audience. When those instances come along, it seems he has no choice other than to give the world a story such as—

Folly

The committee was just beginning the long but pleasurable task of some well-deserved self-congratulatory back-slapping. For some one hundred and twenty-seven years they had held the tide, kept the doors barred, repulsed the fearsome foes of humanity, and for the most part lived to tell the tale.

"Friends," said the rotund man at the head of the table, "we are come together once more ..."

They were not warriors. They did not brandish guns or blades or fly devices into the skies loaded with bombs. They carried not sword nor shield. And yet, warriors still they were.

"And from all I have heard this evening ...,"

They were a battalion of the mind. They were scholars, librarians, men of science, men of enlightenment—they were humanity's first and last line of defense. They were thinkers.

"It seems that once more we have upheld the sacred trust passed down to us by our noble founder."

Many a head turned at the words, gazing on the picture hanging over the doorway at the opposite end of the room from the speaker. It showed a man at the end of his years, his strength and body diminished, but his eyes as sparkling as they were in his younger days when the horrors held just beyond the veil of mankind's understanding had first been revealed unto him. His visage bespoke a lifetime of erudition. The somewhat tarnish bronze plaque just below his portrait read simply: Dr. Henry Armitage,

A.M. Miskatonic, Ph. D. Princeton, Litt. D. John Hopkins.

"There have been tales told tonight, reports made of triumphs which some might feel were, perhaps, a trifle embellished;" many around the grand table chuckled, several pointed, the one figure who was their target, of course, affecting not to notice any of it; "and others still which, if I know their tellers at all, were most likely woefully modest."

Again, much under-the-breath commentary passed about the room. Heads nodded and whispers filled with frank admiration embarrassed those whose recent life-threatening heroics were something which, frankly, they wished everyone would stop making such a bother over so they could just try to forget what they had seen and get back to the serious work of teaching the next generation.

"But regardless," the speaker added, "it must be stated that every man and woman here is deserving of their share of praise and self-satisfaction."

The man stopped, tilting his chin downward for a moment, staring at his chest. Rubbing a meaty hand across his face, he looked upward again after his thoughtful second and said;

"It has been our solemn duty to protect the world, the galaxy, the universe—"

"Reality," Coruthers barked. "It's a shared belief in a confirmed timeline. That's what we guard."

"Oh, leave it to a poet scientist to gaggle us with sophistry."

The speaker was a woman whose mane, some twenty years earlier had finally given up the last strands of a scarlet which at one time had been as red as a beating heart and as thick as tension. She was silver gray now, and trimmed to a respectable length for her advanced years, but she had stood on a broken and blistered field once, and she had chanted from the book as prescribed while all about her men were torn apart by color and roasted by laughter.

She was Katherine Flynn, everyone's darlin' Kate, and as good a man as any of them. Coruthers laughed with the rest. They needed laughter. Healthy laughter, not the kind that started while they were driving, or sitting on the toilet, or trying to sleep. The unbidden laughter, the unconscious chuckling that ... what could you call it? Put people off? Made folks nervous? The childlike ability to fall into titters or giggles, or full blown hysterics. Often then replaced by the most mournful of tears.

"All right now," started Dean Haskell, leading them all back toward sobriety once more, "we are here for a purpose, you know. Why don't we all focus our attention and take a look at this thing, shall we?"

They had outwitted the Tindilosi. They had closed the gates at Mankali and Golubchik Bay. They had shattered the mirrors in the halls beyond darkness and sealed the boxes of Thon'Zala. Their membership had charted the stars and watched the skies and reacted when they saw their duty was clear decade after decade. They fought with their knowledge and their wits, and so far, they had held the line.

"All right, then," the Dean continued," just to make certain that we're all on the same page here ...,"

At a cost.

"I'm going to go over the facts we have."

Hundreds of those enlisted in their cause had died throughout their on-going campaign. Often those mercenary forces they brought in to serve as their protectors became humanity's protectors, giving their lives in service of all rational things.

"Young Fergeson, the assistant professor that disappeared last week," he reminded them, "he left behind the paper he was preparing for us which some think might be a clue toward discovering what has happened to him."

"You know what's happened to him," said a balding man with a thick brown moustache, "something's got him. Fried his brain or et him whole. He's wandering around in an alley or a field some where, groping his way along, or he's already worked his way through some horror's bowels."

"Freddie," snapped Kate fondly, "you're as charming as ever. But, everyone else," she said to the assembled, "just because Freddie's annoying doesn't make him wrong. Did this kid get himself served up as the blue plate somewhere along our lovely Massachusetts coastline, or is he just sleeping off a drug bender or whatever people in their twenties do these days to hurt themselves."

"Mostly for that they just watch television."

Coruthers smiled as those around him chuckled with him that time, but Dean Haskell said, "Sadly, that was Dan Fergeson's proposal. Part of it, anyway."

The hall of heroes grew silent. To those outside their circle, the thought of an artist being driven to acts of madness by one of his own creations was a notion to be ridiculed. But these people knew truths which lay several gossamer layers beneath the surface of the knowledge possessed by the man in the street. There was none among them that could not believe a man could begin some sort of study of this or that aspect of the reality which they understood and suddenly disappear off the face of the Earth for his troubles. Not a one.

The Dean went through the printout before him, his copy of the Fergeson study, leading the others in an analysis of as much of the document as had been completed at the time of its author's disappearance. They read it together as a team, trying to simply absorb the material, until finally Dr. Muriel Phelan snapped;

"This, this is nonsense." Her tone was brittle—annoyed and resentful. "He says mankind is insane. That we're all self-deluding morons—cows. *Cows*—that's what he called us—*cows!*"

"Stop it." Haskell's voice was low and commanding. It shook with a gravity that reminded rationality of the fact it was always on duty. Phelan stiffened, her emotion pulled in and forced into place by a practiced hand. "Fergeson makes an interesting point. If you take all the prophesies we govern our field of study around, the end times really should have come by now."

"It's true," Professor Phillips joined in. "We've danced around it for years. But we're overdue, really. Christian, Norse, fifty more—it should be all over."

"But," sputtered Doc Reily, barely in his thirties, the youngest of them, "isn't that the point of this group? To forestall the end times? I mean, seriously, yes, a baseball game is supposed to last nine innings. Everyone in the stands can predict that it will go no longer, but if the underdog team rallies and pushes the game into extra innings, then into extra innings it goes."

"I'm not saying he was correct," the Dean responded, "I'm saying that there could be some angle of the idea he was pursuing which disturbed one of these entities we know so well. I think we all need to devote some time to this paper in the coming days. Read it over, try and see beyond it, to what clue or direction might have been just beyond Fergeson's grasp..."

"For that thing he was about to discover," interrupted Freddie, "that something would have killed him to keep him from reaching."

Dean Haskell agreed with the sentiment expressed, then wrapped up the remainder of the group's business as quickly as possible. Gathered within the room were not only the leading faculty members of Miskatonic University, but some of the best and brightest figures in the world of business, politics and the arts. They all had lives outside of protecting the world. Fortunes to make, windows to wash, bills to pay, papers to grade, et cetera.

As the group finally abandoned the room, Coruthers found himself the envy of all the others. Katherine Flynn had chosen to descend the stairs at his side. They chattered about the past and the present and other trivialities, and for the poet it was a moment of joy. When they reached the outside, however, away from the others, Flynn announced her ulterior motive. Maneuvering them to a bench, she asked;

"This lad, Fergeson. Did you know him?" When Coruthers admitted he did, she continued, "then what's your gut feeling on this? Was he likely to lose himself on a bender? Do you think he was onto something?"

"Honestly, Kate, I think, yes—Freddie may be onto something."

"I know," she said softly. "I think he is, too."

"But the paper itself," the man answered, "it's so, so ... defeatist. I mean, to even consider that the end times might have happened as long as a hundred years ago, maybe more. I mean—"

"Your a scientist as well as a poet," Flynn reminded her companion. "Let's think as scientists for a moment."

Together they debated Fergeson's theory point by point. All the warnings humanity had given itself over the centuries did indeed point to moments in their past. The end times should have come about by then. The decision one had to make for one's self was, had they prevented the breakdown of dimensions as they had always worked to do, or were they somehow deluding themselves.

Fergeson's facts were interesting to play with. He showed how all the things needed for self-delusion had all sprung into being during the same time. Atomic theories, the cinema, television, all crawling into being in the 1920s, all beginning their destructive weave at the same time. The threat of nuclear destruction had, of course, as Fergeson proposed, turned a once conservative, suspicious world into a place increasingly eager for each new thing that might come along. The world of entertainment jumped on each new fad and rushed it headlong to the markets waiting for it. And somehow, a civilized humanity that had moved at a staid and steady pace for a score of centuries suddenly burst forward, flew ahead in a wild and uncontrolled headlong rush to any distraction it could find.

Scholarship and self-control had been tossed aside as nonsense. Self-pleasure, self-centered never-ending stimulation had replaced them, gimmegimmegimme becoming the mantra of the masses from the United States to Timbukto.

"Still," ventured Coruthers, "to think that we're all living in a fog of self-delusion, that reality is not, not ... well ..." the poet reached out and rapped on the bench, "not solid, not supporting us as we think—well, I mean, then what is there?"

"It's just food for thought, I suppose," admitted Flynn. She turned her head away from Coruthers for the moment, unconsciously silhouetting herself against the setting sun. The glorious red of the evening sky reflected against her silvered crown and for an instant the scientist poet saw her as she had been in their past, and his heart skipped a beat. Smiling, he said softly;

"It's all grist for the mill. And worth exploring. After all, we've had Thomas Gray's warning for quite some time. It would be terrible if we were to abandon watchfulness now."

"'Gray's warning?'"

His smile unabated, he quoted one of his long-time favorites to the woman sitting next to him.

> *"To each his suff'rings, all are men,*
> *Condemn'd alike to groan;*
> *The tender for another's pain,*
> *Th' unfeeling for their own.*

> *"Yet ah! Why should they know their fate?*
> *Since sorrow never comes too late,*
> *And happiness too swiftly flies.*
> *Thought would destroy their paradise.*
> *No more; where ignorance is bliss,*
> *'Tis folly to be wise."*

And suddenly, Coruthers had a thought of his own. Being a man of science as well as the arts, much like young Fergeson, he looked at the idea they had been debating from both angles at once. What if mankind had accelerated its collective interest in distractions, embracing each new performer, every new craze, no matter how infantile or debased or ridiculous, simply as a way not to see life as it really was? What if all activity were conducted within one's mind, and that the wooden slat he had just rapped upon were no more a solid construct than a quart of irony.

Closing his eyes against the glare of the sunset, the poet shuddered for a moment, horrified that their noble work could all be a sham, nothing more than a pathetic exercise in avoiding the truth. In all honesty, the idea terrified the man. It shrank his soul and robbed him of ego, allowing the all-knowing back of his mind to laugh at his pomposity.

It was too monstrous a notion. Not that humanity had been the plaything of black and shambling gods, but that he himself might be wrong about some thing.

Any thing.

And then, the glare pierced his eyes as his defenses finally fell. The breath rushed out of him as he realized consciously at last that there was naught about him but terror and failure and the laughter of cold intelligence raining down on him from the center of a chaos that held the sum total of everything within its twisted and crushing grasp.

Coruthers screamed, then opened his eyes.

"What's the matter with you?"

The poet stared at Flynn, shaking, spittle flecking his lips. His eyes darting, head turning, hands jerking, he pointed this way and that, took note of the setting sun, ran his hands over the worn bench, rubbed it hard until splinters tore his flesh and drove the wretched notion away from him that he was not in control. Not master of his fate. Not the pilot of his destiny.

Holding his bleeding hand aloft, Kate took note of his plight and as she had for decades, she comforted an ally in need. Taking his bloody palm in her own hand, she took it to her lips and kissed his wound.

Ah, thought Coruthers, soothed once more, bliss.

And dark laughter roared in ears which could not hear.

Last but not least, we have a story introducing CJ's latest supernatural investigator. Newly created for Tor/Forge books (first novel available in early 2010), museum director Piers Knight is our author's purest investigator yet. Many of CJ's characters have a foot in two worlds, mainly the mystical and that of the hardboiled tough guy. Knight may be something of a magician, but there is little of the pugilist about him. In fact, he's just about the perfect person to bring into a situation concerning—

A Puzzle Well Made

"Oh," thought the man standing in the ancient doorway, "damn all the fools who plague me so."

The air which flowed forth from the cold, black entranceway, standing uncovered after an eternity of neglect, was more than simply stale. There was a dank fetidness to it, a sense of utter stagnation which chilled the figure breathing it in, leaving him both frightened and angered.

"What's the matter, doc," asked a younger man standing behind him, "isn't this the right place?"

"How," wondered the man, the question an honest attempt to unravel the jumbled fragments of his life so that he might make some sense of its lack of structure, "how ever do I allow myself to become in involved in these things?"

It was, the back of his mind insisted, a question worthy of a touch of reflection. Closing his eyes, he allowed himself to do so for a moment.

Although it was beginning to feel like years since he had seen his home, it had been less than three weeks since he had first met the younger man. He had been sitting behind his desk, desperately attempting to empty his in box when the outer door from the hallway had opened, and the younger man had strode into his foyer and on into the professor's office itself—unannounced and uninvited—boisterously declaring;

"You're this Piers Knight guy, aren't you? Doctor Knight ... the big expert on everything. Right?"

Knight, one of the main curates of the Brooklyn Museum, looked up at his intruder, wondering where he had seen the man's face before. He was certain the grinning, weak-chinned visage had stared at him at some time in the past—from a magazine cover, perhaps. Not a proper scientific journal, but glaring outward from some glossy dreadful meant to distract the masses, such as *People* or maybe *Time*.

"Might you be Randel Anthony, inheritor of the Anthony gold interests somewhere down in the lower Americas?"

"I see my fame precedes me."

"'Fame,' yes ..." mused Knight, wondering exactly what would bring such a person into his life. "There's just the word I would have chosen if I were thinking of being polite about someone shoving their way into my office."

"Ouch," answered Anthony, "you're just as smoking as they said you'd be."

"'They,'" the professor quoted the younger man once more. "And which particular 'they' do I have to thank for this, so far, pointless interruption?"

"Your name came up more than once during my research, but it was the recommendation of a friend of yours, Dr. Otto Strassen, that finally won me over."

"Oh," thought Knight, smiling sourly at the mention of his long-time colleague, "damn all the fools who plague me so." Realizing he was not going to be able to continue with the inordinate amount of paperwork awaiting him until he dealt with Anthony, the professor said;

"Well, if Otto thinks so little of my time that he would inflict you upon me without hesitation, by all means, tell me Mr. Anthony, what is it that brings you to my innermost sanctum sanctorium this day?"

"Doc, I'm going to lay my cards on the table. My family's fortune has been a modest thing for decades. When the reins were handed to me I used what extra capital I could move around into exploration. I've always kept our operations in Guatemala, branched a little up into Mexico, over into Belize, even Honduras once—"

The younger man recited a quick laundry list of attempted digs set up by Anthony Minerals & Gems throughout the last few years. Most of them related to the discovery of new deposits of chert and serpentine, jade, obsidian, amber—even salt. A number of them proved out as completely worthless, but none of them gave up the much hoped for silver or gold that might revitalize the Anthony family fortunes.

"Then, about two months ago," young mister Anthony said, his voice dropping into a tone that promised revelation, "we found something different. Something incredible."

"Incredible comes in many forms," responded Knight dryly. "Could you be even a trifle more specific."

"Yeah, actually, I think I can." Reaching into the hard-cornered attaché case he had set at his side upon his initial intrusion, Anthony pulled forth a thick envelope of photos. Handing it over to the professor, he encouraged Knight to look through them as he continued to speak.

"We'd come to the point where I figured we had nothing to lose. I had the discretionary funds left for one more reasonably sized exploration. So I thought, why not gamble? Really give the goddamned dice a toss for once—you know what I mean?"

Having taken more than a few perhaps unnecessary risks in his time, the professor nodded, indicating that Anthony should continue. Moving the chair he had appropriated closed to Knight's desk, he said;

"I thought, why not go into an area that's never reported anything? A remote spot, no commerce, no people—some place where a guy might find diamonds just laying about, if he had the guts to go look for them."

As the professor continued to thumb through the photos he had been given, he nodded quietly. It was obvious that Anthony's story was going to explain what it was he was seeing in his handful of photographs, and that was something that Knight wanted to hear more greatly with each image he examined.

"Are you familiar with Palenque, doc?"

Piers Knight stopped studying the photos in his hand. His head snapping upward, his mind raced even as his mouth made ready to spit out an answer. Of course he knew what Palenque was. No one in his position could possibly be ignorant of one of the greatest of the Mesoamerican cities. A sprawling, remarkable site in the hills outside the Mayan lowlands of Guatemala, it epitomized the social and artistic achievements of the classic period of Mayan civilization.

"Familiar enough," Knight answered finally, "to know these photos weren't taken there. This isn't Mayan architecture. Nothing like it. In fact..."

The professor shuffled through the stack once more, looking for one image in particular. Uncovering the shot of an ancient doorway, one obviously only recently uncovered, he held it out to his visitor, declaring;

"This is possibly the finest example of Incan architecture I've ever seen."

"Right you are, doc."

"Mr. Anthony, the Incas maintained their civilization in the mountains of Peru. We're talking not only a difference of thousands of miles, but a thousand years as well. Two completely different civilizations, peoples that knew their peaks in two entirely different eras. What exactly is it you're trying to tell me?"

"That doorway you're looking at, doc," answered Anthony, his excitement level clearly growing despite his attempt to remain collected, "we found it under fifty feet of dirt and rock. In the side of a hill, one with trees growing on it, someone over a thousand years ago decided to bury something. Is a tomb, the entrance to a crypt, a mine, a treasure house—who knows?"

"And exactly," asked the professor slowly, his mind trying to wrap itself around the implications generated by the bafflement with which he had been presented, "how many people, other experts, have you brought in on this?"

"Doc," answered Anthony, his tone that of a fisherman confident his hook had been securely swallowed, "I start at the top of a list and work my way down. Outside of my crew and our guides—all of whom, coincidentally, are still on site—you're the first person in the world to know anything about this."

"Well then," responded Knight, still staring at the impossible door, his trademark half-smile beginning to curl one side of his mouth, "perhaps we should keep things that way."

The professor had taken a stance in front of the massive obsidian doorway, studying it in silence. He had concluded that the intricate carvings which ran across its entire width and breadth to be Incan from the photographs he had seen back in Brooklyn. His first few seconds in their actual presence confirmed his original pronouncement.

At that moment he was searching for not the "who" of the mystery. "How" and "what," as in how was what he was looking at build, and what exactly was it, were certainly good questions. Ones, however, as far as Knight was concerned could be answered later. No, the professor was concerned with the "why" of the unexplainable structure.

Why had it been built? Why had the Incas traveled across thousands of miles to build it?

Such a mission held for the professor the same absurdity of the American moon missions. Billions of dollars spent to travel to another world. Why? To gather some rocks. To plant a flag. To go for a while and never return. Why?

Of course, Knight told himself, there were reasons. Political power, research and development. Win the hearts and minds of the free world and get Tang, Velcro and the personal computer out of the deal.

"So," the professor thought, his eyes narrowing, inspecting each inch of the quite solid surface carefully. "Why did you do it? Why this? Why here? Why?"

No answer sprang to his mind.

Closing his eyes for a moment, Knight rubbed his face, running all the known facts over in his mind. Anthony's people had been drilling, looking for anything with a profit connected to it. When their contact bit had begun send back obsidian, the crew was happy to have turned up something of at least a minor value. But, when they began to realize they were looking at fragments of glass that had not only been polished but worked by human tools, they grew understandably excited.

Drilling had stopped immediately. Under orders from Anthony, a shaft was to be sunk to the deposit discovered. Once it had been reached, the entire surface of the deposit was to be cleared. All concerned were fairly certain this would be a quite time-consuming endeavor. While this was done Anthony had proceeded from his native Georgia to the site, dropping everything he had been doing in order to see for himself what his people in the field had uncovered.

What he had found upon his arrival was a sight out of a science fiction movie. To reach their objective, the crew had needed to remove much of the hillside where they had begun drilling. What they found perplexed them greatly. What they found was the massive doorway Knight was standing before, as perplexed as any one else who had so far stood before it.

The professor was beginning to believe the word "doorway" might actually be a misnomer, for the slab of glass before him possessed no hinges. There was no handle or lock or knob, no winch hooks or handholds, no spaces where prybars might be placed—nothing, in other words, that would allow the massive slab positioned at an odd, *67 degree* angle to be easily open. Or even uneasily opened, for that matter.

"Mr. Anthony," Knight said over his shoulder, his left hand absently pulling at his chin, his right making useless circles in the air before him, "I believe you have a problem."

"That much I know," responded the younger man with a chuckle, "That's why I brought you in, doc."

"Yes, quite." Knight continued to stare, telling his employer, "What I'm trying to tell you is that whomever built this ... whatever it is ..."

"What do'ya mean, doc, 'whatever it is?'"

"Try to understand, Mr. Anthony, I hesitate to simply call what we see here a door, because to do so sets up in our minds the idea that a door is what it is. And, given what little we can count on as fact here, I am becoming more and more convinced that a door is what this is *not*."

The younger man held himself in check for the moment. Yes, he certainly wanted to know what the professor meant by his statement. But, he had learned something about handling people running his family's company, and one of the things he had learned about academics was that they dearly enjoyed the sound of their own voices. In the long run, he knew not asking questions would get him the answers he wanted quicker than if he did.

"If anything," mused Knight, rewarding Anthony's patience, "I believe what we are looking at is a plug."

"Like a cork," asked the younger man, breaking his own rule.

"No," answered the professor, moving closer to the great glass slab, "corks are meant to keep something in, but only for a time. A plug is something that is meant to keep something sealed up forever. You cork a bottle. You plug a leak."

Running his hands over several yards of the breathtaking craftsmanship before him, the intricate play of serpents and fish and round-eyed, thick-fanged jaguars, Knight continued speaking, his voice growing lower, more withdrawn, with every passing second.

"If I'm interpreting the message here at all correctly, I don't believe the builders wanted this structure disturbed. By anyone. For any reason."

"So," responded Anthony, his secret hopes finally coming to the forefront of his thinking, "this is a tomb, or maybe a treasure house of some sort."

"No."

Knight said the single word quietly, but did not turn away from the great slab. Continuing to move along the complex lines of figures carved within the dark glass, puzzling over the unprecedented use of inlaid turquoise and silver, jade and amber, he rubbed a hand across his face, blinked several times, then finally turned and said;

"No, I don't believe it is."

"I didn't bring you here to try and out-think you, doc," answered the younger man. I won't argue with you, but I have to ask, if it's not a tomb, if it's not filled with riches someone was trying to protect ... then just what the hell is it?"

"That, my dear young Mr. Anthony, as they used to say, is the 64,000 dollar question."

The remainder of the day did not go as the owner of Anthony Minerals & Gems had envisioned. His thoughts when bringing Knight on board his project had been to enlist an unimpeachable reputation which would lend instant credibility to his find. He had thought to dismantle the doorway and every scrap and shard he found behind it, selling it all off piece by piece to museums around the world.

However, his bought-and-paid-for academic was now distressing his plans with vague misgivings and unfounded theories. To be fair to the professor, Anthony had to admit that the man's apprehension seemed not only genuine, but mayhap not even misplaced. The area had seemed a bit disturbing to him ever since his arrival. Not only to him, but to everyone who had worked on the dig.

Looking across the clearing at Knight in the rapidly fading daylight, the younger man wondered if there was any possibility the professor might be working some sort of angle on him—attempting to curb Anthony's interest in opening his find for some ulterior motive. Might he want to sabotage the dig in order to return at some later time to empty what lay beyond the glass slab for himself? Or his museum?

It was possible, Anthony told himself. People did do such things. It was not as if the world was made up of selfless Samaritans who did nothing but roam the countryside performing good deeds.

But, another part of his mind whispered to him, Piers Knight had the kind of reputation for honesty and impartiality that was generally reserved for saints, and maybe the occasional pope. Not only was there nothing in his background to suggest he might be so inclined, doing such did not even make sense. The main thing the professor had insisted upon had been the right of first refusal of anything discovered for the Brooklyn

Museum. He had also insisted the Guatemalan government be made aware of the find.

That had lead to the arrival of a Ms. Rosell Montiquero, who so far had done nothing but imply that she did not appreciate the presence of imperialists in her native land. Oh, she was happy to admit that Anthony legally owned the land upon which he was digging, and that he had cleared all the legal channels for the exploration of either mineral deposits or antiquities. But, she did so in a way designed to imply that by playing by the rules and doing everything up and above board that Anthony Minerals & Gems was somehow proving they were nothing but thieves and lowlifes. So far, the expedition meant to greatly enhance his family's fortunes was looking like nothing more than a colossal disaster.

Smoking his pipe, still staring at the glass slab outside of camp despite the rapidly descending darkness, Knight was inclined to share his employer's outlook.

"So, tell me, professor, what are you thinking about this discovery?"

The professor looked up to find Ms. Montiquero approaching his resting place. Not having the personal stake in matters Mr. Anthony had, Knight did not view the administrator so much as an adversary to be suspected as he did a somewhat attractive young woman. Removing his pipe from his mouth, he exhaled a thick cloud of smoke, responding;

"Senorita Rosell, I thought you had retired to your tent after dinner?"

"I did, for a while. But it is hot, and I am not tired, and there is a mystery some sixty feet away from us that calls to me. The Director of National Antiquities picked me to oversee what happens here. He also did something quite unprecedented as well."

"Indeed," answered Knight. Taking in a deep lungful of his special blend, he held it down while asking, "and pray what might that have been?"

"When I asked which of our authorities I should bring along to preside over whatever is found, he said that if the Brooklyn Museum's Piers Knight was here, that there was no need." Sitting in a folding canvas chair next to the professor's, the young woman stared at him unblinking, watching his face—his eyes—as she added;

"He said that we could trust your rulings, and he implied that he trusted you to act in our best interests, possibly moreso than we could some of our own people."

Knight nodded, his face showing a mixture of surprise and flattery. Then suddenly, his gaze focused on Montiquero as he asked;

"Excuse me, but you're not saying that old Diego Ortiz is still National

Director, oh my ..." Slapping his hands together, the professor ended up knocking a slug of still lit tobacco out of his pipe's bowl and onto his trousers. Slapping the fiercely glowing cinder to the ground before it could scorch his pant leg, he laughed gently, exclaiming;

"I don't believe it. I haven't seen that old ratcatcher in ages. Is he still the only free thinker at the National Institute, eating Chinese food in his office, still with the bottle of oyster sauce in his bottom drawer—"

As Knight's face broke into an uncharacteristic full blown smile, his eyes glazing over with memory, the young woman sitting next to him dragged him back to the present, smiling slightly herself as she said;

"He has made a few converts." She waited for the professor's full attention to return, then added;

"He also lead me to believe you would be an older individual. You look much younger than I expected."

"I have been well blessed by God and all his saints, my dear," Knight responded. "I also exercise every day and eat nothing but the right foods."

"Professor," the woman said, her eyes narrowing with suspicion despite her smile, "I watched you at dinner. You had two helpings of the barbecued pork and black beans. You ate a small mountain of rice and peppers, to which, despite being drenched in oil and butter you added more of each. And, if my mathematic skills have not fled me, that bottle sitting next to you contains your fourth beer." As Knight blushed, she added;

"I've also been here most of the day, and I observed no exercise program being maintained."

"Why," exclaimed the professor, moving his pipe to his mouth and inhaling, "I've been sitting here doing my bicep repetitions for a half-hour now." Switching his pipe from one hand to the other, he exhaled another warm cloud, adding;

"See, it's time for me to start on the other arm."

"Senor Ortiz also warned me that, outside of the matters of antiquities, you were not to be trusted."

His eyes filling with the innocent of a newborn puppy, Knight touched his chest with the mouthpiece of his pipe, saying;

"Moi? Oh, I hardly think so. But then again, considering the luster of your hair, the fascinating glimmer of your eyes, that ever so wonderful way your lips curl when you laugh, if could be that I am somewhat prejudiced in my own behalf."

"You are a devil, Piers Knight," laughed Montiquero gently, "and I will do nothing more to encourage you." Rising from her chair, the young woman stood still for a moment, giving the professor a final glance, then turned and walked away in the direction of her tent, saying;

"Pleasant dreams, Senor Knight."

"Well, bless all the tiny monkeys," said the professor, loud enough so only he could here. Grinning at the view of the departing Montiquero, he reached for his fourth beer, whispering to the wind, "The only way I can think to make this evening's dreams pleasant would be if I were to visit you within one of yours."

Lifting his no-longer-cold bottle to his lips, Knight downed the last of its contents, then tapped out the last ashes in his pipe. Grinding the embers under his heel, he decided his brief companion had the right idea. With evening spilling over into night, heading for his own tent seemed like the best idea.

"Besides," he thought, "how will I ever be able to visit your sweet dreams, Rosell, if I don't go to sleep?"

Oddly enough, Knight had no way of knowing that he would indeed be visiting Ms. Montiquero in his dreams. Or that there would be nothing sweet about them.

Rosell Montiquero looked about herself, not understanding what had happened to her. The more she thought about it, the more the young woman felt she must be dreaming. But, never before had she known such a dream.

She found herself standing on a great, featureless purple landscape. Flat, unbroken by trees, structures of any kind, or even the slightest tuft of grass, the plane before her reached onward for what seemed like miles, until it ran up against a bluish-black mountain range. An violent draft raced down out of the mountains, stirring a fine scarlet dust which revolved around her in awkward whirlwinds. Lightning flashed down out of the sky above the mountains, shattering their peaks.

As Montiquero turned, surveying the odd vista all about her, she discovered that despite the incredible size of the open area in which she found herself, that she was surrounded by the sinisterly dark mountain range in all directions.

"What," she wondered, "was in those beans? I've never dreamed anything like this before."

"You're not the only one."

Startled, the young woman turned to find Randel Anthony standing behind her. A look of intense appreciation on his face, the man pointed toward Montiquero, saying;

"As much as I'm enjoying the view, the gentleman in me is thinking I should point out ... ah, your current state of ... undress."

The woman shrieked, her arms desperately moving to cover herself. While the controlling part of her mind fell into panic, another questioned her actions. She was dreaming, was she not? What did it matter if she were naked? And, if it did matter, then why did she not simply dream herself up some clothes.

Calming slightly, Montiquero focused on the first image of herself she could remember, the graduation photograph of herself which sat atop her television back in her apartment. Back in the real world. Wherever that was. Instantly she found herself outfitted as she had been that day some seven years earlier. Looking at Anthony, she realized he was dressed as the lead character in the old Indiana Jones movies.

"Well, I see everyone is here."

Montiquero and Anthony both turned to find the professor standing behind them. Knight, oddly enough, was in the same clothes the others had last seen him wearing. He was even still smoking his pipe. As he walked forward to join the others, the woman asked;

"I don't understand this. I am dreaming—yes? But why...?"

"We are *all* dreaming, my dear," responded the professor. "This is not the type of dream either of you is used to. We have crossed over to the dreamplane."

"What?"

There is, for lack of a better word, Mr. Anthony, a dimension surrounding ours where all minds meet. Some call it the ether. There are other names. Simply put, those who reach it can accomplish all manner of miracles. Astral projection, predicting the future, et cetera. Most go insane, or at the least suffer some form of mental breakdown."

"But how? I mean, what has happened to us? Why are we here—together?"

"I believe," answered the professor, "that someone else was here before us. Someone who left the block of glass we have been studying as an invitation, as it were, to join it here."

"But, the doorway, it's a thousand years old," insisted Anthony.

"Older than that."

All turned at the sound of a new voice coming from behind them. As they stared, a man dressed in brightly colored robes off-set by a number of bracelets and necklaces of polished stone walked forward toward them.

He was small in stature, possessed of a hard body graced by thin, tough appendages. His hair and eyes and skin were all dark. That, along with the shape of his nose, the size of his lips, placement of his cheekbones, immediately marked him as possessing Incan blood. As the thought entered the minds of the three dreamers, the figure said;

"I am Topakuti. I am your guide. When you make your decision, I shall be aware of it."

So saying, the Incan walked away into the swirls of red dust dancing across the plane. The trio of dreamers looked one to the other, then not knowing what else to do, followed their guide into the mists. They did so for only a few minutes, finding themselves suddenly delivered into a clearing. The shift did not come gently, crashing down around them instead, flooding their eyes with a brilliant sunlight and their ears with the horrid sounds of violent industry.

"You are where you wish to be," Topakuti told them. Doing nothing further other than sitting down on the grass-covered ground which had suddenly appeared, he said, "You must now decide."

"Decide what?"

"I don't believe he'll be telling us much more, will you, Mr. Topakuti?" The Incan ignored the professor's question.

As the trio watched, all about them the scene began to fade, rapidly being replaced by another—color breaking down, falling into a smudging darkness, then reforming itself anew, the dream world Topakuti had summoned liquified and dissolved, replaced by another. One somehow vaguely familiar.

"We're outside," said Anthony. "Back at the door."

"We're at the site," agreed Knight, "but we're not outside. Our bodies are still asleep. But our consciousness, our souls, if you will, are here, together, on the dreamplane. And if I am correct, we are all about to be tested."

"Tested?" Montiquero said the single word in a tone run through with panic. "How—why?"

"What does it matter," asked Anthony. "It's just a dream—right?"

"Wrong," spat the professor. "I told you, we're not merely dreaming. One's actions on the dreamplane have repercussions. This is the realm of Nod wherein, if you die while dreaming, you die. Period."

"You must decide."

The elder Incan's voice resounded across the scene although he no longer had a physical presence any of the trio could detect. Indeed, all they could actually see, all they were able to comprehend, was the massive square of engraved black glass which had drawn them together. In most respects, it was the same monument they had examined during the day. There were, however, certain subtle differences.

For one, all the noises of the Guatemalan countryside, the call of the birds, the rustle of the constant breeze—all sound had vanished. For another, the glass seemed somehow brighter, more reflective. Beautiful.

Knight stood back, observing, his mind racing. He knew something of the dreamplane, had read about it extensively, traveled it a few times. But this visit was different from his previous journeys through the realm of night and nightmare. He had been pulled to this site unwilling.

"This must be some sort of trap," he thought. "Or test. The old man, his chatter about deciding something. This was all set up some time in the past. But what was it all about? What is supposed to be decided?"

Standing next to Knight, reaching out toward him unconsciously for support, Montiquero stared forward at the pulsating black glass as well. A part of her desired it greatly, knew that such a magnificent find would draw the attention of the world. It would mean research grants, visiting scientists, streams of tourists, all things of which the Ministry would heartily approve.

The woman smiled at the thought. She would be at the center of it, credited with bringing such new fame and glory and mystery to light. Diego Ortiz was a fair administrator. He would protect her interests. Her life would improve in all ways.

Even in that same moment that Montiquero's hand reached out toward the professor's arm, Randel Anthony was also considering the black glass. To him, it was no mystery. It was not a thing meant for the masses. It was salvation.

Anthony Minerals & Gems was not in desperate straits, but it was not the company it once had been. The gold and silver of the region long gone, "Yanquee Exploiters" only begrudgingly tolerated, the company had limped by for the last two generations. The young man's series of explorations had been a desperate roll of the dice, gambling the company's future on the hopes of uncovering some fabulous strike.

And, as far as Randel Anthony could see, he had accomplished exactly that. The door before him by itself was worth millions. The inlay work, broken out and sold piecemeal would bring a sultan's ransom, but intact, offered as the first great object darn of the ancient world discovered in centuries, there was no telling what price it might bring. And, that was only the door.

"What," he wondered, "was behind it? What king's body lay in state here? Surrounded by how many tons of golden treasure? Bricks of it, chests of it. Scepters and crowns and endless strings of beads. Hand beaten pots, chairs made of gold, daggers of silver, piles and mounds of precious metal. And, why just gold and silver? Why not rubies and emeralds? Sapphires and diamonds, black pearls, bags of them—all of it sitting there, hidden in the darkness for centuries ... waiting for *me!*"

As Knight continued to stare, he turned his full attention toward the purpose of the obsidian square. In his heart he knew he was not standing before the resting place of some king. For one thing, all the great Incan rulers were known—well documented. This was something else—but what?

And, as he continued to wonder, Montiquero's fingers touched his arm. At the moment of contact, suddenly the two were of one mind, their thought's intermingling. Agreeing that whatever it was that stood before them was not the tomb of any Incan ruler, the pair of academics turned their thoughts toward what it might actually be.

"Why would the Incas travel so far to build it for one thing?"

"You are thinking only of the center of the Incan empire. Remember, at their height, they had conquered what we now think of as Peru, Bolivia, Argentina and Chile."

"But still," one of them thought to the other, "this was still placed a thousand miles to the north. Why—for what reason."

"It's glyphs tell us nothing. They make no sense."

"Or maybe," thought the other back to the first, "we not capable of seeing the sense they do make."

Next the Montiquero and the professor, Anthony was no longer wondering. His course had been chosen. Needing to know what lie hidden behind the great glass square, he reached his hand out, moving toward the obsidian block.

"We've been reading them in the traditional sense, trying to interpret this thing as the gateway to a shrine or temple or tomb. But, what if the reason we can't determine what's behind it is because—"

"We've never seen the words being used?"

"Because the Incas had no words for what is behind it—"

"Because they themselves didn't know what it was."

And then, in their moment of revelation, the dreamplane responded to their united desire and created for them that which they wished to see. Suddenly, Knight and Montiquero were standing before a gaping hole, one leading downward some terribly long distance. Though they made no movement, still they found themselves hurtling forward, down over the lip of the square, descending into the sheer darkness, the temperature dropping rapidly, falling faster and faster for what seemed like miles, fear clutching their minds, squeezing their nerves, freezing their breath within their lungs—

"What is it? What's happening?"

"There's a light—"

"It's getting warmer. How far could we—"

"There's something moving. I see something moving—"

"It's reaching upward. It's reaching for us—*for us!*"

Unaware of the descent of the others, Anthony's hand grew closer to the dark glass. The cool of it shimmered upward from its surface, inviting, entrancing. The young man smiled. Everything he wanted, everything he desired, would be his in a moment.

"And why not," a voice within his mind whispered. "After all, didn't he deserve it?"

did he?

Montiquero/Knight screamed. The thing, the howling madness, all burned flesh and ruptured organs, the horror that had fallen from the skies, shattered the atmosphere, plowed into the face of the Earth, shattering the mountainside it struck, throwing rock and soil and everything for a half mile circumference into the air, the disgusting maddened beast was reaching for them.

The professor/administrator could feel its desire, its insane hunger. All it needed was a morsel, just the slightest bit of life force, and then it would be able to rejuvenate itself. To rebuild its damaged flesh, to live again. To free itself. To climb to the surface. To consume—

The insane hunger at the bottom of the endless trench reached out for the mind of Randel Anthony. For more than a thousand years it had lain there, buried. Hating, hungering. Lusting for another worldful of flesh to consume. Wanting its blood and meat and life. Desiring it. Needing it.

Ignoring the others, it concentrated on the mind closest to it. The one most easily reached. Most easily entranced. It filled his mind with righteous certainty, promised him everything he had ever wanted, made certain he believed that all he needed to do was touch the doorway before him and that it would open and shower him with all the treasures he wished for—

Come to me

In the pit, the long-buried horror salivated, squealing in terrible excitement. Their minds joined, Knight and Montiquero struggled against the pull of the hideous thing, fought desperately to escape its nearing grasp, strove to reach Anthony—to warn him, thwart him, stop him—

And, as chaos loomed forth, threatening to destroy all, Randel Anthony did as the memory of the long-dead Topakuti commanded, and made for all mankind the decision required.

Piers Knight sat across from Anthony, marveling at the fact he was still alive. As Montiquero came to join them at the flimsy folding table holding that day's breakfast, she reached for an orange, asking;

"Is there any coffee?"

"It's coming." The woman nodded in Anthony's direction. Her hands began absently peeling the fruit she had chosen, but the hollow look in her eyes screamed out her need for steaming caffeine.

"Did you reach the Ministry," asked the professor. Nodding slightly, Montiquero answered;

"I told them all they needed to hear. The area will be made off limits. They are sending workers to fill in the pit. They are also going to cover your expenses, Mr. Anthony."

The young man responded with a smile. After escaping the dreamplane, once the realization sank in that they had survived the nightmare experience the trio had worked out a hasty plan. Those men on site—they whom had already seen the obsidian lure—they would be paid handsomely to cover the abomination back over. They would also be told why. After that, men and machines would be brought in to bury the monstrosity deeper than before, with everything possible being done so that it might never again see the light of day.

"I must admit, Randel," said Knight, "I'm most impressed that you turned your back on the promises being made to you by that thing."

"Listen doc," answered the young man, "I've been hustling for a long time now, trying to keep Anthony Minerals & Gems afloat—okay? Let's just say, I know a con when I hear one. Much as I wanted the payoff being promised, I just wasn't buying the vibe the whole set-up was giving off."

"Still," insisted Montiquero, "it showed great courage, to turn down your heart's desire."

"You see, that's where that thing read me wrong. My heart's desire, it really isn't so much too be rich, as to do right by my family. Before my dad passed on, he would always say, 'you get what you pay for.' Good thing, too, I guess."

"Indeed," offered Knight. As he pulled his pipe and pouch from his pocket, Montiquero said quietly;

"Actually, I'm kind of amazed that we're sitting around calmly discussing having faced down a monster."

"Oh, more than a mere monster," added the professor. Loading the bowl of his pipe, he continued without looking up, saying, "from the images we saw in its mind, it was an alien, a thing that would suck dry the life force of an entire planet, then leap outward into space and onto another."

"Okay, sure," said Anthony, his eyes wide, his mind still reeling from all it was being forced to accept, "but if it landed here during the time of the Incas, why didn't it do what it does? Why weren't we all sucked dry?"

"The Incas studied the skies, knew something was approaching." Knight paused to light his pipe, then in between pulls to get it burning, he added, "their priests warned that what was approaching was a terrible danger. So, the king sent observers, and when that wretched thing landed, the shamans divined its purpose and kept everything away from it upon which it might have fed."

"And so to keep their world safe, they buried it without letting anything living touch it," said Montiquero. The professor nodded, enjoying the first deep pull on his pipe. Letting the thick cloud he had inhaled blow forth slowly, he said;

"Apparently so."

The trio sat quietly for a moment, each of them still trying to deal with their experience of the night before. Knight, who had lived through more than a few such bizarre situations in his time was not nearly as greatly effected by the events as his companions. Still, he was grateful for the quiet of the morning and the comfort of his pipe.

Still, as shaken as they were, both Anthony and Montiquero felt a noticeable stir of relief when they saw one of the crewmen approaching their table carrying what they all knew, or at least hoped, was their morning coffee. As they reached for their cups, checking them to make certain no insects had nestled within them when they were not watching, the woman asked;

"Out of all the things we learned, while our minds touched the spirit of Topakuti, or ... that thing ... there's one problem I have. Why the door?"

"What do'ya mean?"

"I mean, Mr. Anthony, I understand the Incas covering over the pit, hiding the creature from humanity. But, why the door? Why hide something, then leave a marker so close to the surface? What was the point?"

Both the younger man and woman turned to Knight, their twin stares letting the professor know they expected him to have an answer. Exhaling another delicious cloud, Knight sighed slightly, then offered;

"If we knew when all this happened, we might be able to make a more proper estimation. But, my guess is, the Incas decided to use this horror as a type of fail safe device. Let's remember, at the height of their civilization, they were the product of a race that had enjoyed a continual communal existence for some four thousand years. A race that mature begins to come to a greater understanding any of us in the modern world can hope to achieve."

"So ..." Montiquero's tone was alive with interest. As the workman dropped off his tray, indeed containing the hoped for coffee, Knight continued, saying;

"I think perhaps the Inca placed the lure there for future races, for anyone that might come along after them. They were wise enough to realize they might pass from the face of the Earth, and were willing to accept that fact. But ..."

"But," interrupted Montiquero, "they could accept being superseded by outsiders only if those who came after them could make the same choice they did."

Knight nodded, confirming that he was of the same opinion. As the woman smiled in return, Knight offered to play 'mother,' pouring everyone's coffee. The trio then turned their attention to their mugs, each downing as much of the steaming black relief as they could bear. Sighing with satisfaction, the three all suddenly relaxed, the tension of their experience finally beginning to break apart and drift away from them.

Their self-imposed silence lasted for a moment longer, then Anthony, a wicked grin spreading across his face, said;

"Hey, doc—"

"Yes?"

"Last night, on the dreamplane ..."

"Yes?"

"Before you arrived ..."

"Go on."

"I saw our Rosell here naked."

As Knight blinked, Montiquero sputtered, then began pelting Anthony with orange slices. His eyes going wide for an instant, the professor then relaxed, sitting back in his folding chair. His mouth curling into his trademark half-smile, he sipped at his still-too-hot coffee once more, then returned to his pipe, thinking;

"Children."

And then, unable to resist the joy of being alive, he allowed his smile to spread across his entire face, chuckling as he did so.

CJ Henderson

CJ Henderson is the creator of numerous series, in the world of supernatural detectives and in many other genres as well. He has, to date, completed some seventy books and/ or novels. He is also the author of hundreds and hundreds of short stories and comics, as well as thousands of non-fiction pieces. The first novel featuring his character Piers Knight (star of the last story in this volume) will be available in early 2010 from Tor/Forge books. CJ makes numerous personal appearances at conventions and shows around the country. If you can not wait for him to stumble into your neck of the woods, however, you can always visit him at www.cjhenderson.com.

Ben Fogletto

Illustrator Ben Fogletto began his career as a political cartoonist at the age of 15. During his college days he continued in this endeavor, while also producing art for children's literature and teaching aids for Scholastic (while contributing cartoons for men's magazines under a pen name). After college, he turned down an artistically stifling offer from Marvel Comics, choosing instead to be a full time newspaper staffer. Today, Ben is a staff photographer at The Press of Atlantic City. Since the early '90s he has worked in steadily in comics on the side, also contributing numerous covers and interior illustrations for various paperback and hardback publishing houses. Ben lives in Egg Harbor Township, NJ, with his wife, Cynthia, and two sons, Conner and Chase.

Bruce Gehweiler

Bruce teaches seminars and offers consulting services to writers, new publishers, and self-publishers. He is the creator of *The Wordmaster Series* which includes *Profitable Publishing, How to Start a Home-Based Publishing Business* (Second Edition) and *Breaking Into Fiction Writing!* (both co-written with C.J. Henderson) His clients include the authors of the number one bestsellers *The Elf On The Shelf* and *The Starboortz Fish*. He has guided many new publishers through the business start-up process and into profitability.

His own writing career began in 1992 when he began winning or placing in international writing contests such as the Dragon*Con Amateur Writing Contest and the Writers of the Future Contest. Since then he has been published in magazines such as Space & Time, Inhuman, and Tales of the Talisman and anthologies such as *The Dead Walk Again, Crypto-Critters* volumes I & II, *LAI WAN—Tales of the Dreamwalker*, *New Blood, Warfear*—a Collection of Strange War Tales, *Barbarians At the Jumpgate, Hear Them Roar, Frontiers of Terror* and *New Mythos Legends*. He is the co-author with C.J. Henderson of *Where Angels Fear* and *Atlantis—Sea Dragons of Atlantis*.

In 1996 he founded Marietta Publishing which has published over forty-three titles including the bestsellers *Bad-Ass Faeries* volumes I & II, *Breach the Hull*, and *Four and Twenty Blackbirds*. Books published by Marietta Publishing have won the 2007 Dream Realm Award for Best Anthology and the 2009 Eppie Award for Best Anthology. To contact Bruce visit www.mariettapublishing.com or email directly at bgehweiler@comcast.net.

Rich Harvey

Rich Harvey is a New Jersey-based writer, graphic designer, and small-press publisher. His Bold Venture Press imprint specializes in pulp fiction reprints and new hardboiled fiction books. Bold Venutre recently published *Deadly Dames* — an anthology starring some of the toughest women you'd never want to cross, also featuring a story by C.J. Henderson. www.boldventurepress.com

LaVergne, TN USA
11 March 2010
175628LV00003B/5/P